ALSO BY LARRY WOIWODE

What I'm Going to Do, I Think   1969

Poetry North: Five Poets of North Dakota   1970

Beyond the Bedroom Wall   1975

Even Tide   1977

Poppa John   1981

Born Brothers   1988

The Neumiller Stories   1989

INDIAN AFFAIRS

6/26/92

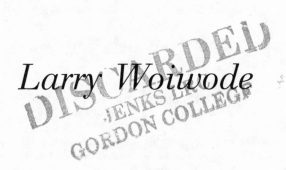

INDIAN

AFFAIRS

A   N o v e l

Larry Woiwode

A T H E N E U M
NEW YORK   1992

Maxwell Macmillan Canada
Toronto

Maxwell Macmillan International
New York Oxford Singapore Sydney

Atheneum   Maxwell Macmillan Canada, Inc.
Macmillan Publishing Company   1200 Eglinton Avenue East,
866 Third Avenue   Suite 200
New York, NY 10022   Don Mills, Ontario M3C 3N1

Macmillan Publishing Company is part of the Maxwell
Communication Group of Companies.

Grateful acknowledgment is made to Doubleday and Co., Inc., for
permission to quote lines from "The Longing" and "Frau Bauman, Frau Schmidt, and Frau Schwartze," by Theodore Roethke,
poems found, respectively, in *The Collected Poems of Theodore
Roethke* (1966) and *Words for the Wind* (1956), copyright by Be-
atrice Roethke and Theodore Roethke.

Library of Congress Cataloging-in-Publication Data

Woiwode, Larry.
    Indian affairs: a novel / by Larry Woiwode.
        p.   cm.
    ISBN 0-689-12155-5
    I. Title.
    PS3573.04I53   1992
    813'.54—dc20   91-30540

10 9 8 7 6 5 4 3 2 1

Printed in the United States of America

In memory

MARY SOPHÍA WOIWODE
(1895–1990)

For your waste and desolate places,
And the land of your destruction,
Will even now be too small for the inhabitants;
And those who swallowed you up will be far away.
The children you will have,
After you have lost the others,
Will say again in your ears,
"The place is too small for me;
Give me a place where I may dwell."
Then you will say in your heart,
"Who has begotten these for me,
Since I have lost my children and am desolate,
A captive, and wandering to and fro?
And who has brought these up?
There I was, left alone;
But these, where were they?"

—Isaiah 49:19–21

Book Two

THE
NATIVE
SON

1

THEY CAME FROM another country, it was clear, considering the way they entered the General Store. He even opened the door for her, like an old man part pansy, or so it seemed to the Indians encamped on different levels of the snowy steps who turned to watch. He had on a camel hair coat and Russian fur cap, and his wife, exactly his height, a gray-tweed Chesterfield and an incongruous fox-fur bonnet that enveloped her head and was held by velvet ties at her throat. They went to a grocery cart inside, each placing a gloved hand on its handle, and then he tucked the other behind his back like a boulevardier, and they wheeled away down an outer aisle, giving off erotic indolence like a fog of perfume. The shuffle he had to adopt in his new overshoes put a crimp in his style, or they might have been promenading down Madison Avenue, New York City, U.S.A.

He regretted his city clothes, though he still wasn't sure how long the two of them would have to remain in the woods, and now he felt stunned by the heat of the store. It was mere idleness being here to begin with, he thought, since they'd driven in to see whether any mail, care of general delivery, had arrived from the university where he used to work. Or from her grandparents.

They didn't notice the Indian. She picked up a jar of anchovies and read its label like the morning news, and then, as they went abreast past a display of mayonnaise, Chris saw him, inside the double doors at the back of the store, his hands in the pockets of a red-and-black-checked mackinaw, as if he'd just now surfaced at the end of the aisle, in the way Indians appeared beside a road they were traveling down. Chris first perceived him as Abraham Lincoln, beardless, his face as seamed as Lincoln's and bronzed over one-half from the street-side plate glass. Then the cast of his features altered into Red Cloud's, but with a Chippewa's higher forehead, and Chris recognized Johnny Jones, a patriarch who would have been a chief in a different age—a loner who lived in a neat white cottage at the edge of town.

Johnny was staring at them and perhaps smiled. Then the brim of his matching red-and-black cap, set on a mass of white hair glowing yellow at its ends in the light, dipped down. He'd acknowledged them.

Chris held up a hand, palm out, and was suffused with the museum sadness he felt after studying a statue too long. He would buy a bottle of wine or a six-pack before they left, he decided, and saw a hunched figure come around their end of the aisle, backside first, with a feather duster wagging from its rear pocket like a rooster's tail as he lugged a carton along the floor—the shopkeeper. The man turned and saw them, flushed with collegiate ebullience, though he was forty, the second generation in the store, and said, "There they are, Chris'n'llen." His patter was so hurried they had to listen hard to hear him.

He put his fists to his hips, encountering the feather

duster, and slapped at it. "Ooo, umbuggers'll gitchafrom behind!" he cried, and laughed as if he expected them to join in, clasping his hands over his chest.

"So, VanEenanams!" he said, and Chris flexed inside his coat, feeling he'd emerged from a straightjacket at the way the shopkeeper, whose name was Art, kept examining how he was put together. Art's round and rapid eyes reminded him of an animal's; though they were merry, one kept straining askew, and now his smile also looked off-center, chock-full of big teeth and beaverish. "How's the bluffs?"

"Delightful," Ellen said.

"Gram's gone, no? S'weather's not furan oldster."

"Oh, yes. She was here only that weekend."

"Beback soon?" Art asked, and put his fingers to his high, neat wave of hair, calibrating its effect, and nearly knocked the pencil from behind his ear.

"No," Chris said, realizing his fist was clenched.

"Jatouch base with that Nagoosa? I tolya, he's an-alumna ma alma mater."

"Indeed," Ellen said, and gave her widest smile.

Art winked, then bent and ripped open a flap of the carton with an explosive menace. They wheeled past, closer to Johnny, who wouldn't speak to them here, Chris knew. Art had suggested to them, in the fashion of family advice, to stop giving rides to Indians. His accompanying merry look also suggested that he, like a wise father, was withholding the worst: that Chris bought beer and booze for them. "They gittaexpect more," he said, "antha'snot good!" Several local Indian families bore Art's Anglo-Saxon name, Kitridge, and Chris was ready to view Art's solicitousness as a guilty mind on prowl. He would have to extend his research to cover that, he thought, and withdrew his hand from the cart. So far, his research, as Ellen remarked this morning, hadn't moved beyond staying up all night with Beauchamp.

"Oh!" a voice behind cried, and Art dashed around to the front of their cart and gripped it with both hands. His face, pulling in several directions, was wide-eyed with reverence. "Jahearabout the fire lasnight by Johnny's? A flashup—not Pocahontastown, Indian Shores." Art was the vendor, also, of news, and Pocahontastown was his euphemism for the Indian village down the highway. "Aguyzole shack was up beforewecouldgitit—I'm fire chief—withrpumper." He unthreaded his fingers from the metal basket and said, "Well, Chris, youknowhow those'r constructed, doncha?"

And Chris pictured, along the highway to the nearest town, a curve lined by buildings of rough-sawn lumber, some covered with tar paper held in place with wood lath, where wrecked and dismantled automobiles rusted along-side deep freezes—all hemmed in by firewood stacked through the yards like hasty corrals—and hallucinated a smell of woodsmoke.

"Johnny was quiteahelp, and so'as Johnny's brother, Jim, wasn't he, Johnny?"

Art performed big nods as if encouraging a dimwit, and Johnny stared out with benign indifference and a beginning smile. His hair was yellowed, Chris saw, from a singe.

"Yes, Johnny's at Jimmy's, and he gotinair and dragged aguy out. Jimmy's a war hero." Art placed a hand on Johnny's shoulder, then swung around behind him like a ventriloquist, nodding at this feat. "He gottaguy out! This guy's boy wasairtoo—well, hezis boy once, I guess; these families, yaknow, all change." Art wrinkled his nose.

Johnny stared at a wedge of floor dusted with sweeping compound, and his elbows lifted in a seizure that looked involuntary. "This little boy," he said, "lived way out my way there but now lives there by you. Gay-land."

"Gaylin Perrin!" Art exclaimed. "Oh, you!" He tapped Johnny's arm, giving them a look of glee, and was back at his carton, working so hard his feather duster waggled.

Chris stepped up to Johnny. "Good," he said, meaning to diminish Art. "That was probably dangerous."

Johnny shrugged and looked up with his same slight smile but a softened consideration. "You," he said to Chris, "come see me. We'll celebrate. Jimmy'd be dere."

Art was behind him again in a flash. "Did you hear that?" He had a purchase on Johnny's mackinaw as if to climb him like a totem pole. "It's probably gonna be special! I mean, Jimmy is kinuh a hero, Johnny, right?"

"Jimmy just pulled Gayland's dad out," Johnny said, then smiled at Chris. "Come see me."

"Do you and Ellen know Johnny?" Art asked, and Chris saw that he looked troubled.

They assumed Johnny's silence.

"Because I didn't think Inyuns asktus to celebrate withum, or whatever," Art said. Chris thought he detected a tone of accusation but couldn't trust his senses on this and felt so displaced he said to Johnny, "A ride home?"

Then he noticed a pair of Johnny's relatives, with a dozen children between them—didn't these children ever go to school?—outside the double doors; they were beckoning to Johnny; one got behind the wheel of a dilapidated car.

The old man touched the bill of his cap, a salute to Ellen and Chris, and went out the door.

*   *   *

"DID YOU have to get a six-pack?" Ellen asked. "You'll just drink it, probably in one sitting, and it's Tuesday!"

"I know it's Tuesday."

"Well, what a way to start a week!"

I thought Monday started the week, he almost said.

She was at the wheel of the Volkswagen bus they had borrowed from the fleet at her grandfather's brewery, and her profile flowed in complementary lines over the snow-covered hills. Most were bare from cultivation that couldn't be sustained on their slopes without horses and bore dark valleys and domes furred with hardwoods. An orchard in regular rows, a geometry of plumes, formed an insignia on a far plain. Ellen's face was flushed with a purity of color usually present only in children, and the cheek he could see from his side of the bus, with muscles bunching at its base, projected the only red across the snowy landscape. He wanted to reach over and pull a tie of the bow that indented her throat and have her shake her hair back in its rose-blond mane. She slowed for a curve, with a gray barn off to the left, and then signaled for their turn.

"Do you think we should go?" he asked. "To Johnny's."

"He's your friend, isn't he?" This was complacent.

"I thought you said you liked him. You know I don't know his brother."

"How would I know that?"

"You don't, then. I don't know his brother."

"Go, if you want to."

He felt like throwing the six-pack out the window. The waste, he thought. The litter. He bought for brothers like Philip and Carlyle when they couldn't get served, but he'd also bought for some teenagers recently graduated from high school, and that was his mistake. No more. He would cache this six-pack to keep from buying for the kids when they came— Then he realized that lately he was thinking more about what he was going to do than doing anything.

She shifted down. The intersection of their gravel road, like every county intersection, was marked with a black-and-white sign like a street sign, an incongruity out in the sticks: *Clausen Road.*

She drove between snowbanks piled as high as the bus and striated at several levels from plowed-up gravel, then along an orchard that had lost its Oriental aspect during a recent thaw, to a road that turned right toward Clausen's farm. A two-track path went straight up a wooded hill, and at its crest he could see, through webbed branches, the glint of their pole light against a pink sky. She parked parallel to a plowed bank and shut off the bus.

"Here, again," she said, and drew the keys from the ignition and let her hands, bare and chapped from working outdoors, rest in her lap as if she were old and had given up. She wouldn't drive up the hill, as Chris had attempted a few times once his buddy Beau broke a trail with his four-wheeler—an antique 1950 Dodge Power Wagon, painted army green, with protuberant headlights mounted on flared fenders that gave it the aspect, seen frontally, of a goggling frog. It wasn't proper for Chris to exert the bus in such a way, Ellen had said; it wasn't theirs, she said.

He slid down the high seat out his open door, grabbing the six-pack along the way, and tugged at his bunched-up coat. At least she'd refrained from mentioning that the road wasn't theirs, or the cabin, or the bluff it sat on; he had to grant her that. She stepped into a pair of wooden skis with ancient leather bindings she'd left leaning against the branches of a tree at the beginning of their trail. His were in the snow past her, splayed out as he'd left them at the finish of his snowplow.

She drew the straps of a backpack, containing the few groceries they'd got, onto her shoulders, and he hurried to help her arrange it, then placed a hand on her hip.

"Don't," she said.

"Of course," he said, and kicked one ski around so he could step into the two without doing the splits.

"It might be interesting," she said.

"I would suspect so."

"I mean at Johnny's. What will they do?"

"Celebrate, I guess. I would suspect so."

She appraised him, about to add something more direct, then asked, "It isn't one of those peyote cults, is it?"

"Ha! No, I don't think." Her naïveté amused him.

She stared across the sun-glazed snow as if measuring his response against its texture. "If Johnny goes to church, as Art the purveyor says, he must be a Pshawbetown Catholic. Why is it that Catholics get together no matter what happens, with medicine, as Johnny might put it, to celebrate?"

"Beats me." She was mimicking her grandmother, but his Catholic background had never been the sprightliest topic between them.

She took off, skating in long strokes of her skis, gaining momentum from the push she added to each beginning stroke with a pair of old wooden poles, and glided into an area reddened by the setting sun. He glanced around for any unusual footprints. He had seen a person prowling through the woods last night and the person, he was sure, wasn't one of the teenagers he'd offended by explaining why he wasn't buying for them anymore: "Somebody's going to get hurt."

He looked up and saw her high on the hill, diminished now, sailing onto a slope where her outlined shape was ignited at its edges by the sun, as if she'd traveled to the outer boundary of his utmost fear while he stood unmoving, unable even to call out a warning, watching from the distance as she went up in fire.

BACK AT THE cabin, he checked his rifle, which he once feared for its potential. Since the incident at the town dump with the breed's wife, however, when the other Indians had warned him about "The Henderson," he was afraid it might be stolen while they were away and turned on him. But it was where he'd hid it, leaning against the log wall beside the dresser in their bedroom. He hung up his topcoat, pulled on the quilted jacket he'd found under a seat of the bus, and walked through the chilly, echoing building. In the back porch, an enclosed porch also built of logs, he grabbed a chain saw and went through snow stained by the low sun to the edge of the bluff, where a wind sent his hair straight up from his head as if in fright.

Hundreds of feet below, at a level too dizzying to contemplate, the sea-green expanse of Lake Michigan tumbled chunks of ice between collapsing whitecaps. Closer to shore he could make out mounded palisades of ice, dingy from sand, that the chunks kept knocking against and sensed a damp fishing day on a creek bank stalled dead within him—a smell of fish and the fish slime scraped off with scales. The lake never froze, though some mornings it was overlaid as far as they could see with platelets of ice, and now he noticed smoke along the horizon where an ore boat plowed through a patch of open water gilded by the sun.

The island of Manitou rose beyond the boat like the ridge of an emerging turtle's shell, while South Manitou, at the edge of visibility on the horizon, was the turtle's ancient head craning back. Then it was gone, quick as that, by a change in the light.

He stepped into the woods, looking for a tree easy to take—it was almost freezing in the cabin; he hadn't kept up—but anything dead enough to cut after a month of burning wood was farther in. He slogged among thick trunks through snow half as deep as it had been, near his hips once, and spotted some crowded stem oaks, then passed these up for an ash, aware of how ash split and exhaled solid heat. He put a hand on the bark, clinging in flakes as if in a race to the treetop, mottled near his glove with gray-green medallions.

"Sorry," he said. "We have to keep warm."

The chain saw had a spongy action and resisted choking. He took hold of the starting cord and flung the housing away from his body as much as he pulled, and with the second fling the woods parted up their center from its rale, and close trunks trembled with wooden ringing in the growing din. He set the bar into the bark at ground level, and moist grain poured over his boot. The undercut and backswing, as the engine dug, then the crawling cut straight in to form the notch. Done. He tipped the saw out, using the pawls on its housing, and stepped to the tree's offside, foot braced.

This cut higher and angling near the upper notch. But before the teeth were there, the tree went—twiggy branches snapping in its leap from the stump, its length clipping past lines of trunks, limbs breaking in its bucking roll, all dimmed by overtones of the saw winding down, then its *whump* into snow. Half-buried, a serpent. Slashes of the

bar up and down its length to delimb it. The lowered
engine muffling at the slices performed with the tip of the
bar, arms gyrating, into the freedom of snow beneath.
The cuts into stove length all from below, steady lifts, the
rollered teeth hissing, starting to steam and going jerkily
into an uneven climb. What to watch. Then the battering
of the final rev before he shut it off.

In the auditory hollow, he stepped back, off balance,
and heard the engine of a truck approaching from behind.
He turned. His imagination. No. More than imagination,
that truck. Its sound accelerated in his inner ear until he
was inside it again, jostling with its noisy action down a
rutted road. On the cracked vinyl of its seat was the jug,
as Grandpa called it. He looked up at his mother's father
at the wheel, the grandpa he seldom visited, and watched
his face flashing black and brown from sun through trees.
Then he was inside the silence that always arrived—was
he asleep?—followed by a shriek of brakes and the smell
of woodsmoke. He sat up on the floorboards where he'd
fallen and found his grandfather gone, the driver's door
wide, the knob of the floorshift twitching with the engine's idle, and got up on the seat to see a blackened
landscape where spires of burned trees and felled logs
sent up dark plumes past lighter smoke. In the rearview
mirror, like a window on the actual world, his grandpa
was embracing a soot-streaked man in leather leggings
with a woman's long hair.

His grandpa steps back and holds out the jug, and when
the man continues to stand in dejection, his grandpa
strikes his own chest, hand in a fist, and says a word that
troubles Chris more than anything since he rose from the
oily rubber of the floorboards: Lakota, *Lakota*.

Chris turned now to check behind. Coppery-red illumi-

nation was streaming over the surface of the lake, lighting
the trees from beneath, gilding the undersides of all their
limbs, and in every direction he turned, he faced a luminous stretch of creation in which he stood all alone.

"NO," ELLEN said. "We can't do that."

She was on the phone, at the other end of the hall to
the great room of the hunting lodge, wearing the flannel
nightgown she always wore at home, whatever the weather.
Chris paused a moment to allow her to signal to him,
even with her eyes, whether this was a young Indian, but
she turned her back. He went across the kitchen, bearing
his armload of ash, and let it roll in growing thunder into
the woodbox.

"Of course not," Ellen said. "It's more wood."

It was as he thought; her grandmother.

"Maybe it sounded like somebody falling on the floor,
but it's the wood he just carried in for the stove. We
have to keep warm. Nana, we're not destroying the
place, for God's sake, or you wouldn't let us stay here!
No," she added after a long pause, and then again, "No,
that's not true."

Her grandmother was grilling her about him. Nana had
been Ellen's legal guardian, along with Der Alte Strohe,
from the time Ellen's parents separated in her childhood
until they died together in "the accident," as Ellen called
it. He opened the lid of the cookstove, saw coals, and
placed three of the thinnest pieces of ash in a pyramid
over their glow. Then he got on his hands and knees and
crawled under the old sink—supported at an unhandy
height by green-painted two-by-fours—and padded
toward the hallway where Ellen stood. Her back was still

turned, and the last of the sunset at a far window outlined her figure in silver under the nightgown. When Nana visited and noticed Ellen wearing the nightgown throughout the day, she said, "I see you lead a tragic life, dear."

He set his eyes on Ellen's nearest foot, large and rigidly corded, encircled at its sole by an orange callus like a clinging slipper, with a big toe that flexed mightier than his thumb, and began to stalk it. He got to it and kissed it before she discovered him; she jerked away but managed to keep talking. Her feet were her most sensitive avenue. He kissed the other and got kicked in the neck. He fell on his stomach and tried to get his tongue between two toes, but Ellen started dancing. He rolled on his back, sending chinked logs and varnished beams—the supports for the log rafters—tumbling into his vision. He edged toward her nightgown; comely calf, white thigh, then blackness, as a foot came over his eyes.

"Don't!" she whispered. "Stop!"

"What's he up to now?" descended from the receiver into his blindness as clearly as if he were in the same room with her grandmother in suburban Milwaukee.

"Oh, nothing," Ellen said, wriggling her toes.

"I can imagine," the old woman said.

"I doubt it," he murmured, and listened, but all he could hear was a noise like an animal gargling.

He pulled himself from under Ellen's foot and went across the room to the couch and sat, his back to her, facing a fireplace of fieldstone. He'd blocked its mouth with a piece of plywood. Far above the half-sawed log that formed its mantel, the mounted head of a moose hung from a hardwood plaque by a dusty wire, its fur bedraggled and beginning to part in spots, particularly around its yellow eyes. If Chris were younger, he would

have to see if he could remove an eye and use it as a
marble. The way up was indicated by the mantel, at each
end of which, on a peeled and varnished limb pegged into
a log, a pair of raccoons were stilled, via a taxidermist's
feat, in their stealthy act of climbing. Their apparent
goal was a group of tacked skunk skins rayed above the
moose like a representation of a rising sun.

"Yes, he checked that," Ellen said.

The pump was out. For two weeks they'd been hauling
water and using a latrine he'd hacked into the frozen
ground in the woods—brass-monkey heaven.

"The man from Maple City who was here— Then and
last week and yesterday, and we still have no toilet. Water
is one of the essentials! Of course he does. We get it from
the Clausens in cream cans. *Cream cans.* I can hardly lift
one! Kitchum—the well man—says he fixed this pump
before but now is the time to put in the new well he says
you talked about. Why didn't you say he already called!"

This poor man had traveled thirty-two miles one way
three times, caught between the pair, and still hadn't
earned a cent. He kept eyeing Chris as if to say, Can't
you do something about this? Ellen's grandfather had suffered a stroke last spring and wasn't able to make deci-
sions; he scarcely talked. When he was happy, he cried
"Strohe!" with a limp-wristed accompanying wave, and
when he was unhappy or confused, he said, "Jeez damn
sunnunnabastard shit to hell." He was confined to a
wheelchair and had gained so much weight that Nana, a
wisp of a woman, had to hire a nurse to trundle and lift
him around their suburban mansion, which they had
built, unfortunately, on five levels.

"I'm not sure, Nana. Kitchum said it was the whole
long thing that pulls the water up, the pump core or—"

"*Rod*," Chris intoned from the couch.

"He said the pump rod had broken off somewhere way the hell down in the pump and— No, those weren't his words. He's a nice man. He said it's hard to get it out because it's down there about two hundred feet and connected to a plunger, or some damn thing. I'm sure he thought of a magnet. He said he's never heard of reaming one out. We did wrap the faucet on the pipe by the meadow, I told you, but it froze anyway. No, it has nothing to do with the well. Kitchum said over and over: 'The pipe freezing there has nothing to do with your well, ma'am.' I don't know how long it was frozen. It started spraying through the old shirts one day when it warmed up— What would you wrap it with? *Heat* tape," she said, and he could sense her attention revolve to him.

"Naturally we'll have it fixed, but not till there's a pump. I'll see what— We'll go out as soon as I hang up and see what we can do. Of course he doesn't!"

"Make you do everything," Chris mumbled. "Hardly makes you do anything. Hardly has a chance to talk to you."

"*What?*" Ellen asked, and he turned and found her facing him, a hand over the receiver on her shoulder.

"I'm mumbling."

"Please! This is difficult enough!" She threw back her hair, as he'd wanted her to in the bus, sweeping this half of it with one hand from her ear, bright red, and raised the receiver again like a tiny, weighty barbell. She began again the story of how they were walking in the meadow on one of the first sunny days when she saw water spraying through the old shirts.

He got up and went in quick strides to the antique sewing machine at her side that served as a table, grabbed a pad and pencil, and wrote, "I hope she's paying for this," and held it up to Ellen's face. She gave a vigorous nod, setting her mane into the action it took when she was above him, head thrown back, eyes squeezed on tears. He dropped the pad and went down the hall, past the defective bathroom that faced an open closet, to the kitchen.

It was already warming up. He started for the dining table but noticed papers spread across it—his work from last night—and stopped short, as if somebody had grabbed the front of his jacket and twisted it in prelude to a barroom punch. He eased back until his hams struck the cookstove edge, then lowered his butt onto its top. He knew his last sentence went, after a semicolon, "and so we see him then in his deepening age altering 'I'll be an Indian / Iroquois' to 'Ogalala,' " and realized that this was inaccurate. The actual alteration was of the final word itself, not the entire preceding line. He folded his arms in resistance to fixing even that.

There were times at night when a storm of words, or the interconnected correspondences that language contains, overtook him like an electrical charge, gripping his head along the hairline, but he was convinced he could never complete this dissertation.

"Ph.D., eh?" Don Jones had said. "Dr. Van Eenanam. And poor Jonesy just a diddly LPT." Jonesy was Nana's name for her nurse—this fellow lying in a white smock on the bare mattress of one of the many beds in the Strohe home, next to the fitted spread he'd jerked aside, his crossed feet up on the footboard and his Wellingtons tumbled below. He kept running an emery board over the manicured nails of a hand cupped at his chest, and Chris realized that after Der Alte died, it wouldn't be beyond Nana to sign the estate over to this crew-cut shyster built like a football player out to pasture. She would sign it over to Jonesy, Chris thought, for the mere satisfaction of cutting him off, no matter how things fell out for Ellen.

"Come see me," Johnny had said, and Chris pictured the Lincolnesque cast to his features, corduroyed grief.

He went to the aging Kelvinator refrigerator, an oblong that stood on high legs and had been painted copper, and peeked down the hall where Ellen stood; her back was turned again. He went to the door and got through it and into the enclosed porch without a sound. There was a tricky lift latch on the outside door that tended to react with a clatter when the door, swollen with weather, was released from its catch, but he got that open, too, without a noise. The power of the cold, that freezing force that sealed up the countryside for months, assaulted him like a slap after the cookstove, and he realized how he loved being bound by a fire, held within the radius of its heat.

The slab of concrete outside, recently swept, glittered like mica, the snow at its edges bearing sandy grooves from her broom. Both sets of skis leaned against the logs like fillets of ice under the bare bulb above the door. The pole light, a bulb affixed by means of a two-by-four bracket to a tree across the drive, was off. He picked up the pair of skis nearest the window where Ellen stood and walked with them over his shoulder up the drive. In the moonlight he could see the upright pipe that the two might still be talking about, with a wadding of old shirts at the core of so many layers of ice it resembled a snowman.

He stepped behind a stunted fir, its limbs irregular from the grapevine strangling it, and stepped into the skis. There was a crusty scarf of ice at the edge of their trail that the tips of his skis had a tendency to trip up on, but once he got into the woods at the head of the downhill road, he was going so fast the hairs in his nostrils stiffened like Brillo. But no poles. He tucked in his arms and leaned toward the tips, a Swiss army regular headed for the bottom of the jump on his first Olympic run, and the schuss of the old wood accelerated so much that he felt on fiberglass. Trunks and branches scintillated silver from the moon, and then he was in the open, under stars—crests and sweeps of silver to his left, all the way to Clausen's light. The exhilaration of a bird! At the bulk of the bus he went into a snowplow and almost wept at the sheet of crystals that whipped so full across his face he couldn't see for a second; then their instant melt conveyed the exact sensation of bleeding.

He looked up the hill, but the yard light was still off. No sign of her. Some of these phone conversations went on for an hour. He could run into town and try the hotel bar, once the watering spot of choice, until it was taken over by a restaurateur from Detroit who disliked the slow drinking habits of the locals and catered to tourists, as Beau said. So the locals planned to boycott him out of business this winter and congregated across the street at a bar that had received a recent facelift—but not Ye Olde sort, like the places taken over by entrepreneurs from Chicago and Detroit.

He put a hand into his jacket pocket and came up with snow. He tried the other pocket, his pants pockets, his back pockets, and felt over his shirt through the jacket. He'd forgotten the keys.

He sucked in cold air to scream out against this idiocy that seemed the most perdurable part of his character but at that moment sensed something in the woods. Then he saw it. An animal, a large one, a bear, from the downward dips and unexpected sidewise shamble it adopted. But it had a human shape. It moved through the trees at the top of the hill toward the cabin, paused behind a trunk, then scurried to the next, heading in the direction of the window where Ellen stood.

"Hey!" he yelled, and his voice went ringing over the angles of icy slopes. "Hey! *You!*"

He kicked off his skis and started up the hill as fast as he could run, centering his concentration on the pole light that suddenly came on above the back door.

ELLEN WAS on the slab, still barefoot and in her nightgown, the bare bulb making her outlined body glow. "Get in," he tried to yell, out of breath, the snowy drive exploding under him as he ran. "Get in the *house!*"

"Ow!" she cried, batting at the snow. "What's this!"

He couldn't get his breath to talk.

"Where were you? The skis are gone. I thought I—"

He took her upper arm, which felt frail under her gown, got the door open, and got her into the porch. He leaned against the logs and felt the veins in his neck pulse with such force his mind went off and on. The university had accustomed him to such underhanded pettiness he'd forgotten what it was like to face actual physical violence.

"God!" Ellen cried. "You act like men in big black cars are after us!"

"Maybe."

"I heard you call and turned on the light and went out and saw you running through the woods—"

"Where?"

"Right there!" She pointed in the direction he'd seen the prowler.

"Which way was I going?"

"*I* don't know! You were hardly out of sight, and the next thing I knew, you were coming up the hill!"

He opened the inside door and went through the hall

to the main room, which had assumed the look of a cathedral with a fire in its nave; she'd switched on the yellow-gold candle bulbs set in brackets beside the windows. Their glow had the raccoons' eyes shining with the hollowed-out red of eyes in headlights. He went to the dresser, bumping the log frame of their bed, and reached past the agitated drapes for his rifle. Much as he hated to have this handy for access, now he had to.

"There's somebody out there!" he yelled at the wall of rough-sawn boards at the head of the bed. Then, through a crack between boards, he saw her step in his direction across the kitchen, vulnerable even through walls.

"Who?"

"How should I know!"

He strode through the main room to the back door.

"Chris! What are you up to?"

Outside, he cocked the rifle—its magazine was loaded to the hilt from the heft of it—and hurried under the light into the dark of the woods, restraining himself from firing a shot. Then he imagined the sound of the report and its echo, as if he'd fired one off after all, and pictured himself crouched in the woods, where Ellen had placed him, attempting to dodge a slug.

The hilltop was scoured of deep snow, even among the big trees, and beyond the reach of the light he could make out footprints. He located the snooper's trail, edging closer to the cabin as it moved from trunk to trunk, and then saw a scattering of mulch and twigs across the crust, as if a scuffle had taken place. Startled by his shout? He got down on a knee. Ribbed treads spanned the bulky prints of snowmobile boots, and the loop of prints led back the way they'd come, stepping into the trail already laid down. Why? It would only be easier to follow.

He stood. Farther ahead, the prints swerved aside in a lunge, off course, as if the person had heard him coming up the hill, and then in another explosion of mulch, the right print turned black and continued on, growing fainter and fainter with each stride until it was merely an outline again in the surface of the unmolested forest snow.

2

"WHO LIVES IN those shacks south of us," Chris asked, "in that narrow neck of land past our old orchard—on past Doc Steele's hill property?"

"Indians," Beau said.

"I figured that, but who?"

"Half a Kitridge bunch. The Hendersons."

"I followed the tracks there, and they got scrambled up with a bunch of others. There were lights in every window and so many people inside I headed back."

"Too many to keep track of, huh? There was some from town, too, a big celebration."

"You were there?"

"A while, before things got thick."

"How come?"

Beau turned from the cookstove, where he was preparing breakfast, and raised a greasy spatula. "I was invited, buddy. I live on the road. I'm brother to them. Neighbor, if that's how you like it."

"The road south of our place runs into your blacktop?"

"You know, you surprise me. At the first curve past my place"—he pointed with the spatula—"you go straight,

and that road runs past their shacks to your wife's property." He shook his head, the skin so tight over his face
Chris couldn't decipher his expression. "We're a mile and
a half off, going crow, and you didn't know that!"

Beau swung to the cookstove and tossed his ropy ponytail, bound with beads, over a shoulder of his green-plaid
shirt. "Like a tourist—blind to everything but scenery."

"I was only here for a length of time that first summer."

"Plus some visits since."

"Nana or the old guy always had jobs for me, and they
conveyed this territorial imperative about property here."

"*Their* property. That's how they come across."

My attitude, Chris thought, was probably implanted by
my father, who always said, "Don't set foot on a man's
land," which had the force of The Man's Land.

"I saw you in the grocery store. That first year, and a
couple times after."

"I never noticed you."

"I had a Mohawk." Beau turned, grinning, and his old-
coot kickshaw laugh, a *hoogah-hoo* behind the square
teeth he held clenched in a smile, started going. "I figured
you as pork-fed Establishment."

"If you only knew."

"Do I now?" Beau asked, and with his *hoogah* Chris
raised a hand to cover his own gapped front teeth. Laughter! Was it Bergson? The round oak table where he sat
held reflections of the kitchen windows, with mullions and
panes bent in curves toward him; he and Ellen were offered the cabin for their honeymoon, although the honeymoon sometimes seemed an ordeal the Strohes were
meting out, and over that summer he bought the rifle. But
it hadn't occurred to him that a native like Beau, or a
dozen others, were observing him from home ground.

"When I was trailing this person, at one point a footprint turned black. Even there in the woods, not knowing what was up, I had to laugh. Whoever it was ran kerplop into our latrine. Recently used."

"You weren't scared."

"Maybe some."

"Sure," Beau said, easing out a squeaky thread of gas.

"Why were you at the party?"

"So I could sneak a peep at your wife, a*hooga*! That's what you're getting at, no? Beau peeps!"

Chris folded his hands over a mullion's shadow.

"Di Kitridge has a son who might be interested in seeing if whites are up to what his mother is," Beau said.

"Who says I'm so white?"

"Okay, who might want to know if a guy trying to pass, like Henderson does, is up to what Henderson is, but with a white wife."

"Who's this Henderson?"

"He worked in Detroit, but's been trying to get back to Indian ways." Beau poked in the pan with his spatula. "That makes it worse. He leaves his wife when he's in Detroit, then gets wrung about her. He was in at least one fight last night. Too loaded to have snuck over."

"I wasn't saying I thought he did."

Beau set the spatula on the shelf above the stovetop and turned with crossed arms. On either side of the stove was a doorway leading to the only rooms Beau had finished—an old milk parlor where his dog slept, to the left, and a room of shelves whose door, on the right, was usually shut. It was open now, and winter light entered both eggshell-painted rooms with such brilliance it formed of them a separate outer space beyond the kitchen—the simulacrum of a shell on the beach. Beau said from the center of this hollow, "You take things so

far, then let them drop. People figure you got other things
behind what you say you're up to."

"You mean you do."

"I'm saying what I see from here." He banged his butt
against the cookstove top. "*Here.*"

The yellow-enamel stove was as tall as Beau, ornately
monumental, and so far the house's only source of heat.
Beau had taken over this farm down the blacktop from
the ramshackle mansion where his father, Emile Nagoosa,
ran his house-painting and carpentry business, and Beau
was attempting to restore the house himself—"a floorboard at a time," he'd said, "and about a floorboard a
week"—although he also claimed it was too far gone to
restore.

"You want breakfast?" he asked now.

"We ate."

Beau grinned, a clear, straight smile with no trace of
ambiguity. Then he set the black-metal frying pan on the
table, on a tinned asbestos pad, and prodded with a fork
at the pieces of cut-up sausage encircling three eggs,
sunny-side up. "How about some of this sausage? It's
homemade—from that farmer past the curve you can take
straight to your place."

"All right."

Beau dumped some onto a plate at his side of the table
and shoved the plate and fork across to Chris, then pulled
up the frying pan and ate from it with a spoon. He hadn't
shaved in days, from the curling whiskers on his chin, and
yolk ran from his mouth and caught there as he sat bolt
upright and stared at Chris while he chewed. There was
a groaning yawn from the incandescent shell of the milk
room, and Ivan, a graying elkhound with a silvery bib,
came tapping into the kitchen on taffy-furred paws.

"You later," Beau said, and Ivan went to the door that

led to the porch and sat on his haunches, his ears up and alert, studying Chris.

"Why would somebody backtrack on his own trail?"

"To throw you off, then double back again so he could come up behind you with a coup stick and goose you!" Beau's grin sent wrinkles streaming around his eyes.

"I'm not that out of it in the woods."

"Once you got a boom stick in hand, you're in another world." Beau grabbed a twisted plastic bag and pulled out a crust of Sweetheart bread and started mopping up his eggs. "Tell me what happened with Henderson's wife."

"I told you."

"You think you did."

"I met the Nagonawba cousins."

"Brothers. Philip and Carlyle."

"They're different as night and day."

"Could be crossed paternity, but I doubt it. Their ma was an Omena Christian and their dad a gentle little guy that drank himself to death."

"They were with this crazy Denny Wing—"

"They asked you to buy them a bottle of Top and Bottom."

Chris heard the word again in their voices as they crowded him to the side of the street behind the General Store, breaths pluming: *Topm Bah-um.* He wasn't sure what they meant until they explained; a bottle-mix of liquor.

"See, I did tell you," Chris said.

"They ask everybody that."

"They were broke."

"How naive can you be? You got 'em pickled worse!"

"They wanted to drink in the bus."

"Or the cop might arrest them, they said. I know it by

heart. We got no cop since last summer. Those two are turning to lushes. Liars. Philip used to work all year out at Fox Island."

"He told me."

"Oral history."

"They had me drive around, and then Philip asked a couple guys to join us—one was this hulk who sat on his hands and wouldn't say a word. Gojum or something."

"Joejim Standing Bear."

"That's it."

"He's the cousin—wanted in a dozen states."

"Wanted!"

"Usually assault. His son Horse, who lives down the road with his mother, is worse."

"Right away this silly Denny Wing—I can't figure where he got this—started talking about shooting his dog."

"It's an old expression," Beau said, his lids half-closed, weary, and Ivan barked once.

"But Wing got into how if he had a good enough rifle, like mine—it was on the floor between the seats—he'd get the sucker right off, one shot."

Beau shaded his eyes with a hand. "Good God."

"He started swinging it around in the bus."

"Loaded."

"It's loaded, he's loaded. 'Go to the town dump!' he yells. 'Let's see how good a one you got!' "

Beau waved his hand and looked off, and Ivan barked again, a sharp rap that rang through the empty rooms.

"Shouldn't you let him pee?" Chris asked, turning to the dog, whose dark eyes, trained on him, sparkled amber.

"A purebred like him'll go through a window before he shames himself."

"I got the rifle away from Wing, mostly to empty it. I was half-loaded, too. We had a bunch of beer in the bus everybody was having, and there was a big to-do when we got stuck down at the harbor, or must have been, because the next day Art at the store said with a wink he understood I had to have quite a bunch push me out when I got stuck. He said I should stay away from Indians. Ha! 'Shoot the rats,' Denny Wing said. By now the Nagonawbas are whooping. I didn't notice anybody at the dump, so I backed the bus around to shine its lights on a pile of garbage. 'Look at the rats!' they were yelling. So I . . ." He prodded open the door with the rifle barrel and slid onto uneven ground, more garbage, into mealy light, off balance. There was a watery swim in his vision and a wash of the nausea of intoxication. Was that a movement where the headlight beams burned? He raised the rifle, an orange streak gilding its barrel, and fired, startled to hear a shriek. A swarm of rats gathered beyond the beams, backs humped, rising on their haunches to fight over the squalling wounded one. He fired a swift series into them, shell casings clattering off the bus as he worked the lever action, and then a voice behind him yelled, "Hey! What are you drunk Indians up to?"

He swung around, ready for blood, as he'd been the only other time he'd been called a drunk Indian, in a bar, and then a woman sailed into sight, higher up, like phosphorescence in the dark, and a child appeared to grab her leg. Had Chris raised the rifle? "You crazy-drunk, dumb-nut Indian!" she yelled. "You could've shot me!"

"God," Beau said, and shook his head above the frying pan, his ponytail crackling as it rolled over his shirt.

"But she was behind and way above, at the edge of the dump. I turned and emptied the magazine into the rats.

I must have blown away a dozen—anyway, Denny Wing claimed that. When I got back in the bus, the guys were saying, 'Oh-oh, that was Betty, the Henderson's beef. She'll tell Dick.' The Nagonawbas were trying to scoot down and hide.''

Beau sat up. Sunlight off the snow burned through a window behind and surrounded him with light of such substance that blue-gold corpuscles appeared to cling to his hair.

"What was your dad like?" he asked.

"My dad? Oh, do this, do that, don't do that—the usual, I guess, but unremitting. Why?"

"When I was a boy, my dad said, 'Champ—' He always called me 'Champ.' "

"Good for you."

" 'Champ, you want to come smear paint on some boards today?' Some days I did, some not, and then didn't at all. I was free." His eyes were so intent they appeared to be looking through Chris to the house beyond. "I ain't Amish or a Luddite," he said, as if his lexicon had burst. "I ain't about to destroy what I got. I'm going to keep this property. You've probably done yourself up real good. Keep away from Henderson. It was a bad second there when you turned on Betty."

"Okay."

"Don't let any Catholicky past get you so guilty you try to make it up. Henderson won't know what you're talking about. You'll be stepping into a story of Betty's. She invents the worst to keep him on edge. You might be the guy who's after her when he's away."

"Oh, come on."

"This county was half Indian when I grew up. Now it's less than a third. It's those retirees and weekenders from the cities. Imagine if we could run them off and get that edge again! We could handle problems right. One thing for sure: no more guns."

Beau was past the side of the stove, into his shelf-lined room, before Chris registered his rising, and came back carrying a bottle of Wild Turkey in one hand, a pair of tumblers pinched together in the other over his shirtfront. He shoved one in front of Chris, pulled the cork from the bottle with his teeth, and held it in a corner of his mouth, like a cigar stub, while he filled the tumbler half full; then he filled his own to the same level, put the bottle to his mouth to cork it, and shoved the frying pan aside as he sat.

"Let's have this," he said. "Let's not talk. How about a cigarette."

It wasn't a question. Chris pulled a pack from his shirt pocket and slid it over to him. Beau lit up with a wooden match, staring down his nose and applying the flame until the entire cigarette end was evenly lit, then exhaled a sigh with the smoke, his grainy lids nearly closed, and whispered, "Too much damn sweet wine last night."

Chris watched him sip in a nibbling way at the whiskey and then lifted his own glass and with the first taste was inside the moment when he turned to the voice that called him a drunk (or included him among the Indians Betty knew), and then she appeared in the downward sweep of that night, giving off ocher illumination, and at the vision of her he had to smile.

"What's that about?" Beau asked.

"Betty made me belong."

"Don't romanticize the trouble you're in—like futzy Wordsworth, or worse, Fenimore Cooper. Your sins will find you out, as Dad says, or the past finally gets you by the neck. I said that. You want that 'rustic innocence,' but you been in the other world too long. One, there's no innocence, and two, you're educated out of my world."

Chris knew Beau went to Michigan's best university for four years, on a minority scholarship, but never took his degree; he got involved with a group of Marxists and spent his last year "writing poetry and reading in a coffee-house," so he said. And Beau had lived in New York for a while, he said, at the fringe of the underground, at the same time Chris was there—one of the junctures in their pasts Chris preferred to keep ambiguous, since he was then at a brokerage house, and it was not considered kosher, in this liberated decade, to have served the Establishment.

To him Beau's talk often argued against what Beau had become. Chris might even be tempted to question Beau's blood, if it weren't for his father down the road, and Beau's pokes at education, he felt, were jealousy. Chris never pressured the academy for special treatment because of his blood, a point of pride to him—even though he took pains to evade being identified. He wanted to pass. So perhaps he had become more white than Whitey, from his convoluted hiding, as Beau once claimed.

"That's one less for me this week," Beau said, nodding at Chris's empty glass. "I pour out one drink at morning, one at night, and make it six days, to Friday. Then I go for my next bottle and have some beer to get me through the seventh. So I measure my week."

Chris was puzzled, since he'd taken to heart Beau's injunction not to speak, and then Beau leaned forward on both elbows, dark eyes direct on him, and said, "It's the only way to keep from being a drunk Indian."

Beau pushed back and stood at the window overlooking

the porch, his fingertips inserted, palms out, into his back pockets. Chris eased from his chair, and Ivan stood, his claws clattering on the linoleum as he sought his perfect balance, and Chris felt a dusky, twining effect of the whiskey deep in his brain.

"Later," Beau said, either to Chris or to Ivan, his back still turned and sunlight seething at his outline as if he were being welded in one stroke to the panes.

Chris put his hand on the oval knob, its filigree worn smooth, and glanced at the tarp covering the kitchen door; he'd never entered the main part of the house. "If you think—"

"That's enough," Beau said. "Go."

Chris stepped onto the porch, blinking against the bitter winter light that never made good on its promise of heat, and the bright red bus he'd parked beyond the turned posts of the porch seemed to erupt with noise against the winter landscape. Ivan hurried past, nearly knocking Chris down the pair of wobbly wooden steps as he bounded toward the bus's closest hubcap; done, he padded down his sunken path to the barn and woods beyond.

Chris turned, but the window was bare. Then he heard a steady thump of sound, like a hammer striking something dull and giving, rise from an inner room.

THE ROAD was dusted by morning snow, with ribbons of black raying into lanes. Chris turned on the heater, which wasn't working right; metal channels conveyed air somehow from the putting engine, but surely not directly: carbon monoxide. Volkswagens. "The people's car," Nazi Germany dubbed them, and in the past years, hardly two decades from the end of the Third Reich, you saw these buses or Beetles everywhere in the States, as if the *Volks* had emigrated en masse. Memory that short.

It was fitting that Ellen's grandfather owned a fleet of them and for a wedding present had let Chris and Ellen drive a Beetle, a gift to Ellen, to his Black Forest hideaway. The reclaiming of that Beetle (a true case of what whites called "Indian giving") was a story to tell Beau, who liked facts stacked up against those he scorned.

At the first curve, a ninety-degree angle to the right, Chris slowed. Sure enough, a two-track lane led straight along a fence and entered a stand of trees, spidery against the sky. He stopped. In a lower level of land, where the trees dipped down and then mounted a hill again, he could see plumes of smoke swing off in strands with the wind. A hill farther on, cleared of trees at its top, looked yellow in the light, and he was sure it was the highest hill at old Doc Steele's, bordering a hay field where he and Orin Clausen had once worked hauling bales. He thought he could also see, in a winking wedge of silver far below, a slice of the lake, and imagined smoke rising above the cabin from the fire he'd laid this morning in the stove while Ellen slept.

"Like a tourist," Beau had said, "you notice only the scenery." Or something to that effect.

Why not, when the scenery was so magnificent? Aspects of it drew him in so far he felt a part of it. Either details stood out as he hadn't noticed anywhere else, or he was entering a change in life that caused them to appear to. A few months ago, he'd passed the age of no return: thirty. Obsolete. Anyway, retrograde. A whippersnapper grad student actually said, "You're getting so old, man, I'm not sure I can trust you." No matter where he drove on this peninsula he kept getting lost. It wasn't that he couldn't make out the forest from the trees, but often, as he examined the bark on a particular tree, spots of fungus of so many colors sprang into view that they merited translation or deciphering of a kind he couldn't explain. He was aware that he was coming as close as he would to the land as it once was. A sweet ache weakened his knees at this prospect, and his foot trembled on the accelerator.

He was afraid he would somehow reveal to Beau his tenure at that brokerage house, although all he did was take orders and put in a couple hundred phone calls a week. Which he had to interrupt whenever his overseer, a fifties Cornellian who wore a Phi Beta Kappa chain, shouted orders at him, always as offensively as he could. One day a client on the phone mentioned a stock and said, "What do you think?" and before Chris thought to cover the receiver to ask the Cornellian what he thought, which was procedure, he gave the client his opinion; he'd been investing and had a sizable portfolio, nothing compared to these people, but enough, and felt competent to give advice. A week later, the Cornellian stormed in and said that the customer, one of their best, stood to lose twenty grand on the bum tip Chris gave him without approval; then claimed he *did* lose it and started calling Chris an "upstart spick" and worse—but that was what stuck. "I'll have your ass!" the man yelled.

But Chris walked out, bearing it away without violence, when the Cornellian wasn't watching. During the drive home, he decided to go back to school and get his Ph.D. in the most humanitarian, honorable, and self-abnegating area of study he could hit on, the classics. Or maybe English. He had put enough aside to see them through three years, at a lower level than the one they were enjoying now, true, but Ellen would concur. She disliked the brokerage work and was beginning to act as disaffected as the crowd who had let loose a summer ago up near Woodstock. He'd noticed he was low on gas and pulled off the FDR into a line that looked a mile long—the beginning of the gasoline shortages that would get worse, but this was the worst he'd seen, and then he noticed a plump man in the car beside him twirling a finger for him to roll down his window. Chris pressed a button, and its blue glaze glided down on the sodden and tangy, oily-tasting air of Manhattan.

"Nice having AC on a day like this!" the man yelled. Chris smiled and tapped the steering wheel of their new car, the last they'd have; they now drove a rusted-out Renault that chuffed so badly he wasn't always sure it would make the hills in the hundred-blocks near campus—the reason Nana had insisted they borrow the bus, to spare her the shame of the Renault at the cabin. "What helps, too," the fat man said, leaning farther in his seat toward Chris, "is figuring those guys washing windshields up there, those pump jockeys, probably all got Ph.D.s!" There had been a story about this in a recent *Times*, and the man was laughing so hard he could hardly continue, but choked out, "Probably in English! Oh, God, *haw!*"

His window smothered his shaking laughter, and Chris smiled as his rose past his eyes like water drowning him. Whenever he looked up during the wait, the same fatso was grinning like a messenger of Satan, slapping his wheel as he laughed, and finally Chris punched up his favorite FM station and decided, Still, I'll do it.

He was aware of what to expect from the academy. When he was working on his master's in math, he became so obsessed with a problem in topology, he couldn't sleep, and one morning, as he drew Ellen closer, hoping her

heated body would pull him under, he saw through a series of Escher-like designs to a pattern so simple he knew
he had the solution to the four-color problem. He ran to
his thesis adviser, who listened to him for an hour with a
blank look, doodling on his desk blotter, and then suggested that Chris stick to the topic his committee had settled on: a theory of the pedagogy and methodology for
introducing topology to the lower grades. Chris went
home sunk, did his work, and two years later read that
the four-color problem that had baffled cartographers for
centuries had been solved by a pair of colleagues working
in tandem. One was his thesis adviser.

He shoved up in the seat of the bus. A troupe of vehicles
had traveled the road last night, from the tracks under the
snow. He could make it through. Or was it drifted neck-
deep in the valley past the settlement? It wouldn't do to
have to seek Henderson's help, with nobody along to push
or serve as character witnesses, as it were.

He noticed the rosary on the dash, half its beads down
the defroster vent, and pulled it free. Der Alte wouldn't
touch such with a shockproof pole. Some employee must
have left it, perhaps the one who mislaid the jacket Chris
discovered under a seat and kept wearing. He shoved the
rosary into his pocket, reminded of his father, who was
devout, or was adjudged to be by local standards, but was
cruel. Or was to Chris, his only son—only child. His father
had a Blackfoot's pure complexion, a beard only on his
chin, and was Dutch, or this was what he claimed. *His*
father had traced the family to New Amsterdam—New
York, now that the Brits had had their way with it.

"Oh, we went to your ma's church a while," his father
once said, and shrugged, as if giving the only explanation necessary. Rock Creek was Chris's hometown, a

Wisconsin backwater with families so interrelated every relationship had the aura of incest. It supported an Indian mission that later became a church, then a chapel, and finally an antique shop deconsecrated by a pair of bearded gays. Chris's paternal grandfather was once well-to-do, so Chris's father claimed, with hardware stores from lower Wisconsin into Michigan, but Chris had never glimpsed him or his beneficence; he'd died before Chris was born.

"Heartbreak," his father said, and stared at Chris's mother across the room with a mellowness that seemed to blame her. "He cut me off and gave it to his brother, who ran it in the ground. One of his sons was that dumb-ass uncle you stayed with the summer I was sick."

The words arrived with such precision that Chris felt the whiskey, in a fresh wash far away below his consciousness, spread brimming tears over his eyelashes as if he'd been slapped. He often had and was often accused of untruthfulness. "Don't lie!" his father would shout. "Don't lie to me and don't lie to your mother! Don't even try! I won't stand for it!"

After that, the company of women became so necessary he was sure Ellen despised him for it. Before he met her, he was connected with a dozen others, mostly for sanitary reasons, as a professor who disapproved of his promiscuity put it. Chris never made any promises, as if to keep the relationships at the level of his need, and if one grew too demanding, he disentangled himself and turned in another direction, always ascending, it felt. It was the lowest side of shadowy cowardice to lay the blame elsewhere by employing Freudian terms. He was responsible. All he'd lived for was women, and once he'd met Ellen, all he lived for was her, until she seemed merely grateful. But she didn't take his decision to return to graduate school well; a fool's trek. As a graduate assistant, he had to over-see bonehead composition courses, after a couple of which, if you could look at a sloppily typed page without gagging, as one wag in the department put it, you had a vocation.

Only two women, from what he'd heard, thought they were ill used. "You can't do this to me!" one cried. "I won't let you!" She was young; the women usually at-tracted to him were older, often nurses, and one who kept him for months called his looks "primitive Cro-Magnon"—to evade his true identity, he later decided. But this young woman, whose name was Michelle, was an authentic screaming hysteric, once wound up, and he didn't have the grace to know how to handle hysteria. It had the same effect on him as his father.

Michelle once appeared at the campus theater, where he was working props, just as he stepped into the lobby with an elegant actress who had been holding forth on Schopenhauer in the greenroom and then had asked him out for a drink, and he was always willing to listen to any philosophy. "You can't do this!" Michelle cried. "I'm a human being! I deserve you as much as her!" When he claimed they were merely going for a beer, Michelle said, "What do you *mean*? We've been dating for months! You were at my place last week! You were in my *bed!*" The actress, who was as hard as nails and a head taller, said, "Oh, go home and dry your ears." She gave the girl a shove, and Michelle attacked her with such fury he had to restrain her—dark hair spilling from her stocking cap over his arms as he held her pinned. Theatergoers gath-ered in the lobby, aghast, and the actress finally exited out the swinging doors. "You'll never hear the end of this!" Michelle assured her audience. "I'll kill the bitch!" When

Chris was finally able to subdue her and started after the actress, Michelle kept at his side, jerking at his jacket, yelling, "Don't you dare go near her! Don't you do this to me!" So he stood and watched as the actress took off in a miler's strides down the dark street, and never saw her again.

He fumbled for the cigarette pack in his pocket, under the rosary he'd stuffed there. He couldn't remember when he'd had a smoke, this morning or late last night. He hadn't had one with Beau, and he'd left that pack on Beau's table, since Beau wouldn't buy tailor-mades. He rolled his own.

I might as well quit, Chris thought. If it doesn't mean any more to me than that, I must be ready. He cranked down his window and gave the pack a toss, trying not to register where it hit. Then regretted the act. In the last year, he'd become a revolutionized ecologist, along with Ellen. He wouldn't toss as much as the cellophane strip from a pack out a car, and he and Ellen carried used paper bags to the store and loaded up their groceries themselves, saying, "Save a tree." They avoided products in expensive packaging and separated their garbage into containers of aluminum, tin, and three hues of glass. They buried organic garbage around a tree in the yard of their apartment building, and he had cardboard boxes filled with envelopes he intended to turn inside out and reuse for his own mail. They wouldn't buy stationery that wasn't recycled, though it was gritty and gave off an odor that made him wonder about chemicals in the recycling process. Animals were of equal worth to certain human beings; endangered species worth more—the earth a continuum of living tissue akin to God.

His breath was fuming so much he felt he had to suck

up a cigarette's heat. A kind of sovereignty of separate rights had come into effect: Whatever anybody wanted most was valid. He hadn't seen the potential holes in this until one of the group of graduate students who met to play softball decided he most wanted another student's wife. The wife was willing to acquiesce, and her husband, silenced by their rights, left before the semester was up.

Chris popped open the door and slid out. The pack was in a rut in the ditch, where somebody had missed the turnoff. He bent for it, feeling vulnerable, as if the tire tread might contain a clue to their prowler, and remembered his father saying, when they were deer hunting, that if it looks like somebody's shooting at you and you hear the shot, they missed. He got in the bus and backed in a spinning hurry from the road, and when he was a ways down the blacktop, near a granary with a rusted tin sign advertising hybrid seed corn—his landmark to the road that cut across to their blacktop—he thought, Sure, quit. He punched in the cigarette lighter and took his usual long way back home.

3

E LLEN WAS AT the cookstove in her nightgown, ladling through an iron pot, and Chris, just inside the door, eased his weight against it. He had parked the bus at the foot of the hill and walked up, and at the edge of the woods had seen snow-filled footprints, his and the prowler's from last night, and then a new set next to them, and knew he couldn't leave Ellen alone again.

"I was at Beau's," he said, out of breath.

"I thought you weren't getting along."

"Why would you think that?"

"He hasn't been up. He used to be here every day."

"We should get your grandpa to come."

"Grandpa?"

"For protection."

"He's in a wheelchair and can hardly talk!"

"Nothing terrifies people more than big bucks."

She plopped the ladle into a bowl on the stove and swung to him. "How about a global nuclear fry?"

"Peanuts. The people I worked for, their life and religion, their *identity*, was money. They'd face a hangman or the holocaust rather than pass up a good deal. Look how many took the leap in the thirties, or suicide now over the shame of being broke. There's nothing that affects people as much as money."

"So why don't we have some?"

"You're a nice person, and I'm a graduate student."

She ran a wrist over her forehead and held it there, squinting, as if studying him across a sparkling vista. "Are you all right?"

"Beau wasn't friendly." He looked down, wondering why he'd said this, and saw a furze of melting fringe across his snowmobile boots. "His usual morning mood—you know, like he's having his period."

"He's that way nine-tenths of every month!"

Chris placed a hand on the electric range, balancing himself to remove his boots, and drew back. Their first day here, after he'd got the electricity going, Ellen was sitting with her feet in the oven when there was a screech from the stove, then the hum of a high-voltage arc being struck as sparks sprayed from a burner. "Stand back!" he yelled, and a half-dozen mice scattered out of the stove. He shut off the juice and unplugged it, but a few days later the burner started to smell, so he removed it and found the skull of a mouse attached to a wire fried copper-green.

"I had to tell him about last night."

"I'm not exactly sure what happened myself," she said.

"The voyeur—that peeping snow queen!"

He looked down, trying to picture the moment, but could only see the form's furry correspondence with their woods; then its bulk, as if it had no legs, which led him to think of a bear. "Not his face," he said, and sensed an undertow of intuition drawing him toward her, as if they were about to touch. He looked up and found her studying

him. "Did you know the road behind the old orchard here
runs south, past an Indian settlement, to that curve in the
blacktop just before Beau's?"

"Of course, didn't you?"

"Of course, didn't you?" he repeated, jogging his head
in his mimicry, and heard his voice take the tone of a
mincing seamstress. "Sorry. No, I didn't."

"Beau's been coming here that way."

He assumed his surprise would suggest an explanation,
but she said, "I hope you didn't try it with the bus."

"I wouldn't think of trying it with that bus."

"So did native-boy Beauchamp have some sage advice?"

"Why don't you like him?"

"I'm not sure I don't."

She continued to stare evenly back, and the sensation of heat against his front, he realized, was from
the stove. How far did rights go?

"What should I do with the soup?" she asked.

"Eat it. *Woof!*" This bark, once out, he recognized as a
copy of Ivan's and was surprised to see her jump.

"All right," she said. "Set the table." She picked up the
ladle, gathering one side of her nightgown in the other
hand, and turned and thought, Now I'm hardly able to
ask a question without that look on his face like he'll fall
apart. This is about his thesis, I'm sure, which he could
finish in a week if he tried, but instead worries about
getting started—even worse since he got involved with
Beauchamp, and now he has to keep up, he has to! he
can't quit, not on this!—until he's starting to act like he's
seeing things, going around with that look that had me
so scared the first night here I figured I had to hold him
in the sleeping bag to keep his brains from falling out.
Well, I've about had it!

She slammed the ladle down and beet-colored soup bubbled in searing lines across the stovetop.

HE PICKED at the soup, chunks of potato stained red but only partly cooked, and thought they had to speak soon or spend their days guessing who the other was. Manners had brought their marriage to an impasse, a means of skirting the past: his women, her parents. He stared at the blurry plastic over the window behind her, where shadows of birch limbs gathered in shifting tines, and tried to imagine the dissertation finished. But at a place with so many duties and discomforts he hardly had time to think? There would be privacy, she'd said, but they'd already seen more people than they had over the last year. It was her wish to winter in the cabin, which she'd never done, that had really brought them here, and he suspected this had to do with her parents. Then he'd had to build bird feeders and suet cages before he could even start his dissertation; then the pump went.

"I liked the trip," he said, as if they'd just arrived.

"Mmmm," she said, as she had on the ferry.

They'd taken it across the lake from Milwaukee on Valentine's Day, through a storm so vicious the crew roped down everything that wasn't bolted in place. Below-decks, in a cabin of solid mahogany sadly battered, a place barely wide enough for them to stand between a sink and the bunks—upper and lower, like a kid's camp—they crawled into bed together, banging against the walls and the bunk above from the force of the gale, and managed the valentine she'd promised by clinging to each other as the ferry threw them into a violence of motion unlike anything they attained on their own. "Mmmm, I never get seasick," she whispered in conclusion, striking a steel bulkhead, and as the storm got worse, he pulled on his pants and tottered down a passageway to the head and stood at a urinal that ran from his bare feet to his nose. For big guys, he thought, and at that moment a six-foot-five sailor dashed to the neighboring one, groaning as he unslung himself, and then they both went stumbling backward as if propelled by their streams and crashed through the doors of the stalls behind into a sitting position on the cans—if the sailor ended up like he did. "Remind me never to take night duty," the sailor said from next door, as if Chris could. "God's mad!" The storm seemed more a clangorous accident in progress than weather, and when Chris made it back to their cabin, Ellen was vomiting into a pillowcase she took to be a garbage bag.

He stirred at his soup and stared at her until she looked up. "Something's occurred to me."

"An idea for your thesis?" She had its name wrong again and smiled so eagerly he was shamed by his detachment.

"Well, in a way." He set his elbows on the table and swung off on another course, like Beau. "The main reason I can't get anything done—and I don't have much done, I'll admit—is because I've been trying to work at night, and that's when the distractions come. With the light staying longer, I ought to be able to get the wood and water in, and all the rest done before dark, after my own work."

"That's wonderful! Forget about everything else and start right now. I'll clear the dishes and take a nap."

"Well."

They turned toward a sound like rough-toothed gnawing that came from the hall, beyond the army blanket they'd hung up to help hold the heat in the kitchen: the telephone.

"Nana," he whispered, as if the old woman might hear.

Ellen strode across the kitchen through the blanket, and he carried their dishes to the sink—a rust-stained oblong enclosed in a wood frame painted green. There was no place for anything; stacks of crusted plates and bowls filled the sink. The woodbox was empty. He reached to remove the cover from the nearest cream can, and it rose off the floor, weightless. The can next to it, with CLAUSEN BROS. painted on its collar in purple-crimson nail polish, was empty, too. One of the brothers was Anna; or, rather, her husband was a brother but had died, and Anna had inherited his half of the partnership. The other was Orin, who was up on his skis last Sunday, in a sheepskin coat and fur cap, to see if Chris and Ellen wanted to go to church.

Which reminded Chris that Clausens attended church on Wednesday for a prayer meal, or whatever, and wanted them to get their water earlier, and today was Wednesday, already past noon. He lifted the stove lid and saw gray coals. He threw down the lid lifter and jerked open the refrigerator door: the six-pack. He ripped out a can as Ellen went on behind the blanket and downed it in four gulps, or wanted to. No, the wood first, he thought, and then Ellen stepped through the blanket looking dazed— had Der Alte died? She placed a hand on his sleeve and said, "It was Nana. Kitchum is coming over tomorrow to start putting in a new well."

"Terms were reached."

"Apparently it means drilling down three hundred feet or more. She's putting in a submersible! Part of the problem, she claims, was knowing where to put it."

"I thought down at the pump house."

"Oh, no." Ellen pointed in the direction of the army blanket. "There. Just beyond that corner of the cabin."

HE CUT WOOD to length at the trestle he'd built over their honeymoon summer, sawdust streaming in yellowy spray over violet snow. Beau had loaned him a saw—auxiliary number one, Beau called it, used only for rush orders. Beau cut and sold wood, and Chris, for the use of the saw, had let him cut up the brush that stood in piles down the center of the meadow—the old orchard trees, seasoned cherry they could have used, Ellen said. So now Chris had to take down old trees and deadfall from deep in the woods, cut it into lengths, and lug these to his trestle. Perhaps he'd have to adopt a night schedule, too, if a drill rig was running all day. He laid a log across the trestle, sliding the bar deep, and with a buck of the saw suffered an internal glimpse of blood soaked into the fresh snow.

He set the saw down, and its bar tipped into a bank, hissing and sending up an oily stench, and the clearing around the cabin brightened as sunlight angled through the treetops to where he stood. Then he saw somebody coming toward him along the edge of the woods, a young man, it looked, who stepped down the drive with the alacrity of a person on familiar ground, past the stunted fir and icebound spigot, toward the back door. This door opened, and Ellen stepped out, an empty cream can in each hand, and stopped at the sight of the boy, blocking Chris's only quick route to the rifle. He grabbed up the chain saw.

"Hey," he said, to let the young man, an Indian who didn't look over fifteen, know he was there.

"Yeah," the boy said, and walked past Ellen without

acknowledging her, through snow whose surface was taking on a mirror's shine in the light, up to Chris—a rocky
little fellow with an Arab look and one eye half-crossed,
his hair sleeked back in a pompadour. He shoved his fingertips into his pockets, below a jeans jacket, and said,
"Some help?"

"What?" Chris asked.

"Cut you some wood or something, Beau said. Me and
Beau's tight." There was no pleasure or humor in this.

"He told you to come and help me?"

"A week or two ago—more, maybe—he said something.
I thought about it."

Chris glanced at Ellen and saw her slowly set the cream
cans down in the snow. "School isn't out, is it?"

"School's for peckerheads to learn white ways."

This sounded like a lesson learned from Beau, and drew
Chris's attention to the boy's head: stunted, with a narrow
forehead and hair recently trimmed at its edges with a
razor; there was a cut above one ear where a black bead
of blood had congealed. "All I got's this," Chris said, ro-
tating the bar of the saw toward the boy, and was
ashamed; what he meant was most of the Indians he saw
cutting wood outside their shacks used a bucksaw.

"Yeah," the boy said, "Beau's. I used it lots."

Chris felt worse that the boy had sensed his meaning,
and shifted the saw to his left hand, going for the pocket
where his cigarettes usually were. A purring sear came
past his face, and a lit farmer's match, produced from
behind the boy's ear and ignited with a thumbnail in the
downswing of a dagger thrower, burned in front of his
lips. "Always ready, babe," the boy informed Chris.

"I'm out," Chris said, meaning out of cigarettes.
"You're from one of the houses down the road there,
right?"

"Those are scalawags. I live on down the blacktop, past the curve before Beau's, on the right in those woods."

Chris had never noticed a house there. "You walked all this way?"

"A mile, about." The boy shrugged, then said, "Oh," as if he'd remembered, "I'm Gaylin." He placed a hand over his jacket and for the first time smiled, revealing steel caps over his eyeteeth. "Beau's buddy." He extended a hand.

Chris bit off his glove, braced for mischief, and gripped a hand so warm it was damp. "Chris," he said.

"Yeah, I saw you once. I was a kid, walking down the beach here. You and your woman"—he didn't glance at Ellen—"were down in a hollow by this dune, humping."

Chris looked at her, and she stared away, a flush climbing her cheeks. "Gaylin, I don't have dough to pay you."

Gaylin raised a shoulder and rolled his head over it, a kind of shrug that indicated money wasn't the point.

"I need the exercise," Chris explained.

"Good," Gaylin said. He turned away and went up the other side of the drive, away from the cabin, toward the road that ran south. He was past the fir before Chris realized the interview was over. He watched Ellen pull off her mittens—the green ones she wore to Clausens' rather than for working—with a deliberation that suggested she meant to throw them on the ground. Was she that offended, he wondered, or did she have it in her, consciously or unconsciously, to issue Gaylin a challenge?

Gaylin was now nearly out of sight; only his shoulders and pompadour bobbed along the brush. He probably figured he'd done his duty, as he perceived it, and would report to Beau that Chris was such a wooden-hearted peckerhead he didn't stand a chance. Ellen hadn't looked up, so Chris grabbed the saw and said, "Well, do you think we can get through the interruption of getting water without getting interrupted?"

ANNA INSISTED they use a spigot in her entry. "It's still too cold for you dears," she said, referring to their first night here. Orin always directed them over to the hand pump near the barn for their water, and though they were late arriving with the cream cans, Chris started to help Anna clear a way to the spigot.

"Ya," Orin said in the doorway to the house, his hands beneath his overalls bib. "There's one there."

Clothes were piled over other cream cans—Orin didn't milk anymore but had pigs in every building—among cartons of canned goods and fruit and implement parts. Chris went at it with his head down, used to all the clothes needed on a farm: the layers to work outdoors in different seasons, the changes for machinery repairs or working stock, besides clothes for town—though some farmers became unconscious of themselves and walked into a store ragged and unshaved and grease stained, smelling of manure. Chris held such farmers in contempt, and finally farmers as a class, once he got to school. In the five years his father had farmed, Chris couldn't remember a day when his father hadn't been frustrated or furious, and once Chris looked out a window to see his father going at a tractor that had broken down in the field with a crowbar. His father started back to the house, and Chris hid upstairs, to escape the wrath that at these times was like a torch over him, and heard his father say from the kitchen in a quiet voice, "I quit."

Anna and Ellen moved into the kitchen, talking about

the terrible weather the night they arrived, and Chris pictured the clusters of flakes adhering to the hull of the ferry as railroad cars emerged from its maw into a gauze of snow—wheels shrieking under the tonnage—and then their Volks bus descending a set of switchbacks and stopping where they stood, the driver getting out and rising along with other drivers, sailors from the ferry, on an elevator of sorts, a revolving chain with footholds, up into snow that engulfed them before they reached the walkway to the deck above, where cars were parked.

The snow fell as fast and thick during their drive, and the temperature dropped so quickly he was sure the heater had died. When they finally slogged up the hill to the lodge through drifts thigh-deep, their faces turning so stiff it seemed the rattle of the bag of groceries he was carrying was his skin, the thermometer in the main room read twenty below. The only wood he could find was in a bark carrier in the main room—a few sticks Nana might call logs. He coaxed up flames in the fireplace, but the draft only drew a deeper chill through the room. They both squeezed into a sleeping bag on a couch in front of the dying fire, their clothes still on, and he lay stricken with the fear that they'd be found in this posture a week later, frozen to death. If it was true the dissertation had put them in this fix, and if the dissertation were a man, he'd shoot it.

"Isn't that right, Chris," Ellen said now.

"Uh . . ." He had kicked over a carton of cherry juice and was restacking the cans. "Six," he said, and realized he'd been counting each one, so thick tongued with thirst at the thought of that night that the word arrived in his worst Wisconsin accent, as "sex." "I mean, I guess."

"No, ho-ho-ho," Orin said. "The boose."

"This?" Chris held a can over his shoulder without turning. "The label says cherry juice."

"No, ho, in you."

"I was just saying how grateful we were" came from the kitchen; it was Ellen, still trying to connect with him. "I was terrified we'd freeze."

This was news to him and the reason, apparently, she gripped him so tightly she scared him even worse.

"Well!" Anna sang in emphatic concision. "I had thought I'd seen headlights go by and not return, so when I woke next morning and saw that red thing parked across your lane, I said to him here at breakfast, 'I'm afraid we have an accident! Or unexpected visitors! You go on up to that cabin and look!' I meant vandals or worse, seeing how this generation carries on. So when it was you, dear, the only proper thing was to invite you down, at least till the weather broke. I still think of you two as honeymooners!"

"Yes," Chris said, and realized that what he'd found under a blanket-lined coat was a half-eaten apple, now dried. "That was thoughtful of you."

Orin had skied up just as the wind caught a sheet of plastic Chris was trying to fasten over the windows and carried it like a kite past the bluff, high over the lake, and in the midst of his amusement Orin managed to suggest that they might come down and warm up. Anna insisted they stay, and Chris overheated himself so much at their androgynous kitchen god—half cookstove, half electric range—he felt in a swoon, and then Anna conducted them to a side room where she stood at a door with her hands clasped at her breasts, over her heavy cardigan, as if to contain herself in the way the heavy braids coiled around her skull seemed to contain her, and announced, "Here is our bathroom. I was at wit's end to know how to persuade him to install it, after all these years, when this fall I said, 'What if the weather turns bad and your *lawyer* has to stay over.' He's been working on his will now for a year. So you may bathe, dears." It was the hottest bath Chris had had, and as he soaked to a thaw, he thought that to live with somebody in the same house and be so alienated you couldn't even refer to each other by name was—what? A worse affliction than he could imagine.

"Ya," Orin said, and Chris, nearing the spigot, could picture Orin's lips twitching back from his gold-inlaid front teeth in his peculiar smile. "Ya, that Indian that was here, too, you know, he's the kind to watch for. He was— Well, he worked for us years back, a real corker, you bet!" Orin clucked his tongue, and his gray head, with tufts of hair sprung at every angle from the most recently removed of his many caps, continued to wag. "No, now in the hay-mow and silo still, you know, I dig up these bottles. Boose."

Have you found one here? Chris was tempted to ask.

"That young fella, though, Gaylin, he did some picking for us last fall, our cherries south, and I don't know!"

Chris straightened to face Orin, who was once more shaking his head, with the skin under his jaw in a pinch between forefinger and thumb; then he nailed Chris through his metal-rimmed glasses. "Him I'd hire. That Beauchamp that keeps coming up, though, him I'd tell— I'd say, 'Git!' "

Chris turned to Ellen to see how she translated this, but she was trying to take in something Anna was saying.

"Gracious!" Anna cried, and clapped her hands like a

child, then drew them clasped to her lips. "Look at that! How good of you, dear. Bless you!"

Chris looked around to where the rest of them were looking and saw that he had not only cleared the way to the spigot but had set the entire entry in order.

THEY WERE finishing dinner, a roulade of beef she had marinated and cooked on the stovetop with hot peppers and carrots, when he said, "There's a light."

"A light?"

"Over the treetops behind you—a pair of headlights, maybe." He went through the porch, working the rattly latch of the outside door, into cold that reminded him of last night. The rifle. He could hear her clearing dishes inside and then faintly, far below, a sound of voices, several it seemed, whispering with intensity. He went back into the kitchen and said, "I think it's the kids. Do you want to hide in the other room?"

"It's too damn cold!" She stood at the cookstove and rubbed her upper arms at the thought. He shut off every light but the yellow bulbs between the dining-wing windows, then propped an elbow on the refrigerator and rested his head against that hand as if his head would otherwise fall off. Heat from the cookstove climbed his back, and he considered going for the rifle when he heard the voice of Marty Sturgis, ringleader of the group, intone something the others found funny, from the clamor of laughter. Then such a loud rap rattled the back door that its latch, which he'd forgotten to lock, clacked and hawked like an adult with whooping cough.

He went through the porch door, jerked the other open, and said through the screen, "All right, what's up?"

"Ah, we're kind of in trouble," Marty said, and the others—the fat Anfinson kid among them—scattered farther back. "Philip and Carlyle said we should come up. They tried to buy for us, and that dink wouldn't let 'em. Hey, I know you said don't bother you, but Philip and Carlyle, they said, 'Go see the man on the bluffs.' "

"I'd say you've had a bit already, Marty."

Laughter started up from the group, but at Marty's look it stopped. There were five altogether.

"Look," Marty said, "tomorrow I'm twenty-one and won't bother you no more, but see, Bobby's brother here"—nodding at Fat Anfinson—"he's getting off tomorrow, and Bobby said we'd pick him up and have a case with us, and now the dink won't sell to Philip or Carlyle. It's straight-out prejudice!"

Chris flipped the switch beside the door, and hands rose and heads bowed as they blinked against the bulb overhead.

"Hey, baby, we're cold, huh?" Fat Anfinson said, and hugged himself in his thin, shiny jacket. "Mama!"

"We lef our car down below so we dint bover you." This was a tall one Chris had never seen before.

He opened the screen door, and they trooped past, reeking of beer, into the kitchen, and he almost ran into them where they huddled inside in yellow light, as if struck dumb at the sight of Ellen. She was still at the stove.

"Hey!" Marty said. "You're starting a creamery!"

Chris had attempted the hill with the bus because they were carrying four extra cans from Clausens' but spun out near the top and had to carry all six from there, and now they were lined beside the sink, like a palisade between the group and Ellen. Chris turned on the lights and gestured at the table, in a dining ell off the kitchen. "Sit."

They took every available seat, including his piano stool, filling the wing so full its log walls appeared to bow out, and Chris leaned a hip on the burned-out range.

"Would anybody like some coffee?" Ellen asked from the cookstove, arms still crossed, studying him in anger.

"Coffee?" somebody asked, and more laughter went up.

"Look, you guys," Chris said, "I've tried to be nice, but I told you last time, this is it."

"Tell you what," Fat Anfinson said from a corner, and shoved up his glasses with a thumb. "How about ten bucks?"

"Have I ever asked for money? That's not the point."

"I gotta have this," Anfinson said. "My brother."

"Hey," Marty said, "we were telling Lonnie here"—he punched the tall boy, who seemed to be suffering worst from the beer, on the shoulder—"we were telling him about that stuff you used to read to us."

The first few times they'd visited, when Chris had had a bit to drink himself (the reason he was in this situation, Ellen insisted), he figured he might as well radicalize the young while he had a chance, and read from Vine Deloria. They responded first with huffs of agreement, then cheers and *amens*. "I don't have time tonight. I have to work. Here." He indicated the table and his typewriter.

"I thought it was on that book." This was Anfinson, who usually sat silent, his bland face blank, waiting out the time until the beer arrived.

"Not Deloria's." What view did he have of books? "It's more like one of my own."

Marty said, "I liked that part where Vine said whites shouldn't feel guilty about their granddads killing off all those Indians, because they were doing worse now." He jerked his head to the rest, and they laughed at this communal joke on Marty's cue. He was a witty little fellow, the one to be contended with, and Chris's favorite, for his foxiness—always dressed in gray twills, starched and pressed, never even a jacket, only the matching cap that bore the name of his father's orchard operation, his horn-rimmed glasses giving his lively eyes a mock-professorial earnestness. He had delicate Chippewa features and knew the precise angle at which to cock his cap to set his face apart, in no camp but his own.

"So are you working now?" Anfinson asked.

"I was," Chris said. Then remembered their dinner was interrupted. "I was about to."

"Maybe we should go." This was a retreating sort who looked like Marty's older brother, and his remark got him a scowl.

"Your reading made me think," Marty said. "This stuff didn't bother me till I heard old Vine. I had this teacher in seventh grade, pretty hot stuff." A cheer went up. "I mean, she thought she was, the way she handled us and the migrant-worker kids. She kept saying to me, 'Marty, you could do better.' I was getting into trouble a lot."

"You bet," somebody said, to Yeah!s of agreement.

"She kept me after school once and gave her could-do-better speech. She said, 'You Chippewas are impetuous, I know, but I expect more from you, Marty.' Dig! I should have said, 'Hey, it's Marty, see?' " He placed his hands, crossed, over his chest. " 'I'm this one person, not a gob of Chippewas.' "

"What's wrong with Chippewas?" Anfinson asked, drawing back from the table and thumbing his glasses up.

"Hell," Marty said, and seemed to give up, tracing the grain of the table with a thumbnail that looked manicured. "Nothing, as long as they got a little Ottawa in them so they got some sense."

They all laughed except Anfinson and the tall one,

Lonnie, who had a fringe of straggly hair at the base of his chin that must be a beard.

"I'm sorry, guys," Chris said. "I can't do it."

"Are you chicken?" Anfinson asked, and Chris felt them all bristle at this.

"Concerned. You guys've had some."

"Says who?" a voice asked, again in a threat, and Chris couldn't decide if it was Anfinson or Lonnie.

"There's this," Chris said. He set the six-pack from the refrigerator on the table, and they drew back and stared at it from the corners of their eyes, offended.

"Read us something, then," Marty said, and gave a faint smile, looking betrayed. Chris considered a book he'd found in the local library, *The Report of the Commissioner of Indian Affairs, for the Year 1856.* In it, he'd discovered that an agent and a superintendent of farming for the Sioux had been fired by the commissioner for presenting the Indians' grievances: the government was withholding money and materials owed to the Sioux.

"I don't want buffalo bull with no dessert," Anfinson said. "My brother'll whip shit out of me." He got up and shoved past Chris as if he'd like to shove him down, and two of the others got up and followed him out. The tall one beside Marty, groggily confused, said, "Dint you say we left our car down dere so we dint bover him?"

Marty nodded, and when he rose, the initiate was on his feet, a head taller, swaying as though he might go backward through the windows, and Chris realized the boy was under Marty's control and would do whatever he wanted. "Calm down, Lonnie," Marty whispered. "His wife's here."

Chris wanted to say, You mean you're sparing me because of her, but said, "What's this about Anfinson's brother?"

"They're letting him out down at Pontiac tomorrow."

"I heard that, but out of what?"

"Jail. He's in for assault."

"Assault!"

"He's crazy half the time. But this was prejudice, see, according to Bobby." He gave Chris an aggrieved glance. "Anyhow, they're letting him out." He shrugged.

"You mean you expect to drive to Pontiac and pick him up, with a case of beer in back, in the shape you're in?"

Marty shoved his hands in his pockets and looked up at Chris directly, his face set, and said, "I won't hold it against you, brother."

4

BLANK DARK, A WARNING of more snow, and Ellen in bed. He eased to the end of the dining wing, barely able to get by the table with its four chairs shoved beneath, and stood at the window facing south. Tall and almost as wide as the windows in the side walls, it rose from the logs at his knees past his head, and within its multiple panes a pearly permutation of his face flared and developed folds as the plastic he'd fastened outside shifted with the breathing wind. At night the plastic was translucent, and even at noonday its milkiness dimmed every view, which was why he'd stopped his winterizing with the wing. This end of it was too far around the corner from the cookstove to keep warm, but he'd found an electric heater he kept trained at his feet, whirring now on the linoleum-resounding floor.

He sat at the side of the table, facing the windows that looked toward the lake, and opened his file folder, distracted by a reflection of his head projected across dozens of panes via the bulb above. He'd screwed it into the only fixture in the wing—a wooden reflector, suspended from a log chain, that had the appearance of an inverted salad bowl. His reflection was doubled by the windows behind him, he saw, and then sensed his back facing the woods where he'd followed the prowler. This window was inches from his back, and night cold radiated past the plastic and glass through his jacket.

He glanced over his shoulder. Huge icicles clung to the overhang like a wall of stalactites covering a cave's mouth, dully radiant from the bulb. His desk, a typewriter on a plank supported by fruit lugs, ran above the split-log sill of the window south and looked as he'd left it, books piled on each side of the typewriter, undisturbed.

Damned Castaneda. Though he considered Castaneda's writings about the Yaqui Indian Don Juan fabrications, he'd packed a Castaneda book in the box of essential texts he'd brought and was idly skimming it one night when he came across a passage in which Don Juan tells Castaneda that he'll never be able to concentrate until he's found his "spot," or particular patch of earth to work above. Don Juan says Castaneda has to get on the ground and when he finds it he'll know. Castaneda, who claims intellectual credentials, scoffs at this, and then one night . . .

That night Chris set the book aside, figuring everybody was exploring the fringe these days, and got down on his hands and knees and started crawling around the table, his head low, sensitive to the absurdity of this. Finally, he lay on his stomach with his face to the floor and closed his eyes. He moved slowly, snakelike, the table and chairs grating aside, trying to focus on the conjunction of his forehead with the linoleum, then on its connection to any-thing that might exist below, and got so tired he was about to lay his head on his arms and doze off when a blue spot appeared in his mind as if burning itself in place and then was gone. He raised his head, eyes wide, figuring he'd conjured this out of himself, but noted the spot. Then he went to the player piano in the main room and took its stool, a swivel stool with claw feet clasped over glass globes, and set it above the spot, where it stood now, its circular seat reflecting light, in front of the typewriter.

He'd set up his typewriter on the rigged desk after this discovery so he could reach it from the piano stool, but now, when he wanted to type, he had to fold down the leaf at that end of the table for room. First that phrase to fix—"and so we see him then in his deepening age altering 'I'll be an Indian. / Iroquois' to 'Ogalala.' " He pulled a copy of Roethke's collected poems off his shelf to check the quote. It didn't appear at the end of "The Far Field," which he'd turned to, but at the close of an earlier poem, "The Longing." The print in the unwieldly book looked skimpy and artificial, like a photocopy disintegrating under his eyes as he read

> *Old men should be explorers?*
> *I'll be an Indian.*
> *Ogalala?*
> *Iroquois.*

and thought, Now what's this? He grabbed *The Far Field*, Roethke's last book before the collected poems were put together by Roethke's young wife after he died, turned to "The Longing," and found the ending as he expected:

> *Old men should be explorers?*
> *I'll be an Indian.*
> *Iroquois.*

Where was it he'd seen "Ogalala" substituted for "Iroquois"—in that privately printed book dating from the time of this one? He didn't even look for it. He hadn't brought it; it was too expensive, he'd thought at the time, turning it like a lock of hair in his hands in their bedroom the night before they left, Ellen asleep below in the dim light of a gooseneck over their featherbed. And it was on this exact point his thesis hinged! He hadn't mentioned the point to any of the professors on his committee, suspecting their response, though thinner things had been hung out for inspection and turned up sheepskin.

He let the book fall. And now? He was nearing the middle of his introduction, preparing to state the ground for this thesis. Roethke's question was of course a crack at Eliot, who intoned near the end of one of the Quartets, "Old men ought to be explorers." You could practically hear his porridgy British accent. Roethke had the same distaste for Eliot, apparently, that Chris's father had for Frisian Dutch—"who go around like the pork of the county fair," his father would say, "with names like Enema." It was the direction that Roethke took from there that had led Chris down this route—not the Anglo-Catholic parsonage of Eliot, with its incense and tea and written-out prayers that precluded thought, not for Roethke, but back to the beginnings, to the real people, the two-leggeds: Iroquois first, and then, even better, Ogalala, the bitchiest branch of the Sioux. Crazy Horse!

Chris thought he saw a light and let his hearing extend into the woods he'd walked with the rifle last night. He turned, and one of the icicles, groaning with dripping weight, dropped and imbedded itself upright in the snow, a fence post. *Ogalala.* It was the natural progression in Roethke's work, if you noticed how, in his first book, published when he was thirty-some, he covered adolescence and young manhood and then in his next swung back to childhood, to his father's greenhouse, and began identifying so closely with plants that it started to seem, in "The Minimal" and "The Cycle" especially, when his point of view grew too fractured to trace, he might disappear.

Which he did, in a sense, in "Lost Son," entering the infantile babble of a child trying to fit words to the world. This was picked up in the next book, more artfully but so far from rational sense that the controlling consciousness of an adult was gone, and that's how his next book began. But in the midst of it, with the turn of a page, he breaks into a seriocomic parody of Yeats and finally ends the book, *The Waking*, with music as clangorous as Yeats himself.

The next, *Words for the Wind*, is a search all over the place for what to do, which Roethke at last seems to locate in "Meditations of an Old Woman." But the book after that is nursery rhymes, disappointing, except that they aren't nice—probably attempts over the years at a form that didn't quite work, which Roethke decided to get between covers in order to move to the book that all of this was leading to, his last, *The Far Field*; and in its opening poem he says he doesn't want to take fogy Eliot's easy route but the right one: I'll be an Indian. Ogalala. Back with the four winds busy in their original rearrangements.

And now this read "Ogalala? / Iroquois." Damn.

There was the sound of somebody knocking, and Chris was on his feet, the chair banging against the windowsill. No, a sudden rattling of the plastic. The imbedded icicle leaned, a stream impaled, and gave sideways as he sat.

It was touch and go enough to be able to do what he wanted without misreading. This was his life now! He'd waited as long as he had only because Roethke's literary stock wasn't rising. Roethke hadn't been canonized in the manner of T.S., and whenever Chris brought him up to a professor, to test the waters, as it were, he got evasive looks. Which might merely mean the professors hadn't read Roethke (this was best not to pursue), and then his dissertation director was bumped up to dean of the college, out of reach, until Lowell's *Near the Ocean*. Chris called and made an appointment—for this afternoon, he said, and the dean said it had been a while but all right. On his way over, Chris stopped to see the stodgiest member on his committee, a man in Early Americana who once told Chris he'd never been able to "internalize" Jonathan Edwards or Cotton Mather until he'd "backpedaled" and read Luther and Calvin and Hus and Knox—"the whole schmear"—and now at Chris's news he said, "It looks like you're going to have to research the entire Reformation before you'll really understand the Puritan influence on the American Indian. You'll have to read Luther and Calvin and Hus and . . ."

So he had one on his side. But he was late for his appointment, and his dissertation director, or dean, the one with the real clout, sat poring over papers, head down, for such a stretch Chris felt he was being punished for more than mere tardiness, and then the dean looked up, level with him in the chair he'd taken in front of her desk, and said, "Did you arrange this appointment, or did I?"

"I." He swallowed a lump like lignite.

"Chris!" she said, setting down her glasses. "I recognized your urgency but didn't connect it with your face. It's you, dear! Where have you bean!"

His grin felt gap-toothed, goony. "Studying."

"How you've changed!"

So she did remember him. "Well, I've, uh, I've—"

"Spit it out, this is confessional season across the continent, dear!"

"In Lowell's most recent volume of poetry"—he held it

up—"there's an entire poem dedicated to Ted Roethke."
He had decided he would make this chummy. "And I—"

"Isn't Lowell the one that hung out with Gene
McCarthy?"

"Right."

"Good man!"

Which of the two she meant, he didn't know, but said,
"I always had a kind of interest in Roethke, since you
steered me toward Twentieth Century, and it seems to me
that with the approbation of a poet like Lowell, he
would—"

"Didn't one of those guys get a Nobel?"

"Both received the Pulitzer Prize, I believe."

"Busy at your research, I see. You know, Chris, I'm
going to confide in you." She was heartily heavyset, and
as she leaned toward him, her breasts broadened over the
papers on her desk. "This summer at the Cape I read that
new book *Jaws*, for the buzz factor, you know, the sheer
pleasure of a page turner, and I thought, Where do these
littérateurs get off with boring us to death! My tolerance
for that stuff's kaput. Why be ashamed of *Jaws*, by God,
I thought, when it's the best damn thing I've read in years!
I recommend it. Read it!"

"Have you seen Roethke's Saginaw poem or 'Gob
Song'?"

" 'Gob Song' sounds great. Do it!"

"You mean the dissertation on him?"

"Do it!"

He got up to leave before she had a chance to change
her mind, and she said, "And let's start a new tradition
with this one: under two hundred pages—fast-paced!"

"Great," he said, going for the door, but she pushed
up from her desk and came and put a hand on his
shoulder; she did remember the night they met, years

back. "Chris," she said, "I know it hasn't been easy for you here, so"—she swung one hand in an uppercut and held her fist at his chin, shaking it—"sock it to me!" Then she unfurled her fingers and tapped his cheek in a powdery touch. "Okay, sweetie?"

He stepped to the window again, sure he'd seen a light, and placed a knee on the piano stool and leaned forward to see past the plastic. The most potent dreamers trip on morning light like a rug! But maybe his main point could move past this snag, because after Roethke's journey to his own interior and his young wife's, he enters the continent itself, driving so far inland it seems he won't be able to stop, until fragments like spray fly over the last pages, those hurried closing songs in the sequence sometimes metaphysical, as Roethke calls it, as he ends up against pure Spirit.

Then bring back Eliot, after his earlier catching it in the neck, to signify the dissertation's lack of prejudice, and the way the two arrive at approximately the same place, which Roethke is partly acknowledging in his allusion to Eliot—no matter whether the two could be in the same room without going at each other hammer and tongs. Would an Anglican strain of the hierarchical sort have been better for America's natives, and the continent itself, than the Puritanism that arrived? The Pilgrims viewed the natives as heathens but also held that view of Roman Catholics, which was the traditional Jewish view of the unwashed (the Americana professor had handed him a separate reading list he'd had to plow his way through), and the Pilgrims had lived outside England, in Holland, among the Dutch for so long they felt their children were being taken captive by an alien culture and had to get out for their sakes. The Covenant.

The Pilgrims were sent by financial speculators, not a

church, and arrived with a mix of others, convicts included. If you examined the influence of Catholicism, *pax Jesuitas*, as it traveled from Quebec to this area of Michigan, Roethke's home state, you might not put your money on Anglicanism. And the Spaniards were headed north, after decimating the best of South America, bearing their wooden saddles and gold and incense for Rome.

At this point he could work in references to another modern, Berryman, from his "Homage to Mistress Bradstreet," along with quotes from Bradstreet herself—a true poet whose father and husband both were governors of the Bay Colony. The British of the day nearly canonized Pocahontas, after she converted, of course, but it was hard to tell how they would have handled a household of brown brethren, considering their treatment of the Welsh and Irish. Not to mention native populations in every country under the Empire since—that Empire Brits still hungered after, unable to halt the falling away from the time of their original loss: America. The anti-Semitic side of Eliot, so surprising to intellectuals, nowadays, anyway, was congenial enough to the Anglican culture of his time. Eliot, of course, was an immigrant from St. Louis.

Dylan Thomas, a friend of Roethke's, and Welsh, from the first subdued native tribe in England, would probably serve as best commentator on Eliot, since his mildest name for him was "The Pope." Thomas was ruined by America, his wife maintained, tempted to it by money and, once here, sawed apart by lying praise—his native lyric talent gobbled up. Thomas became such an alcoholic randy during the stodgy fifties that stories of him were still current; when he spoke at the school Chris attended, he pursued faculty wives with such ferocity he had to be carried by four men back to his hotel, where he jumped up and down on the bed like a child, naked, yelling, "I want a girl, I want a girlie student *now*!" And maybe it was in Thomas that Chris's thesis was embodied, since the source of the real problem, as it was beginning to emerge for him, was—

The window at his face went flying in all directions, poised in the air a second by his inability to accept this, and then he heard the connecting wallop and went for the floor. He'd knocked over the piano stool and lay panting above his spot. He started in the direction of the rifle, contemplating a crawl or a sprint, when the noisy latch on the back door clacked, followed by a clumping slam from the porch, and as he rose, the kitchen door swung in, and a head, swathed in a plaid cap with the earflaps pulled down, swung in from the top of the frame and said, "Boo!"

There was a busy clatter—Ivan's claws on the boards as he hurried inside, wolflike and slinking, shedding snow, and went for the stove and dropped beside it, bone on board, *ka-lunk*. Chris was now able to see that the jagged lines on the plastic were radiating away from the point where a snowball had struck.

Beau stepped in, grinning, and slammed the door, his face in darkness above the wobbling lines of light from the agitated bowl. "Did I scare the brave?"

Chris attempted to manage his breathing.

"You got me started today, and I decided not to stop," Beau said, and Chris noticed a gloss to his eyes. "Too cold to work. I had a guest. I got a gift here."

He took a step toward the table; even meant to sit, it seemed—giving off a woodsy scent of fresh cold air from his ragged army jacket. Chris put a hand on the table, trembling, and something crystalline swung from Beau and came down beside his fingers with a slithering impact: a long plastic bag bulging with shrunken vegetables.

"Beau, do you know what the hell—"

"I know." He raised a hand, first two fingers up. "Forgive me this one time, okay?"

"One time!"

"See the dainties." Beau's grin wasn't constrained by qualms. "I knew you wouldn't want to miss out on this. The man only comes when he comes." Beau stepped to the chair across from Chris and sat, drawing the bag in front of him like brownies. "Mescalito, baby! Do you have a cigarette?"

"Beau, I've about had it. I mean—"

"I'm sorry, I said. You'd go for me in spades if I hid this on you. Sit."

"Is that Beau?" It was Ellen's voice, sleep soaked, from the other side of the boards behind the cookstove.

"Yes!" Chris yelled.

"Mmmmm," he heard, and went on, as much for her sake. "How many times have I told you—is this three or four or six times now? Don't bother me at night! I have to get this damn thing done. You didn't even knock!"

"I don't."

"That's the point! It's our place! I mean, it's the only place we've got. I came here to finish this!"

"We got different views on ownership. Didn't you walk in on me today?"

"I knocked. I saw you at the stove, but I knocked."

"Okay, I stood on the hill and saw you sitting here like a post, but waited awhile, anyway. Then you got up and went to the window, staring right at me, I don't know how long, so I thought you knew I was there."

"I'm tired of your excuses and games!"

"Excuses and games," Beau said, and stood, his face so high above the swinging light that it turned black.

"You should put on a dress and run backward!"

They set their feet as the bulb in the bowl swung like an interrogation lamp, and Chris could see Beau's eyes going over his face as if to choose the point to strike and then noticed the dinky dangle of braid coiling from under Beau's folded-down earflaps as Ellen called, "Come on, you guys!" and heard Beau's *hoogah* before he realized he was laughing, too. Beau was so loosened by whatever he'd had he couldn't stop, and Chris felt invaded by a heated rush that brought his imaginative construct of Roethke and the rest down in an avalanche.

"Hey!" Beau cried, "I believe that beautiful lady just saved your life!"

"Is that all it takes?" Chris asked.

"Keep it down, you guys!" Ellen pleaded.

Beau sat, sobered, the tautness in his face drawing up the corners of his eyes, then jerked off his cap and threw it in the corner, where the piano stool lay tipped. He sat with his head under the light, his braid bent up in the shape of a swan's neck. "You know, you're an irritant," he stated. "I'm sick of this."

"Likewise."

Beau looked up so quick that Chris added, lowering his voice, "I mean, the way you walk in when you know I've got this damn thing to do." The rustling peyote quieted him. "What if I did that to you every day, at your place?"

"It's not mine. I'm squatting."

"Oh, for God's sake," Chris said, and sat.

"A family had it, then their kids. The kids moved, but one of them down by Detroit still owns it. Nobody up in years."

"What does your dad think about this?"

"Interesting, he says. He's worked for enough whites, I figure he's fed up. I'm claiming the land as my allotment, and he says if it gets involved he'll help with a lawyer. He bought his place. We're owed this. He figures I should pay the John something for the buildings." Beau nodded with some private thought. "Let's try this truth serum and see if we really want to talk. Do you have a cigarette?"

Chris went across the kitchen to a narrow open cabinet, its top board coped in circles around the ceiling joists, and reached to the shelf where he stored his cigarettes to keep from grabbing one every ten minutes. They weren't there. A bottle of schnapps stood farther back, still capped, and he thought, *No*. He turned to where the wing joined the kitchen, the butts of notched logs intersecting in rough-hewn overlaps, and reached above a shelflike end bright with growth rings: his new cache. He tossed the pack onto the table and sat.

"Who's Gaylin?" he asked.

"One of the real ones. He lived with one of his dads till he was eight. He's with his granddad now, his mom's dad. I been trying to teach him since I got back, but I should leave him alone." Beau drew the zipper down the front of his jacket, parting it warily over a black T-shirt, as if he'd dressed up or down.

"He said you told him to come here and cut wood."

"He didn't say that."

Chris tried to recall, precisely, what Gaylin had said.

"I can't tell him what to do, he's past that, and I didn't tell him to come here and cut no wood." These slips arrived when Beau was relaxed but caused Chris such surprise, as now, his eyeballs bulged. "I mentioned you," Beau said. "If he wanted to help cut wood, it was his idea. Welcome."

"He specifically mentioned you."

"Don't you understand, man?" Beau put both fists to his chest and stomped them there. "The connection! He'd only see you through me!"

"He said he'd seen Ellen and me humping, as he put it—a real nice Sunday-school type."

"What's wrong if it's true?" Beau pulled a hunting knife from the sheath at his belt, his mouth set in amusement, and slid the tip of the blade into something like the shriveled butt end of a prickly pear with its thorns picked off. Its rind was the texture of skin on a scrotum, but lime green. He waved this at Chris from the end of the knife in a threat. "We'll talk," he said, plucking it loose, and began to shave off fine slices. His attentiveness precluded talk. He pared the slices into slivers, then picked one up on a wetted fingertip and placed it on the sprawl of his tongue. He took a cigarette from the pack and rolled its unfiltered end between his fingers, patted one of the slivers he'd cut in the green dust at the bottom of the bag—"The last of the herb," he said—and slipped the sliver into the loosened tobacco and lit up. He drew on it and then held the cigarette out in the fingertips of both hands, a pipe stem.

Chris took a pull, tasteless but for tobacco, and they passed it back and forth until it was down to the filter.

A trembling of relevance occurred to Chris, apparently related to the ghost-cloud of thought built around Roethke, and he said, "Down here among us groundlings, huh?"

"You better believe it, baby."

They were whispering, but Ivan woofed from the stove.

Chris turned to the window, so bright yellow it looked flooded with sun—reflections of the logs, he thought—and saw lines of water trickling from the clump of snow still stuck to the plastic. "What were you doing today?"

Beau shrugged. "Nothing cruel."

A tug at Chris's stomach suggested laughter, but he felt his face draw down in the gravitational lines of weeping.

"Do you see the old world much?" Beau asked.

Chris looked up. The mist of illumination that faces can project spread from Beau's until his features were enclosed in radiance in the vertical—a stone of shadow under the roll of his underlip, whorls and grooves rising from there to his nose, hewn from smoothness, with lines like knife cuts where his eyes rested, dazed, in a trembling fervor that seemed to melt the wisps of hair, missed by his braid, wrinkling out from his skull into the light.

"You mean the world Black Elk sees?" Chris asked.

"Half that book sounds whiteface to me."

"Transcribed."

"Um!" This signified agreement but was meant to urge Chris on.

"It's difficult to see that world."

"Some days I'm the agent's or missionary's boy, not a two-legged human."

"I almost saw it today, after I left your place. I pulled off the road, and my knees got like jelly."

"Mine, too."

"Lugging in water through the snow, the way we had to do tonight, smelling woodsmoke up ahead, I'm there. Or when I walk through the woods toward this place, I can sense my mother a few steps behind. That's enough, I figure. Isn't it?"

Beau shrugged, and the ends of his eyebrows rose as if extending into points of pain.

"Other times I'd kill to get back what they had," Chris added.

Beau whispered through a tangle of saliva that almost clotted his words, "I can dig it."

"My last year in high school I took French. It wasn't enough having a language separating me from them—here was another in Frog dialect. The teacher had been to Paris. She was big, six feet, with curly, chopped-off hair. She used to pose on the windowsill, hike her butt up on it and extend her legs, which were her nicest feature, as she knew, and cross and recross them and kind of rake the calf of one, real slow, over the other."

"I been there."

"Her hair was like nobody else's, black but reddish—dyed, I'm sure. Back then I figured a woman who dyed or bleached her hair was a whore. That naive. Native son of my parents. When this woman called on me, she'd say, 'Now listen to Chris's lovely accent. It's something I want you to shoot for.' Shoot for. I got my accent from imitating her, as everybody in class knew. My first taste of mass hatred."

"Ooo." Beau's eyes closed, and his lips pursed as this went down the scale. Ivan woofed. "What's that?" Beau asked, his head up and cocked toward the stove.

There was no further sound from Ivan.

"You can't imagine how she worked her lips for those French words while she posed. She was new, so they made her adviser for the annual, the worst job, because of the hours. She said I should be an editor, and since nobody wanted the job, I got elected. My girlfriend then—good scout, nice Christian girl—was another editor. At the end of the year we worked on pasteups one whole week, and then on Saturday the teacher called and said we had to review the last batch before we sent them off. She said she wasn't feeling well, and would it be all right with my parents if I brought them to her house—maybe she even asked if it'd be all right with my girl. I drove to her place, a mile out in the country, and she came to the door in a bathrobe.

"She sat in a chair beside me on the couch, leaning over the coffee table where she put the pages, with nothing on under her bathrobe, as far as I could see. I figured she must really be ill. I mean, how else could she be so unaware of how she was practically baring herself? Then she'd take the collar of her robe and grip it to her neck, but that opened it lower when she bent. She moved to the couch, put the pages between us, and leaned over, then looked up and smiled, and I thought, I can't take this. I think I even vaguely considered trying to kiss her, which was all I'd tried with my girl. Poor her! I thought, knowing I had to get the hell out. It wasn't until later, not when I got home but after school was out and this teacher had moved someplace else, that I realized what she was up to. All I wanted was an hour with her."

"That's it?"

"I remembered that when she mentioned *apaches*, the French dancers, she gave me a wet look."

"The taste for a wild one!"

"She knew what she was up to."

"That ambigues."

"Ambigues?"

"Slides a couple ways at once."

"It wasn't so subtle then, or so I see now."

"You came to it the back way." Beau's laugh cracked through such an accumulation of saliva he had to clear his throat. "I'm not sure this is working. Have a sliver."

Chris placed one of the shavings on his tongue and felt a bitterness slide in tendrils down his throat, then swallowed.

"What does your wife think of you?" Beau asked.

"Ask her. Doesn't think about it, I guess. I'm sure she knows who my mother was. She never met her."

"A loss."

This caught Chris with his mouth open, and he had to bite back what felt like the cry of the leader of a drum. "Ellen was brought up Christian Scientist. Anybody who's been in that from the start has real power to 'deny the material,' as they put it—whatever they'd rather didn't exist. Some get so good at it they make sickness go away. There's the same kind of word magic in it as in animism. If who I am bothers her, she's denied it."

"How about her grandparents?"

"Oh." Chris felt himself descend into his worst entanglement of identity. That dark place.

"They must have said *some*thing," Beau insisted.

"Enough said."

"What was your mother like?"

Chris looked up and saw her striding into the aureole of light around Beau's face, her head lowered and her features hidden, a peasant in a smock, and behind her saw the sink where she always stood. "There if I wanted her."

"A squaw."

Chris winced as if her powdery alum had possession of his gums; she packed it over his canker sores. It was only in contempt that his father referred to her as a squaw. "She was religious, I mean, religion was real to her. She was my religion before I went to school—the Virgin Mary."

Beau put his head in his hands and appeared to knead it to size, then laid it on the table. "Oh, Mother!" he cried.

The windows squared and appeared to glide into Chris's sides at his shock. "Mother?" he got out.

Beau spread his arms, chin raised, as though at the edge of their bluff, darkness trembling at his edges. "Planet Earth!"

The watery aquasphere seen in satellite photographs, woven over with clouds, trembled across Chris's vision, and he said in alarm, "Beau, we don't own Asia, do we?"

"You know what I mean. *Her.* I have trouble with my own damn house. I'm paranoid."

"There are Africans. The Arabs. Are the families in Virginia related to Rolfe and Pocahontas of the tribe?"

"Once you go off the land, you're outside the line."

"You left."

"Not my country."

"There was integration by blood even at the beginning, both ways, and then every which way."

"Is that why every other person I meet can't wait to tell me he's quarter Cherokee?"

"Do you know a pureblood?"

"Only me."

"Beau, you're a racist!"

"I couldn't read till I was twenty. I knew the woods and animals first. I talked beaver and dog."

"How did you get to college?"

"Read two years straight. It twisted me. At school I took The Psychology and Sociology of Cultures—or close to that—you know, one of those courses where the John can teach anything that flies. I wanted to learn something, and heard the guy was funny, but he must've got tenure or had a substitute personality. His word was 'identity crisis.' I guess he read Erik Erikson that year, but Erikson at least lived with Indians—they gave him the idea of that crisis to begin with.

" 'Young people of college age are more susceptible to the identity crisis,' this John would say. Or, 'Perhaps the identity crisis so prevalent in youth today comes from all they have to integrate into their minds.' Nobody was integrating anything from him, I'd say. I got so sick of it I stood up in the middle of this lecture hall and said, 'Hey, man, you say identity crisis?' I was real hip then—another layer on the onion. 'Hey, man, I go through worse changes every day. I wake up thinking I'm a pineapple!' People laughed; they didn't know how it feels. 'And I never been to Hawaii,' I said. This was for an East Lansing type in the class who kept craning around, trying to grin at me, when the John lectured on customs in Samoa. She walked up afterward and said in that mealymouthed way dumb racists have, 'Are you from our newest state?' 'I only been to Alaska once,' I said, 'and it was so damn cold I run straight back. That's why us nomads let the Eskimos have it.' I thought those buck teeth fitted with braces would hit the floor. To spend my life mopping up stuff like that! Oogabooga!" Beau made pop eyes.

Chris was lying in a day in Los Angeles, in hazy August heat, back inside the summer he spent on a scholarship unearthed by a friendly professor. He had worked part-time on a shingling crew, setting shakes ahead of a Chicano who worked with a hatchet, and could run a peak or ridge roll like a racetrack rabbit. All the laborers on the crew, in that California culture more race conscious than any in the South, referred to him as Tex-Mex, and he let it go at that. Safe by misnaming.

He looked up and saw the yellow of the window deepen to California gold, and then something sparkled like a spiderweb across a log above. A gathering of miniature particles, insectlike in their strumming, fluttered there in unrest. They took on different colors as their activity speeded up, and he saw tinted currents travel across the space above the joists and lower in swirls into the room and realized that whatever made up the universe was turning visible. The butt ends of intersecting logs looked composed of cork, their age rings spinning around one another in opposing directions. He stared at the table, and streams of similar particles traveled under its surface like colored threads lacing through the weaving of a rug.

"Here, I think," he said, about to point.

"Say it!" Beau cried, waving widespread hands near his ears so they wagged like cartilaginous wings.

"Come on, you guys!" they heard in Ellen's voice, and studied each other with rapid, frightened eyes.

"What was I saying?" Chris whispered, hoarse.

"Nothing I didn't know."

"Those laborers' name for me hid me under what they thought I was more than I've ever tried to hide."

"I knew it!"

"Hold it down!" It was Ellen again, and Chris sensed that if she hadn't joined them yet, around the corner by the cookstove, she was on her way.

"Please, Beau!" he said.

"You, too," Ellen replied, closer, by her voice.

There was a clatter, and Ivan appeared around the corner with his hackles raised in a mane and his gums drawn over bared teeth as a growl started from so deep inside him he resounded. He stepped forward on tense legs, his flared nostrils parting his muzzle, and his stare turned them to the window. Below the point where the snow adhered, through streaks of water drooping in the form of a cape, there was a shadowy black face, with three yellow slits set in a triangle—eyes and mouth.

"Kachina!" Beau cried, and was up and over to the

refrigerator as sounds like gunshots deafened Chris. It was Ivan, barking, black lips back from his wolfish teeth as he edged in jerks of his planted legs toward the window.

The army blanket behind Beau swung aside, and Ellen stood at the fringe of light in her nightgown. "What is this!" she cried. "Are you two *sick*?"

Which seemed to catch Beau where he stood at the refrigerator, his face a lemon shade, one hand to his stomach. She stepped past him—not just in her nightgown; she'd pulled on a coat—to Chris. "Can you explain—" She swung back to Beau. "Get that damn dog to shut up!"

Beau looked draped across the air, suspended, staring at the window. "Kach— Ka—" he tried to say, and then cried, "Ive—*uh*!" Ivan's barking stopped.

Chris turned—the face was gone—then turned back to Ellen, her features so whitened they took his innards on a downhill slide. She was staring at the plastic bag on the table. "What's this, a pot party?" she asked in an even tone of contempt. "You're supposed to be working."

"There was somebody at the window," Chris said.

"Kachina!" Beau cried.

"Who's she?"

"Southwest god of the dead," Beau said.

"You're hallucinating!"

"We both saw a face," Chris said. "Would a dog bark at a hallucination? It was black, with three rings on it." He sketched these over his features.

"One of his cronies in a snowmobile mask," Ellen said.

Chris turned to Beau, whose eye sockets looked hollow. "Is it?" he asked.

"Did you check?" she asked.

"Check what?" Chris asked.

"If somebody is really out there—or who?"

"No," he said, and glanced at the window as she stepped closer.

"Well, why don't you?" she insisted.

He went past her to fetch the rifle, and she said, "Not with that gun!"

He turned to Beau, who wouldn't look at him.

"Please," she said.

They both went out. Musty smoke curled down the shingles with the odor of a fire going out. The dining wing was lit so brightly Chris could see, through the pearly plastic, the four upright rungs in the back of the chair he'd been using and on the table the shapeless bag beside his file folder. Then Ellen glided into view with a hand extended and picked up the bag. There was a hydraulic upheaval, like the sound of a primed pump releasing water in a gush, and he turned to see Beau with a hand on the trunk of a birch and a green liquid pouring from his open mouth. Chris shoved his tongue against his teeth and stepped to the end of the dining wing.

Just inside, bent over the bag she was revolving in her hand, Ellen stood in profile.

"Did you walk up to this window when you came?" Chris whispered to Beau.

Beau leaned farther forward from his handhold on the birch and shook his head. "Agh!" he cried, and drew curled fingers across his lips.

There was a trample of prints in the snow underneath the window. Then these moved, or the shadow over them did, and Chris looked up to see Ellen gone from the wing.

"I ain't well," Beau said.

Chris heard the faint sound of a car on the county road headed toward town, going fast. "See, I told you!"

"I have to go."

"It was somebody!" Chris said, to the air now, and at that moment Ivan shouldered through the screen door and took off up the drive over the hill, silent except for the sound of his paws on their packed trail.

"Keep the peyote, brother," Beau said. "I can't get like this."

Chris glanced at the window, then said in a quiet voice, "Is it okay if Ellen has some?"

"No, don't."

"If she wants it."

"You see what happens!"

"It was the same damn snooper from last night!"

"I'm going home," Beau said, and his "home" had new complexities of meaning now for Chris. Then a further turn occurred in him: "Do you want to stay overnight?"

"Here?" Beau asked, and stepped back from the streaks beneath the angled birch in a stagger. "There's some kind of sick shit going down at this place. I want out."

5

DARK, SHE THOUGHT, as she woke, her head buried. Not only under the covers but the pillow, too. She never slept like this. She couldn't bring herself to attempt to sleep without a window open, though he preferred not. Drafts, he said. But when the fire went out, her hair— now nearly the length she wanted—grew so cold it woke her up. She removed the hand looped among its snapping strands from her breast and pulled a hank so hard her head nodded. To *there*.

She freed her face and found it was still dark. No, he'd fastened the curtains, old drapes from one of her former bedrooms, over the windows—across the lakeside at her feet, and to her left, where he lay. A line of light from a parting in the curtains burned on the boards above him like a smoldering thought going straight up. He was turned away, his head wrenched back as if garroted. How was he able to sleep that way, with the rear of his head against his spine, throat so exposed? She patted his hair, nervous, then scissored a wisp between her fingers.

This year it had gone from chestnut to pure platinum, and when he visited a barber she could see the original color still, at his nape, in the core of each hair. Now it was too raggedly long, and she pictured him as an old man fastening up the drapes (with their ugly flowers that used to remind her of lions' heads) hook by hook along the rod.

Her nightgown was bunched to her neck. Had he? She was breathing so hard that columns went straight up, zero in here, the floor like ice every morning. Stepping on it set her ankles aching. She'd laid down rugs at the side of the bed but couldn't lay a trail from here to the cookstove, could she?

Oh, yes, Beau had been out, and— She slid from the covers and went on her rugs to the dresser beside the door, merely a gap in the logs with a muslin curtain across it, and pulled open the top dresser drawer. Under her nylons was the crumpled plastic bag with green buttons bulging inside. He hadn't asked for it last night. She eased the drawer shut and heard the growl of a big engine shifting down, like a snowplow climbing their hill, and ran into the closet at her side of the bed, pulling its curtain on a deeper darkness warmed by the cookstove on the other side of the wall. She jerked off her nightgown and leaned full front against the rough boards, grabbing a coat hook in each hand, for the warmth she could absorb.

Then she started dressing as fast as she could and was stepping into her shoes when a knock rattled the back door.

HE WOKE sitting poised, blankets in a hand ready to fling, then stood, setting in motion the ungodly drapes he'd hung to foil the peeper. He held still, unmoving, when he saw from a part in the drapes a wilder trampling of tracks under this window than the ones last night outside the dining wing.

"Chris!" Ellen called from the kitchen. "You're going to have to do something to help with these fellows here."

SHE KEPT smiling at them, all she could do. They stood beyond the screen (which Chris hadn't hooked, she saw), the older in rusty coveralls, the younger, whose lady-length blond hair was crowned by a pink stocking cap rolled like a foreskin, in a black snowmobile suit with zippers all over it at every angle. Their legs were planted as though the ground were tipping them in different directions, an illusion caused by the sun coming in a haze through the tree trunks at their backs—and maybe not an illusion, since the snow here was dug up and piled unevenly from shoveling, due to Chris's attempts to drive to the back door.

"Maybe you'd like some coffee," she offered.

"We had some," the older man, Kitchum, said, before the other could respond. Kitchum was angry. Over his shoulder she saw the cab of an ancient truck brown-nosing above the crest of the hill. It was stuck.

"We have plenty of water," she said, and realized her reference to the origin of their problems was not nice. Kitchum spat, a quick jabbing action that set a streak of tan beside a sulfurous crater in the snow, with anxious squiggles leading to it like a fuse, where Chris had re-lieved himself instead of walking into the woods, as she'd asked—unreliable even in this when he was wound up in his work. "We hauled some yesterday."

The young man grinned and withdrew a hand, un-gloved, from a zippered slit at the side of his snowmobile suit and touched the sunburst of yarn crowning his cap to see if it was in place, preening. He had been at the door and had tried to see as far into her as he could the first shot, that sort. When she called to Chris, he withdrew a bit, but now was attempting to act like the kind who could wait. What experience have you had as a sixteen-year-old? she wanted to ask.

Kitchum looked like he'd eat up the snow in the whole yard, piss holes and all, if he didn't kick somebody in the head soon. He was a scrawny redneck, or that was her impression weeks back, but now his face was full, jowls clotted with the blood of serious cursing.

There was a rattle of the lock, and she turned and saw that last night wasn't ended for Chris, from his look. And with an erosion of her composure she understood that with his silver hair sticking out from sleep, plus the reading glasses he'd slipped on, which blurred everything beyond his hand but magnified the bags under his eyes (besides that ratty jacket he'd found in the bus), the blond would figure she'd married somebody so old the guy was losing his touch. Or she was. Then he would notice that they didn't have a child.

"What is it?" Chris asked. "What's up?"

THE DUALS of the antiquated truck were dug in to their hubs and the spun-back snow was stained with rubber Chris could smell. "You can't back it?"

"I'm afraid for the rig," Kitchum explained.

Extending beyond the platform of the truck was a steel tower like an oil derrick. The angle of the truck placed its overhanging end a foot from the ground. Then Chris saw in a blur at the bottom of the hill something dark beside the bus. "What's that?" he asked.

"A Ford 150 XLT," the blond boy pronounced.

"Oh, it's yours."

"Dad's," the boy said, and Chris noticed Kitchum stir with uneasiness. "Brand-new. It won't do nothin' to your rig." The boy laughed too eagerly at this.

Chris pulled off his glasses and shoved them in his pocket. What was he doing with these, imagining a student at the door with an essay? The boy slid his hands into his snowmobile suit and stared down at a boot he was stepping into the snow, and Chris realized he'd gone into teaching for young people like this. No son.

"What I need is a replacement for this crowbait," Kitchum said, and took hold of the side of the flatbed, edged with steel, as if he'd roll the truck. He drew his hand away, and his leather glove remained, clinging like a deflated claw. "Cold," he said, and then to himself, "Maybe this job will finance that."

"Has she paid you anything?" Chris asked.

"No, but she'll owe half once I'm down a hundred feet."

"What about this?" Chris stomped the ground.

"Nothing, that foot or two of freeze, when you consider the rock I expect we'll hit at sixty feet."

"This hasn't gone smoothly."

"Oh, it's run-of-the-mill for this business, I guess," Kitchum said, the S's setting his dentures going like a steam kettle. "A well's a kind of life." He smiled—a rural philospher?—and tinted molecules, like a residue from last night, sprang into the air from his face. "Old Strohe, you know, wasn't so bad to deal with as some say. It was yes or no with him, and that was it. I hear he's about a goner."

"Well."

"Don't they push him around in a kind of high chair?"

Chris studied Kitchum's thin face, with furrows falling from his features in a form of perpetual mourning,
and sensed the concern of a colleague. Jonesy had told
Chris he had had to attach the weighted steel frame to
the rear of the wheelchair and strap Grandpa Strohe in
because the old man would raise a finger as if something had occurred to him, Jonesy said, and then would
try to go take care of it and tip over. "Where'd you
hear that?"

"A few people here, you tell them your bedtime, you
might as well print it in the *Record-Eagle*. There's one or
two, I hear, have better circulation than it."

Chris tried to remember who he'd spoken to about old
Strohe; nobody, not even Beau, so far, and he wondered
who Nana had contacted that weekend. Then a thought
came like a slap in the air, it was so clear: Nana wanted
them to bear the brunt of whatever might arrive from the
locals, such as Art and Beauchamp, once Der Alte was
dead.

MEN, ELLEN thought. Before they could start a job they
had to talk an hour to size one another up. Whereas
women dove in and saved their opinion for the way the
other worked, or didn't, and then let her have it. The
kitchen was clean, and now she had to fetch wood for the
stove, since Chris hadn't even thought of it with Kitchum
and every woman's angel at the door.

Last night had tipped her into her project, her real reason for being here—other than the challenge of living the
way earlier generations had, and his thesis, of course.
She'd been keeping a journal for a year and knew she
had enough for a book, the perfect cottage industry. Let

men bicker among themselves about outside jobs. The book would be in the form of a journal, a season of grief, as she pictured it last night.

She went through the blanket into the main room, to the dresser, drew open its drawer, and took out the bag. She'd read that researchers were concerned about the genetic effects of hallucinogens but she was sure they meant LSD, not anything organic. Southwest Indians ingested this for centuries and were the soundest and most organized, not to say placid, of the tribes. Chris tried to assume that his thesis, or dissertation, or whatever, was scholarly, but she knew he was trying to justify being an Indian (she weighed the sack of nubbins in her palm, wondering what was a safe dose) while living like he wasn't. As if living were intellectual! Nana's treatment of him maybe helped explain his reaction—"Look at him!" she had cried the first time she saw him. "What *is* he?"—but did he think this could extend to *her*, to the point of exclusion?

The week Nana visited, after they'd picked her up at the airport and parked at the foot of the hill, Nana said, "Now what?" So Chris got a length of rope from the cabin and pulled her up on a pair of skis, but when she stepped into the back porch, leaning on his arm, she said, "This simply won't do. You may not store firewood in my back porch, mister."

They would store propane there, he said, if they had a stove that burned it, but he carried all the wood out and had not stacked it there again, maugre the inconvenience—the extra trips and the freeze that had to be steamed from it before it burned well. Nana was upset at the bark on the floor beside the stove, at the way he swept it up, at his use of more coffee in the percolator than her measure, etc. It was so cold that Nana cut her stay to the weekend, and on Saturday they escaped to town, to give her privacy, they explained, and had too many drinks and back here found her in front of the fireplace, which she'd unblocked and fired up, on the couch, inserting flexible metal markers through *Science and Health.*

Chris had read the book as a way of understanding the Strohes and had said when he was finished, "Mary Baker Eddy might have something there." Then he decided to read the Bible, and read it through twice, in his thoroughness with any new project, this time referring to *Science and Health* along the way, and at the end said, "On the other hand, it's clear she's a charlatan. Or bonkers. She ignores the best parts of the Bible." He had asked Nana why she thought this was so, and perhaps that still rankled Nana, because after their ascent of the long stairs to the loft they were using to accommodate her, she said from the couch, "Ellen, you're too involved in the material."

She didn't mean materialism but, in the argot of the users of *Science and Health*, Ellen's neglect of "the spiritual" for "the unreal world of error," which included drink. Ellen undressed in a newfound warmth along the log rafters, and when she got under the covers, Chris came crawling to the bed on his hands and knees and whispered, "I think the Devil's giving me a material erection."

She woke the next morning to Nana's voice in the kitchen, urgent, then heard Chris give a quiet response, and by the time she started downstairs, Nana was yelling, "I've never approved of you and never will! I abhor the way you sneaked off and married her!" Goodness, Ellen thought, that was seven years ago! "I don't consider it a real marriage and never have! I hope it doesn't last!"

Ellen got to the kitchen just as Chris went out the door,

and it was an hour before he returned, carrying an arm-load of split wood. "Ax," he said.

Ellen hid the sack at the bottom of the drawer and slammed it shut. This was her place to work. The city reminded her of men's tendency to stack lifelessness to the limit. Chris hadn't installed plastic over these windows, at least, and she studied the black knobs and rings on the birch beyond the corner of the bedroom, so full in its trunk that it leaned toward the dining wing—had begun leaning so much farther these last years that one of Grandpa's last threats had been that this birch would have to come down next summer; and then, black and gray, like a reflex of the tree, a nuthatch bobbed around its trunk, upside down, and dodged its snakelike head into a suet cage Chris had attached to the bark.

She went into the kitchen and out the back door, heading for the wood at the trestle, and heard the burr of their talk below the hill. She loaded her arms and started back, conscious of the cold and of how she was dressed, in jeans and a cotton shirt, the bark biting through the flimsy material into her skin, and saw somebody like Gaylin heading in an Indian's hurried walk down the road south. No, an older man, the Indian who was helping Orin prune his orchards, perhaps, gone now but dressed the same as that little wiseass.

She stomped her feet clean before she entered, thinking how her stomping was of no avail as a reminder to Chris, and went over and sank beside the woodbox and let the wood roll in. She took a stick and stirred the coals until orange sprang through the ash, then jerked back her hand. The heat had gone through her fingernails like an electrical shock. To be singed in that flesh! She loaded the stove to its top, went into the closet across from the bathroom, and slipped on a sweater. She drew a stocking cap over her ears and stood a minute, impatient, as she tucked her hair inside. Then she took down the pen and notebook she hid on the closet shelf and dragged a chair from the dining wing to the front of the stove. They'd eat later.

She pulled herself closer to the stove by hooking a toe under its iron skirt, then laid the notebook on her knees. She figured they had two months; Nana's term of hospitality would be up by then. Seven weeks, say, and figure five days to a week, for interruptions: thirty-five. She wouldn't consider this if Chris hadn't urged her to keep a journal, and the picture she'd received of it last night placed it at 250 pages. Roughly seven pages per day. She opened the notebook, settled it on her knees, and wrote: "On the night I was brought the news that my first child was dead . . ."

ONCE CHRIS had surveyed the damage, as Kitchum put it, he got out the chain saw and cut limbs from trees lining the road, which needed trimming, anyway, and they laid them in a kind of corduroy down the hill behind the truck. Both of the Kitchums, familiar with work, fell in behind him as if this were planned. The boy started digging around the duals, packed between with snow like a third white tire.

Chris decided to cut chocks so they could back the truck out at a gentler angle. He saw a stunted tree with gnarled limbs and boles of age scabbing its trunk and got down on his knees in the snow beside it, kicking the saw up to full throttle. In the racket through the trees the bar dug past the bark, and the engine pulled to work but barely cut, as if the chain were mush. He rocked the bar, then let the saw pull until its pawls gripped, to give himself leverage. The chain freewheeled uselessly, and he recalled Beau's finicky sharpening and his anger when a blade got dulled and wondered if he'd hit a buried rock or steel post, though he'd kept close watch on—

A hand grabbed his shoulder. The bar popped out as he swung around, everything akimbo, and saw Kitchum draw a finger across his throat. He hit the cutoff switch.

"You'll be sawing away at that quite a while, son."

"What?" His ears weren't clear of the shattering sound that entered in an ache.

"That's hop hornbeam. Ironwood. You can go ahead and take it down. It's trash. But it's not going to do that nice sharp chain of yours any good."

Chris glanced at the boy, who was turned away, and saw bursts of silver appear around his head with his laughter.

"It looked like osage orange," Chris said.

"A bit like, though I think your fibers'd be tighter in this. It's the bastard of the birch family. That osage is a strain of mulberry, isn't it? About as tough, I guess. I heard the Indians used to use it." He studied Chris. "You must be a newcomer to these woods." Kitchum was searching for something. "You've worked in the woods somewhere, though, the way you handle that saw."

This was the opportunity to tell Kitchum in which woods where, but Chris leaned against the tree, silent.

"You don't see real pine and oak, nor anything much else, the way you used to. My daddy worked as a sawyer for the lumber companies till they went so big. Those logs in your cabin came from Cedar Lake. The real woods were pretty much cleared off by then. My daddy and an

Indian took them down the old way, *ee ooh, ee ooh*"—
Kitchum worked the end of a bucksaw—"and the Indian
with only one arm. Some lumberjacks at the Sault said
he got his hand too far in with a white woman, if you
catch my meaning, and those boyos up there held him
down and chopped it off. By a sort of oversight, they forgot
he was left-handed. Well! when Daddy and that Indian
got the logs all sawed, old man Clausen hauled them here
by team and had the two build the cabin where it sits. To
his very particular specifications, I might say. Daddy still
knew how to run one up the old way, notching those big
louts by hand and fitting them *that* tight, and he never
got over the way Clausen kept at him. An ace of a stickler,
that guy!"

"Clausen?"

"The patriarch, as they call him, not the sons."

"You mean this was Clausen's place?"

"Well, it always was, don't you know. About the
whole county wanted it at one time or another, but probably not as much as me—because of the connection to
Daddy. He said old Clausen had them get the place so
true they could drop a plumb bob from any corner and
have it fall dead right. A feat, considering the girth of
some of them logs." He made a circle of his arms that
framed his face. "Once when I thought I was something,
not much older than the boy, I spoke to old Clausen myself. I stood right by that tree there." He raised a finger
as if to point. "Well, it doesn't make much difference, but
I stood by that big elm to the right of your cabin, and I
said, practically down on my knees, 'Mr. Clausen, if you
ever, ever go to sell this place, please let me have a chance
at it.' He wasn't such a bad old giant. 'Charlie, I luf ya
like a *suhn*,' he said. He had the accent thick. 'But dis is

for da boise.' Well, I understood that, or do now . . ." He glanced at his son, who was leaning on his shovel, listening to this story he might have heard a dozen times. "But then Clausen died sudden, and I guess his widow was flustercated, or the boys bickering about it—there was five in all—so your Grandpa Strohe, who'd been coming up and renting the place every summer, he was at the right place just then, I guess, and it kind of fell in his lap. There's a bit of bad blood in the Clausen family about it still, though, huh?"

Chris set down the saw as though it bore the weight of Kitchum's monologue. It was the first time that he had heard any of this.

"WHY DIDN'T you tell me about it?" Chris asked her.

"Did I know?" She pushed away her plate, appalled at the revving of the truck, which was used to run the drilling rig and put out such a throaty clatter she could feel it through the floor. "I would've been pretty young." That wasn't what she intended to say, but nothing was arriving as she intended through the noise. There was so much gossip in this area that she had vowed never to be party to it. "Some things are unclear. The accident." She wasn't sure this was true, either, but knew it would forestall his questions and she needed some relief. This noise!

"It's a wonderful meal," he said.

She had made it in minutes by starting hamburger on the cookstove and shoveling at it while she wrote. Then she noticed how meager it looked as the truck cleared the hill and he came behind carrying the chain saw, so she sliced cabbage into it, along with a green pepper she found shriveling at the bottom of the refrigerator, and the vegetables hardly had a chance to cook before he walked in. She poured the grease into the cookstove hole, causing a *whoosh* that sent soot floating past her face, but the cabbage was already invaded, oily-dark at its edges. She smiled, uneasy.

"Really," he said. "It's perfect winter food."

"How long will they run that rattletrap?"

"Till they're down at least a hundred feet."

"Oh, please!" she said, and at that second the truck shut down. She sighed and noticed she could see her breath faintly, the fire dying again.

"Lunch, probably," he said, and then a smaller motor started in a higher pitch, whining like a drill.

He went over and drew aside the blanket, and flashes like sun sparked over the logs of the main room to a *zzt-zzt* from outside. "The kid's welding the first piece of casing in."

"What does that do?"

"It's the well pipe. I think each piece is ten feet long. Ten of those to hit a hundred."

"Good God."

"Just hope the rock they hit isn't flint."

The thought of that false lightning flashing through the room unsettled her, like a reminder of the jerky progress of her pages; but four finished before he walked in.

He stood at the blanket, studying her, and before he could get out a question in concord with the new motor that seemed more her speed, she said, "Was he stuck bad?"

He sat again with his back to the woods—a black tangle over his shoulder—and stared at her. "What is it?"

She could as well tell him, she thought, and looked at her hands, her fingers, which were her betrayers and lay in such shapely lines in the lap of her jeans she was ashamed.

"All this noise?" he asked.

She felt a paralysis in her limbs at his tendency to take hold of the immediate. She nodded.

"I cut some wedges that made it easier to back the truck out, and once it was out he came barreling straight up." Then he was back to where he'd been. "Your eyes are so misted you look like you've been crying."

She shrugged, already trying to think of where to hide the notebooks as they filled.

"Why don't we get together tonight?"

"How do you mean?"

"A date—you know."

"Oh, stop!" But she was pleased by his indirectness.

"We'll drive to town, maybe have a drink, and then come back and, well, we'll see."

"What about the six-pack?"

"Mollification for the kids. I will not get into their skaggy kind of guilt about drinking. Guilt is the source of alienation."

"Condemnation, I thought."

"That, too—your conscience telling you you've done the wrong thing. In some it's overdeveloped. They read about a dead cat and feel responsible. That's neurotic. Others feel they could be the cause of the Second World War. That's probably psychotic. If they know for sure they caused it, there's no question."

"How would guilt alienate anybody except in that kind of extreme case?"

"It condemns, you said, and to condemn yourself is to set yourself apart. If others condemn you, too, or declare you guilty, you're truly alienated. Guilt on top of guilt."

"Where does conscience come from?"

He pursed his lips and looked out the window, and for a moment his eyes appeared to penetrate to the answer. Then he studied her up and down. "I haven't got to conscience yet."

Their laughter, subdued and intimate, settled her as she hadn't been settled here since they arrived.

"The Puritans were right about one thing," he said.

"The necessity of self-government?"

"The depravity of man."

"Man?"

He gave a suggestive smile. "Women, too."

"That's all you think of!"

"How else can we have one?"

By which he meant that their only child, born six months after their marriage, had died; by which he meant, considering she hadn't been pregnant since, that its paternity was in question, by which he meant, when this got to its lowest, that they shouldn't be married. Probably. He couldn't quite come down on it clean as a guillotine. She didn't want him to, or hadn't so far, which he wasn't quite able to believe, which rendered her assurances meaningless. So she felt worthless. But before she left him, if it came to that, she had to convince him of the degree to which she considered herself a failure, after losing his child, not being able to have another to hand over to him in the midst of the mess of a time like this. That's what her journal was about.

The truck started up, and she couldn't remember how this conversation had led to here; then put her finger on it. "All right," she said, and gave him a smile that aroused even her. "It's a date."

*   *   *

I WILL BE the very model of decorum, Chris thought, as he held the door for her. Then he saw the Nagonawba brothers, Philip and Carlyle, sitting at a table to the side of the empty barroom with somebody whose back was turned. Philip arched an eyebrow and started to wave, then took hold of his beer bottle with both hands and stared at it, his eyes widening with enacted concentration. Henderson? A pair of elderly men at the far end of the bar, near the television, craned halfway around on their stools to take this in.

"Do you want to sit at the table with them?" Chris whispered. "I could bring your drink over."

"I'll wait."

He took her by the elbow to the bar's bumper, and the bartender, with a flour sack tied around his waist and a rosy complexion coloring his bald head to its crown, leaned on one hand as he poured a crystalline liquid into a double-shot glass. Schnapps.

"I'll have some of that," Chris said, and the man looked up as if Chris were equally crystalline, invisible. Okay, Chris thought, and eased himself onto a bar stool.

Finally, the man came over and leaned with both hands in front of him, sad-eyed, and Chris said in a low voice, with a tug of his head toward the table, "Who's that?"

"I thought those were your buddies."

"Not the brothers. The big guy."

"Beats me."

"I'll have a schnapps, please, like that, and she'll have"—he turned to Ellen—"a scotch and soda, right?"

She nodded, looking grim, ready to leave.

Chris hated barroom brawls as much as the bartender seemed to suggest, with his sad, watery-blue eyes. But when the fellow finally brought their drinks, Chris took his over to the table. Philip smiled below his big nose and performed a scooting motion on his chair—chrome metal, not the balsa kind that broke over cowboys' heads—as if to make room for Chris beside him, and said, "Ma'guish."

Chris leaned enough to see the third man in profile, glum Joejim Standing Bear, and breathed more easily.

"El," he said, "why don't you sit over here?"

The men at the bar craned around farther, riveted by the unbelievable, and when Ellen was halfway there, Joejim shoved up from the table and stalked out.

"What's with him?" Chris asked.

"Afraid somebody'll *see* him," Carlyle said, head down, smiling a thin smile that barely exposed his teeth, all badly decayed. He was self-conscious about this, dressed in a pressed shirt with his hair styled like Elvis Presley's, since, like Presley, he had such a luxuriant growth there seemed no solution except to pour on oil and keep combing—sleek black, with comb-tooth lines riding like furrows through its waves. Chris pulled up a chair for Ellen and sat where Joejim had been, on a seat still warm.

"I was telling Ellen about your stay on Fox Island," he said to Philip. "I mean, how good you are with trees."

"Oh, yeah," Philip said, and studied her with his small eyes, cinnamon brown and ingenuous, then gave a nod, his somber business self. A baseball cap shoved back on his crew cut framed his face, small chinned, a perfect triangle. But his nose, broad as a sausage, bowed out from his forehead, then bent to the right, its bottom half bent even farther, his small mouth below like the hull of a boat whose sail had filled in the process of coming about—everything pulled out of kilter by the nose. His tiny eyes seemed to be trying to correct for it with their brightness.

"Yeah, on Fox," Philip said. "We went out in a boat in winter." He swallowed as if to clear his nose, which interfered with his speech, and took a breath that lifted his shoulders. Chris assumed the nose had been broken in the woods where it couldn't be set, perhaps by a tree, from the force that had shoved it so far to one side of his face, and not in a fight, but felt it improper to ask. "They kept us in this shed. Mail once a week. *Guzz, guzz, guzz,*" he went with an imaginary chain saw. "Timber so thick you couldn't walk and we had to get them logs out." He smiled, a light going on and off, then was solemn again. "All these deer and bunnies, I never seen so many. The little bunnies, *bwip, bwip bwip*"—he wriggled a shapely hand—"*bwip bwip* through the snow."

"*Bwip bwip,*" Carlyle said, playful in his imitation.

"Okay, you guys, hold it down," the bartender said.

Chris turned and stared at him, then said to Philip, "So it was hard to fell the trees."

"Oh, mother," Philip said, tiny eyes wide. "Take 'em down that way, the boss said. I had this chain saw—blade three feet." He measured. "*Guzz, guzz,* here and here a notch." He illustrated with his fingers. "Then *beeeee,* straight down on the saw, and this big old buzzard he'd step off the stump, walk walk walk, and fall right there."

"Walk?" Ellen asked.

"Oh, yeah," Philip said, pursing his lips, wet now from the effort to talk, and drew in a breath that threw his chest up, bony shoulders twitching for more air. "We had to walk um so they fell on the exact spot."

"The trees walked?" Ellen asked.

Philip held out his arms and sashayed his butt on the

chair, saying, *"Tesh, tesh, tesh,"* then let his head fall on the table. "Then we brush 'em," he said, upright, slashing where his head had been with the saw. *"Teez, teez!"*

"You say you brushed them?" she asked.

"Wipe the brush and branches off." Philip stood, above a tree now, enacting the procedure with his saw. *"Tzz, tzz!"* he said, and sat, checking the reaction at the bar.

"I stayed home," Carlyle said, drawing his head down in a retreat so shy it seemed a form of grief; he often appeared to be grieving. "Maybe I'm not so smart."

"Maybe it was smarter to stay home," Chris said.

"Maybe," Carlyle said, and resisted a smile, so that his mouth took the prim set of a nance. "Maybe I'm *wise*."

Carlyle and Philip glanced at each other, started shaking with laughter at a joke that must be personal, and then got giggling so badly Carlyle had to cover his mouth.

"Wise old Indian!" Philip exclaimed, and they went into arias of separate laughter.

Chris turned in his chair and called, "Three more beers!" He wanted to disarm the bartender and see if he'd serve them as he served others who took tables.

Ellen said, "There's a couple of old birches at our cabin somebody said we'll have to take down. They lean right over the roof."

"Gotta go!" Philip said.

"I've heard that birches can't support their own weight when they get too big. They might also be punky inside."

"Oh, yeah," Philip said, nodding solemnly, his small lips twisted opposite to his nose as if in counterbalance. "Hey, I seen a snow bring one down last munt, only snow on a tree."

Three clops came down on wood, and the bartender leaned his forearms on the bar, hands folded behind the lined-up bottles. Chris went over and counted out enough money, then threw down a dollar tip and grabbed the beers without checking the man's reaction and started back. Somebody had come in and was sitting at a table in the rear, near the hallway to the rest rooms—a woman with bulky shoulders that looked padded, her back to him, and Chris felt connected to her by a force that seemed to raise strands of her hair from her head, and for some reason he pictured Michelle; and then the actress running down a darkened street.

Ellen was portraying the angle of the birches with one hand, and Chris sat down dazed, passing the bottles. His schnapps was gone, but he didn't want a beer. Philip drew upright, studying Ellen for her authenticity, then said, "Oh, yeah, I can do that. See—" He stood and leaned at the angle Ellen had indicated, then spun as the birch would spin off its stump, *"Thop, thop,"* in its walk, then the direction it would fall. He caught himself before he was all the way over, but the bartender called, "Philip, I warned you before, and that's it! Once more and you're out!"

Philip sat and shoved out his lip, and Chris could see, in his near profile, a protuberance of resistance to his eyes and the shining sclera on this side that yellowed at the corner into a pocket of blood.

Chris got up and headed for the hall to the rest rooms and passed the woman, again with that swirl of connection that set his senses awry. She turned away. Down the dark hall, lined with cheap paneling, to a door where the sign read CHIEFS. It couldn't be. Yes, the door he'd passed read SQUAWS. The bartender's idea of a joke? Did any doors in the Deep South read BUCKS and MAMAS?

He stepped inside and leaned against the wall, then

stepped out, feeling the volume of dark all the way to the back door, near enough to her table so she had to look up. It wasn't Betty, of the Hendersons, as he feared at first, but an equally sad-looking person, with strangely bulbous bags under her eyes, and now her upper lip lifted at the corner in a kind of snarl.

He sat at their table, out of breath, so unsettled he couldn't take in what Philip was saying. Ellen turned to him, and he got up and went over and said to the bartender, "Who's that woman in the back?"

"Never seen the goofball in my life," the man said.

Something's going on between him and that woman, Ellen thought, and he thinks I don't know. Well, by God— She got up and strode to the women's room, closed the cover some slob had left up, and then had to sit to alleviate the numb weakness in her legs. How could he be interested in anybody so ugly and fat? She'd seen the shape Indian women got into by thirty, but she wasn't sure this was an Indian, or anyway, not the Henderson woman he'd shot the rifle too close to, or whatever. Were men drawn by the size of such women? Big Mama?

The door swung in and hit a knee, and Mama stood above her, huffing, mismatched shoulders tugging at her coat, with bags worse than Chris's under her eyes. "Sorry, honey," the hulk said in a surprising voice, not cigarette- or whiskey-soaked but mellow in its concern. The woman worked sideways through the door in a manner that suggested her coat might once have been sable and then backed to the knob, emitting Shalimar in this closet hardly large enough for one.

"I was only sitting," Ellen said, and stood near the sink so the woman could edge to where she had been. But the woman wasn't about to move.

"You've had it with those jerks, right?"

"Sorry, one's my husband."

"How'd you like to one-up him?"

"I'm not sure what you mean."

The woman slid along the wall, away from the door, to indicate the way was open. "How'd you like to meet the intellectual cream of this county? All women. We go over our problems about marriage and men in general. Don't take it as an offense, honey, but seeing where he set you down and how his interest wanders, I feel for you. How much does he let you go on your own? Are you free? Can you come?"

"I'll consider it," Ellen said, trying to leave.

"We meet Thursdays at seven. I know you probably can't make it tonight, but try next week." The woman lunged to check herself in the mirror, and Ellen turned enough to see into it, too, noting, at this removed yet intimate encounter, a youthful tension in the woman's eyes and the botched red mess of her mouth. "We meet at the library," the mouth said to her in the mirror. "That new brick building down—"

"I know," Ellen said. "I hate it."

"Wasn't it just like that pig council to tear down a perfectly good building—could be on the National Register— and put up a Lutheran church? I mean, what's it look like? We discuss these things, too, honey, in a nice quiet room where nobody bothers us. Who reads?"

"I do!" Ellen turned and was surprised to find the woman nearly against her.

"*We* do," the woman said, and put her hands on Ellen's shoulders, breathing so fervently there was a scent of something she'd eaten beneath the Shalimar and whiskey. "Who else in this county does, though, I mean?" She gave a firm shake. "Just don't tell your husband about the meeting. We'll see if we can work something out later, but for now don't let him in on it, okay?"

There was an intensity to this that led Ellen to believe the woman was about to continue forward in a kiss, so she wriggled free and pushed past her out the door.

6

CHRIS GLANCED at her green-lit profile in the pad-
dling murmur of the bus, her fox-fur cap pushed back so
far her hair looped over her face, then shut it off.

"You spent a lot of time in the Squaws."

"It bothered me that you got that beer."

"That was for Philip, there when we left."

He climbed out and took her arm and they started up
a furrow left by Kitchum's truck—blue-black in the blue
snow. Chris found it difficult to maneuver the middle
ground and let her go on ahead. Was it the night he skied
down here that this began? It was true that her clock was
set to daylight time and his closer to the Old Style calen-
dar, or Mayan—more accurate to actual days—but they'd
learned to live with the difference, even here, with no
outside schedule to refer to.

Earlier societies measured a job against the conditions
of a season. You didn't go clamming or out to hunt, no
matter how hungry, in a hurricane or a blizzard. He had
strayed far from that, in the lockstep of a race entirely
different not only from his but from any that ever existed: *globalniks*. The network of bureaucracy, whether

Soviet or U.S., measured you by your willingness to bend to its standards, usually unwritten. The Establishment indeed.

He ran into Ellen. "Goodness, sorry!" he said, and took her gloved hand. "Clumsy!"

"Anything but," she stated as a fact, and he heard her heavy breathing. "You must be thinking."

"I believe I was halfway through my introduction."

"I think somebody's been up to the cabin." She disentangled her glove and pointed; a pair of tracks swerved from the broader set laid down by the duals, and lengths of tread-patterned ice, feathered away in a spin, were sinking into the crystalline surface of pure blue. He looked toward the cabin and felt his hearing extend and probe through the area, ears turning against the fur of his cap.

"Beau," he whispered. "After another cigarette."

"Why are you so rough on him?"

He tried to make out her expression in the light, or lack of light, and saw her lower lip slide out, stubborn. He grabbed the edges of her cap and pressed his lips against hers, then drew the lower between his and ran his tongue inside its inner salt, a slice of the moon.

She set her hands against his chest and stepped back. "You're a savage," she said.

He tried to laugh but felt the force of her statement as a challenge. And as surely as this was snow, he knew his response would affect the direction their marriage was tending. "I come by it naturally," he said.

"I'm not saying it's so bad."

"What's good about it?"

"It's what attracted me. Your intensity."

"The quality you most desired in a husband?"

"A man. It's more that it sought me. You did."

This was going off course, as if a central premise on her part was unspoken. "A man," he repeated.

"Marriage never occurred to me until I met you. I didn't think I'd get married."

"You regret it?"

"It's not that, so much as a picture I get, after all these years, of the way a life can be with only one other person, for as long as I can imagine—eternity."

"That sounds like hell."

"You get to see students and others, at school."

"You're too intelligent to waste your time in school. Is that what you want?"

"I want a *child!*"

The word returned from the woods in two tones, high and low, a whiplash. He'd taken the only medical test a man can take, and she had taken tests that proved nothing amiss, as her first pregnancy suggested. He walked past her, feeling the emptiness, corrupt as a hollow log, where a child should walk. But none now. *Why?* At the top of the hill he saw the lake shelved in silence far below, a mere shine at the bottom of the night from a form of stellar illumination he didn't care to locate. The yard around the cabin, overseen by angled birches, fell away to the bluff, and he could make out a glow in the windows of the wing where he worked from the light they'd left burning in the hall closet. Once past the fir and spigot, he had no doubts about tracks; they climbed the drive from the back door, and there was a tread over the cement slab Ellen kept swept clean.

"It's so ugly!" she cried from the head of the drive.

"Isn't intrusion, invasion of privacy and privates and the rest, always ugly?" He meant to be ironic, but the words took him straight to the sick sense of grief every tribe must have felt when others kept trespassing on home or sacred ground until they claimed it as their own.

"I mean that well rig," she said. "It's like something out of Oklahoma up here in the woods."

Faint light glinted off the girders in rectilinear lines above the treetops. "We'll be grateful enough for it soon," he said. "When we have water. I meant these." He stood over the concrete and waited for her to walk up.

"Didn't you say it was Beau?" she asked.

"He has snow treads. See where one tire cuts over the other? Both front and rear are regular tires."

He gave a quick look at the woods behind and felt hands enwrap his upper arm. "I'm so glad you're here," she said, and tugged at his arm. "I'm so happy we're home."

SHE GLIDED to the closet where the light burned, and he watched from the door as she dreamily undid her cap and hung it on a hook, already headed toward sleep. He went to the cookstove, threw his gloves on it, and found enough coals to coax up a fire, laying down the thinnest kindling available. He shoved the slotted damper at the front of the firebox open, the stove lid still off, and as the kindling caught with a sound like snapping sticks and sent light and shadow jerking up the walls, he held his hands, fingers spread, over the opening, then rubbed them as if to wash them clean.

From the closet he heard a sound like a long zipper unzipping but with a continuing liquidity and cocked his head. "What's that?" he asked.

"Why do you think I spent half the day ransacking the upstairs for a chamber pot!"

"You did?"

"Do you think I was going to walk out in the woods with that teenage ace out there, knowing we didn't have water, waiting for me to? I'm going to keep using this!"

He'd been planning his schedule and hadn't noticed. He narrowed his eyes and made an examination of his bowels to see if a late-night trip to the latrine was necessary; it could wait. When he was nineteen, a bullying queen tried to persuade him to change his ways and said as the clincher to a terrible litany, "All right, then, wait till you're shaving one day and she walks in and has to use the can!"—exposing a dimension of existence Chris hadn't ever considered, at that age, and he couldn't tell his devil's advocate that the prospect only excited him more.

A sweep of illumination, like the headlights from last night, swung across the trees at the edge of the bluff. He hurried into the dining wing to see. "Damn plastic!" he said, and the closet light behind went out. She was in the hall, in a silky white teddy undergarment instead of the union suit of her grandfather's she'd taken to wearing, under her flannel nightgown, to bed.

"Get something on," he ordered, and went through the porch into cold air that reminded him of how the paths at a particular place fall into patterns that become inscribed. He could hear her hurried footsteps and then, far below, voices like last night's. Go home, he wanted to shout, but stepped back inside and, pulling off his topcoat, hung it and his cap in the closet beside her clothes.

"Ellen!"

"Here, in bed."

"I think it's the kids."

"Oh, no."

He pulled on the scruffy jacket he'd found, then grabbed the rifle at the back of the closet, heavy from a full magazine, and was outside, near the woods, when he heard tires wind up in a growling whorl and somebody shout, "Stop, dammit!" There were quiet remarks with an undertone of cruelty, as if somebody were being jabbed, then Marty yelled, "All right, all right! But then I'm going home!"

At the head of the hill Chris stepped to a birch, aglow in the dark, and set the rifle against it, then went over the crest. Marty was coming toward him; he could make out the outline of a car where others milled. Marty paused, aware of him, and Chris stopped in a silence so sudden he could hear wings beating through the woods. An owl? He picked his way past the worst ruts from the truck, and when they met, Marty said in an undertone, "Worse trouble. The dink wouldn't serve me, so they made me come out. I'm stuck bad."

"You shouldn't drive up."

"Hey!" Marty cried, then whispered, "You don't know."

Chris went toward the car, near enough now to count the figures around it, five, one more than last night. Fat Anfinson stood with his fists on his hips, ready for this, and beside him a pair the height of Lonnie. Chris walked past the three, one of whom was relieving himself with a socketing sound into the snow, and sensed their menace. He stopped at the back bumper—a fifties Buick sedan restored by Marty, so he'd boasted, to factory specifications.

Chris got down on his knees at the wheel well: buried to its fancy skirting, the bumper scraping snow. "All right!" he commanded, and felt his voice enter them with the shock he'd intended. "Here's how Beau did it!" He hoped the name would evoke caution. "Marty, get in and start it up and get it in reverse."

As he rose, he heard a whisper with "sucker" in it and

understood Marty held his own by his wits more than he'd imagined; it was clear to him now that Marty wasn't liked. His father owned a successful orchard operation (it was Marty who always had the money), and he had been elected the local county commissioner, mostly by whites.

"You big guys come up front with me," Chris said. "One at each corner of the bumper." He got down at its center and set his shoulder against it. "You others get in the backseat for weight. Marty!"

A window creaked down. "Yeah."

"Once it starts, keep backing till you hit the road!"

"How you expect to push this mother?" Lonnie's larger twin, to Chris's left, asked. "We tried."

"Kick yourselves holes to brace your feet." Chris did this himself and prayed for the wildcat strength available to him at times. The summer he returned from his stint of school in California, with a student from the East who wanted help with the driving, he strayed onto a back road in the middle of Montana late one night and at the sight of a ranch house realized he was in somebody's drive. He braked and backed off the shoulder to turn and felt the rear end bottom out. He ran around and saw he'd backed over an irrigation ditch, both tires spinning in its chasm. By now the owner of the car was awake, and lights were going on inside the house. The icy masses of the Tetons and Crazies had filled him with a certainty of fear that this was cowboy paradise, so with the other fellow at the wheel he ran back and slid under the car, into the ditch, and set a shoulder to the differential as a pole light went on and he imagined ranch hands blazing away at the breed in a ditch like the ditch at Wounded Knee and yelled, "Now!" as he rose in entire weightlessness and watched the car go trundling off. Then he was out of the ditch, beside the driver, soaked to his knees as they spun off.

"Go!" he yelled now. "Back!"

He felt he pushed straight up, and the effect was like a shotgun slam to his shoulder, but there was a tearaway at the other end and he had to scramble to keep against the bumper, Lonnie already flat in the snow, the brute beside him stumbling, and then the car drew away so fast that exhaust poured past its headlights. Chris was upright, trotting now, fifty yards off when the car leaped the plowed ridge at the road's edge, then swung to a stop. He ran to keep ahead of the other two, seeing Marty hop out and dash past the headlights, flashing gray, while Anfinson and the others piled out the back.

"Hey, that was great!" Marty cried, and grabbed Chris's hand, then his arm, grinning. "Thanks."

The oversize pair came chuffing up, and one bumped Chris from behind, maybe by accident. Chris turned, and Lonnie's twin was leaning over him, his face lit from below, a ragged scar above his nose, as though somebody had tried to remove it with a broken bottle, and Chris received a picture of a raccoon's head in profile, snarling, as it was crushed with a boot. He was on the other side of history now, a settler surrounded by braves.

"Fungay!" the fellow cried. "I'm *Horse.*"

"My brother!" Fat Anfinson informed Chris.

Chris held up his hand, palm out, and said, "Well met."

"I could beat your whole damn head in flat," Horse said in the jerky Indian manner that always seemed one-half of a translation. "Then stick a knife in your throat."

Any answer to this was the trigger. "You want beer?" Chris said. "I'll get it."

"Yeah?" Horse asked, and Chris saw his clublike fists clench. "Why didn't you before?"

"So you'd be standing here safe."

"We got plenty beer, anyway, from Johnny Jones," Marty said, like a bucket of water over this.

"So you don't misunderstand me," Chris said to Horse, then glanced at Fat Anfinson, his brother, stepping closer as he jammed up his glasses, "I'm buying." Fats looked like the one to watch for trouble now, able to trip Horse into action, so Chris said, "I can't buy if I'm mauled."

This put it so much in the open that everybody stepped back. "I'll get a case," he said.

"Two." This was either Fat Anfinson or a buddy.

It wasn't a time to quibble; Chris barely had breath to talk. "Just one thing. It's best nobody sees us together. Drive around. In an hour I'll set the cases at the head of Clausen Road."

"How do we know?" Horse asked, and gave a backhand wallop to Chris's shoulder.

Chris turned and started down the road toward the tree where the bus was parked. There was a shuttle of light and shadow as bodies passed in front of the car, and he listened for footsteps, ready to dash for the other side of the bus, then along it and up the hill to the rifle.

"Come on," Marty said faintly, and a car door slammed.

Chris got to the bus, around to the driver's door, and got inside, shoving his door lock down with an elbow, sure the other was locked, since Ellen kept up her city habits. And now, he thought, hearing car doors clump closed as he shoved a hand into his jacket pocket: the key was there.

THE SAME elderly men were at the bar, so engrossed in television they barely gave him a glance, but Philip and Carlyle were gone, and the woman. When the bartender finally extricated himself with a shove of reluctance and came over bearing TV light and neon on his shining head, Chris ordered another schnapps. Only after the fellow had poured and stood lingering for his pay, glancing at the television to keep track of whatever was evolving, Chris said, "And a couple cases of Strohes."

This got his attention. "Continuing the party?"

Chris picked up the schnapps and tossed it down.

"I finally had to kick those two out," the man said. "You saw how they were carrying on."

"I asked Philip about logging."

"Once they get up and start dancing like that, you know you're looking at trouble."

"Philip and Carlyle?"

"Any Indian. So Philip has the gall to come back and ask for a case, as if I'm too dumb to know it's for that carload of kids that's been cruising town all night."

"I'll have another." Chris pointed at his glass and laid a twenty on the bar. "Plus those cases."

The man filled his glass to its mark, then dribbled in a bit more. "I hope it's not for those kids."

"I know a twenty-one-year-old 'kid' you won't serve."

"You mean Marty?"

Chris blushed.

The man scooted the bottle aside and leaned into the tray at the back of the bar. "That's my business, okay? I've lived in this town all of my life, and I know these people. My kids go to school with pigmented children. I know their dads and granddads, and I've seen more hit the skids than I can count. Alcohol and Indian don't mix. Or if it does, that's it for the wife and kids. I like this Marty, and I said I'd buy him a beer on his birthday. I told him he could sit here half the night if he wanted, but

I told him I would not by God sell him a case so he could go out and get polluted and get some underage kids polluted besides. If the county or the state wants to shut me down for that, okay. Two cases?"

Chris saw that the elderly men had turned from the TV for this moment of actual reality and felt a trembling begin in his legs. There was little he hated worse than lying, so finally he said, "It's my party."

The bartender walked past his patrons, under the television, to a cooler door that opened into the wall, and came back carrying a case in each hand. He set them at a gate near the cash register, then took Chris's twenty, glaring, and tossed his change in front of him.

"I hate to bother you," Chris said, "but I hurt my arm a while ago. Could you carry those out to the car for me?"

HE SET THE rifle at the back of the closet and removed the quilted jacket; his arm did hurt from that lunge at Marty's car. He'd pulled the cases out of the bus one-handed, with jingling *ka-lunks* at the head of the road, hoping the bottles sprayed foam all night. An anger like bleeding began inside, and he recognized its source: fear of the worst. He dug the blunt toe of a snowmobile boot into the heel of the other and drew it off.

"Chris?" Ellen's voice, bodiless, from the bedroom.

"Yes."

"Where have you been?"

"They were stuck. I helped them out."

"I thought I heard the bus pull away a long time ago."

"I bought them some after all."

"I hope you didn't have that gun with you. Did you?"

He looked to where he'd propped it and felt a soaking chill through his socks. "You can't push a car with it."

"I'm aware of that."

"Why are we talking through this wall?"

"You are," she said. "I've been waiting."

He remembered the teddy, reserved for special occasions, that she had been wearing in this doorway. He went past the stair of split logs glinting under the yellow lights, into their bedroom. He'd left the closet light on, and dim shafts radiating through cracks in the boards illuminated the mound of her under the blankets.

"I have a dream," he said.

"So do I." A wisp of her breath drifted into a stream of light from the closet, and he rubbed his upper arms. "Let's use up those awful ties of yours, wide as shovels and all flowery, dating from 1969," she said.

"I'm not sure I catch your meaning."

"There's one here." She jiggled her leg at the other side of the bed.

He walked over and saw her foot, free of the covers, with a necktie draped over it. "Who did this?"

"Um, the Devil made me."

"Not without your approbation. Are we getting so old and benighted we must use devices? I have a beaver outfit I can zip myself into. *'Brusha, brusha, brusha,'*" he sang, and bent to lick the sole of her foot, sensitive avenue, then licked between her toes.

"Must you!"

"I'm afraid it's going to take about five minutes on this one and then fifteen or so on the other, yup."

"Please!"

"I have to see if your friendly foot bones are developing that straight-ahead walk."

"Stop!"

"No bondage for you, then, Rowlandson. I won't even carry you off."

"Oh, do."

"I mean, you know—" Then, once started, he couldn't stop, "You know, like, uh, hey, man, I mean, cool, huh?"

"How gross!"

"It's just talking."

"Not really."

"How true."

"Not my foot again. Don't!"

"Okay," he said, and got up on the center of the bed, on his knees, and dragged the covers off her. "This is the thing the Puritans really went for. Though with my hurt arm it's liable to be a little lopsided."

"Lopsided?" Her eyes, luminous below the shafts of light projected in lines across his belly, opened wide as it throbbed into sight, and she said, "You're telling *me?*"

THEN THE wind went wild, and it was the wind that signified a season of change. The wash that dropped from the edge of the bluff in a striated concavity formed a channel for the wind off the lake, and it came over the bluff in booming gusts that collided with wind overhead and knocked them off balance. It could block their breath unless they turned their backs to it, gasping, and the scarves they tied over their faces against it and the mist of blowing sand vibrated so badly they resonated through their skulls or went tearing off in tumbling cartwheels toward the woods.

One morning the phone rang, and the voice at the other end said, "Is it wind enough for you?" and hung up. It was Beau, who seldom said more than a sentence on the phone, as if strangled by technology. Which left Chris wondering how Beau was able to stay in business, since customers had to call when they needed wood.

Everywhere Chris and Ellen went, as they tended to the feeders on trees and added to their supply of firewood, they found themselves blown off course. Dorsal-shaped drifts spread back from the lip of the bluff, turning brown-gold from blown sand and grew solid as sastrugi— branches of an inverted stream they could walk like wood. For days Beau didn't appear or call. Holed up. Once, when Ellen looked up from her notebook at the stove to see Chris slipping against the wind with an armload of wood, she thought, What did that woman mean, "We'll see if we can work something out later?"

The well men tried to work the first day in the wind and then gave up and called each morning to see if it had let up. But it kept sending clouds from the lake tearing overhead at the speed of panic, while here and there sun struck the earth like a cannon, reverberating, until only the thickest of the sastrugi were left, shedding sand over the combed-back grass as they diminished, the remaining snow already drawn into the atmosphere by the wind.

On an afternoon when it was less bad, Chris fought his way down the hill to the bus, to make a run for supplies, and on the road the bus was buffeted so badly it started tilting as Chris went around a curve; then a big gust struck broadside, and he yelled, "Yikes!" sure he was going over. The General Store was like a carton of cotton, and Chris, displaced, felt his hearing strain to check the force of the wind. Then he saw Johnny, at the rear of the place, beside the doors, and whispered, "My God."

Johnny stared out at him with the same slight smile, but his head was wound with bandages, passing even under his chin, mummylike, and above one ear a copper-brown stain bled through. Feathers brushed Chris's elbow with a chilling sensation, and Art the owner was behind Johnny, a managing hand on each shoulder, his head beside Johnny's bandages like a slicked-down ventriloquist waiting to go on. "Jasee what happened?" he asked.

Johnny's eyelids slowly opened, and Chris realized Johnny had blinked or closed them in a moment of pain.

"Hezinahospital three days witha concussion, right?"

"Two," Johnny said, and the bandages above his ear assumed a minty radiance as the wind, rattling the doors fitted with glass, drove the clouds so far off that sunlight entered the store head-on.

"It was actually Indian boys atdidit."

"Horse," Johnny said, and again his eyelids retracted with weary slowness from a blink Chris hadn't caught.

Chris's lips began to quiver with the question he knew he had to ask.

"They brokinnaJohnny's place and tore it up."

"They was drunk," Johnny said in explanation, and gave a slight shrug, suddenly as shy as Carlyle.

Chris saw a rectangular patch of floor beside Johnny's shoes that was lighter than the rest, with four rusty gouges in it, as if a potbellied stove had stood inside the doors on an asbestos pad, and wondered how much of that night this pair of professionals knew about. Before he could ask, Art said, "It was Friday, the day whenay broughtatAnfinson kid in from jail. He beat Johnny up till he thoughtee's dead, a poker or a ballbat. But Johnny, by golly, he crawled out to the road!"

"Stick a wood," Johnny said.

"Sheriff's after him!" Art said, doing his deep nods beside Johnny's bandaged head, solemn.

"Horse is hiding," Johnny said, and his eyes, merry with a sudden shift, came direct on Chris. "Ha!"

*   *   *

WHEN CHRIS walked into the cabin with his full knapsack of supplies, Ellen said, "What's wrong?"

He dropped the knapsack and walked past her to their bed and lay down and remained there the rest of the afternoon.

THE BLOW lasted three further days, and in the sudden calm that came their ears opened to another world. They kept their distance, stepping around the cabin gingerly, and she glanced at him as if this otherworld of absolute silence could invade her life and take over. Blue-gray mist gathered on the lake like a mingling of all of the clouds they'd endured, and then tattered streamers curled toward the horizon, and another snow arrived, slanting down in beads so fine they appeared molecular but were wet as well as icy—a dense, damp drizzle that chilled Chris as he worked to keep up with the wood—and by the next day was six inches deep.

The cabin took on an acrid smell of burned ash and oak, as if they'd plunged flaming sticks of it into buckets of water, and permeated the place with the potential for burning. He felt done in by the continual weather and deadness of winter, and one day at the kitchen table drew his file folder out and started the next sentence of his introduction. Late that afternoon, when she started dinner, he had seventeen pages. The introduction was done. Roethke wavered and soared in the air above him.

"Aren't you going to join me?" she asked.

There was a plate at his elbow. She stared at him, gold wisps of her hair like ragged engraving over the blue of the plastic. Then the blue deepened to black and began to rattle like parchment under a new onslaught of sleet.

"El, I—" Tears, unexpected and stinging, squeezed over his lashes and started down his cheeks.

She placed her hand on his, lying (he saw through a bristling blur) over his last page. "Chris, what is it?"

"That you care for me, I think."

"Why wouldn't I, after all this time?"

"Why should you, after it?"

"The work's too much. It's a job just to keep warm."

"The only time I am is in you, in bed. That heat."

"Cabin fever."

"What?" He'd noticed, in the scattering of sheets at his side of the table, the schedule he'd started months ago, it seemed, as if it had surfaced by this pull of recent work. "Goodness," he said, and ran a curled finger down his cheek. "I'm a week behind. Or was." He smiled at her. "Now I'm almost caught up."

THAT NIGHT he finished five more pages, the beginning of the first chapter, and took his schedule out. He'd allowed himself two months when he'd set it up; now it was March. He would have to finish by the first of May. Mayday! Eight weeks—fifty-six days, divided into two hundred, went roughly three times. He could do three pages a day, certainly, now that their need for wood was about to end, or better be. His hearing returned to the drizzle that drilled at the plastic, and then a log in the cookstove went off like a gunshot.

He stepped to the green shelves and took down his bottle of schnapps, sliced through the blue band of its seal with his thumbnail, and undid the cap. He took down a juice glass with red lines encircling it and poured to the line he judged to be a double shot. He put the bottle back and went to the stove, glass in hand, to the corner opposite the firebox, and eased his butt onto its top—the perfect temperature to warm him in a second, without his having to jump up scorched.

He expected to start chapter one with a recapitulation of Puritan history, and slide from there toward his eventual subject, the American Red Indian, but found himself writing, instead, about a troubling early Roethke poem, "Frau Bauman, Frau Schmidt, and Frau Schwartze." Roethke had included the poem in every collection while he was alive, but it was cut from the posthumous *Collected Poems,* as if it exposed him or his genesis, as it were, too completely. The "three ancient ladies," who later in the poem become "leathery crones," were employees at the greenhouse Roethke's father ran in Saginaw and are central to the collection called "The Lost Son" (or "the greenhouse poems"), since it's their actions Roethke records in his poems of preparing cuttings, weeding, transplanting, moss gathering, and other procedures of greenhouse work.

The trinity of women taught Roethke as a child to relate to the minimal—the hair roots of tiny seedlings, the plant lice clinging to them, the swimming bacteria in wounds; and now they haunted him, "These ancient leathery crones, / With their bandannas stiffened with sweat, / And their thorn-bitten wrists, / And their snuff-laden breath blowing lightly over me in my first sleep."

Chris took a sip of the schnapps, ignoring a sound like scratching at the plastic. The drizzle. If it was Beau, he could knock, though Chris was drifting past human contact in the free-floating state that followed concentrated work. He had stopped in Saginaw last summer to see if he could locate the Roethke greenhouse and discovered that the business still existed, under the Roethke name, although another family owned it now—after a relative of Roethke's had run it into the ground, the present manager, a plump Dutchman with a ruddy-streaked complexion, told Chris, talking past the bobbing, smoky pipe he kept gripped in his teeth as he transported plants, their pots swathed in pastel tinfoil, from a glass cooler to a counter, where a delivery boy packed them in boxes that he carried to a waiting van.

"Ve've kep dee Retke name," the manager said, "becuss— Oh, vell, becuss uf dah *lushter*, I giss."

"Did you know the original owner's son was a poet?"

The man's shaggy eyebrows rose, and the pipe dropped. "Ya, uf course! Ain't he famous tru America?"

"Do people stop in often to ask about him?"

"Off and den, like you."

"Does anybody still work here who might remember him?"

"Iss Ellie out back?" this man asked the delivery boy.

"I giss, Daddy."

Ellie was led in, a tiny white-haired woman bent so badly at the waist her long black dress brushed the floor. Her stubby cane seemed only a foot tall, and she had to crane her head sideways to look up at Chris—mumbling, toothless, a glaze of recognition in the one eye that wasn't dotted with cataracts. She didn't give off an aroma of snuff but a vinegary tang of decrepitude, or incontinence, and when Chris asked if she remembered Theodore Roethke, the poet, she said, "Oh, Teddy. Oh, oh, oh," in a lament of diminuendo and loss, and then grabbed at the air with lumpy fingers blackened by soil.

She was grabbing for Roethke, Chris knew, as if Roethke were present, and Chris remembered the revelation he'd received the week he returned to school, when the director of graduate studies invited doctoral candidates to a party and he arrived late, without Ellen, after she conveyed how unhappy she was at his reenrolling—the lack of income, he thought, as he stood in a dim kitchen where bottles had accumulated and an argument was going on about Barth. The rest of the house was dark and reeked of wine and weed. Students young enough to be in high school sat on couches listening to a folk song turned up high, and Chris was in the living room a while before he realized the group sitting in a semicircle on the floor, off in a corner, was nearly all undressed, staring ahead in silence, as if made of wax, dead to the instinct that suggested such a state meant you were ready.

A middle-aged man walked up wearing what looked like women's hip huggers, with blossoming bell-bottoms nearly covering his feet (a bare big toe, its yellow nail bent over the toe's end, appeared)—so emaciated he seemed drained by cancer or grief, the bones under his wheyey face taking the shape of a skull shorn of flesh, with only hair and the beard attached in a graying fringe. Ahab.

"Doctor . . ." he said, as if searching for Chris's name.

"I've just enrolled in the program," Chris said.

"Yes, Darlene, my wife— She was on the entrance committee. She's awfully sick. She'd like to see you—*so* sick." His eye sockets hollowed until it seemed he'd swoon. "She's—" The man ducked his head, and tears slid into his beard like dew down a web. "Come. Please."

He led the way up a carpeted stairs to a closed door, where a table of vials and equipment rested against the wall, and picked up a surgeon's mask and pulled it on, adjusting elastic straps at its back. "I must ask you to wear this," he said through the gauze, holding up another.

Chris slipped it on, and the man put his hand, heated, on his shoulder and said, "If you'd do it, please." Tears were again rolling from his eyes, darkening the gauze, as he swung the door in. A pair of spotlights beamed down on a woman under a sheet, her dark hair combed back, her face covered by a similar mask—that and no more, from the areas visible through the sheet. "Yes?" she whispered.

"Your doctor," Ahab said.

"What?" Chris asked, and found the man leaning against the closed door, his hands behind on the knob.

"Just be gentle," he whispered.

"Yes," the woman said. *"Quick."*

Chris, unmoored, turned back to the man—glaring out from misted eyes over the mask, as if it would be his privilege to watch—then to the woman, unable to imagine what kind of person would portray such a sick sort of Fatima, and pulled down her mask. It was his dean.

So as he stood over the elderly, crippled woman in the greenhouse, he knew Roethke had been led by her and the other fraus into an animism that drew him so fully into the world of "spirit" he came to see himself as an Indian, just as Chris seemed the one called to say this. Before Roethke was born, American religion took a feminine turn in the Father-Mother-Loving-God of Mary Baker Eddy. Chris knew that Roethke noted this and also how, as the colonists' Puritanism slid into Unitarianism, then Enlightenment thinking, the influence of Indians on the culture became apparent: transcendentalism. Pantheism, really. Thoreau's wigwam in the woods. It was then the covenant breaking, the ignoring of treaties, the outright lies and planned mismanagement of Indians began, not by Puritans but the government, as if it knew Indian life well enough to dictate its course with moral authority.

That life was mainly horizontal—brother deer, brother grouse, grandmother moon—and organized around the family, with the mother, the earth, at its center: all gathered in her lap. The topless towers of theology and literature were as alien to the culture as Westminster Abbey. It was light the fire, be attentive to its spirit, be wary of it. It was take a deer, apologizing to it for its life to sustain yours. Or this was mostly so, except when Plains Indians chased a herd of buffalo over a cliff's edge, sometimes thousands at a crack, and sawed off as much favorite meat as they wanted from the wallowed mass. Squaws sometimes arrived to skin as many as they could, true, he thought, and turned to the window between the cookstove and sink and saw its panes and mullions as the divided countryside, where his fate rose toward him like his reflected face.

The pattern was to apologize to the woods, the birds and beasts, to attempt to placate them as you placated the spirits of men and women so those spirits didn't pursue you after their death. Everything contained a spirit, and any spirit could overtake you, so every confrontation on the horizontal was fraught with life-and-death overtones. Peace talks became massacres. Somebody building a house with boards could be your kingdom come. A woman might swallow you into her for good. The Puritan lives, so ham-handedly opposed to the course of nature and the spirits within it, were viewed as threats. There was no tower of theology to cling to, as the natives of Western Europe had clung and so absorbed the Huns and Mongols and Moors. Not only absorbed them but fit their cultures into the existing one.

Every historical movement unwound backward, he saw

through his reflected face; first religion was questioned, then government and authority, including men as heads of families or tribes, until women took over—first in the most sophisticated branches of society: here, the Iroquois and Algonquin. Then children rebelled against matriarchy (Nero assassinating his mother) and threw society into an upheaval that turned it to nature again, which at least couldn't talk back. The point was to slay or engage it at its own level: ecology. Thoreau's wigwam in mom now. The attempt to meld all material into One. Transcendentalism's amorphous curse. It was Roethke or one of his students—there were so many, Chris had read so many books—who said, "Transcendentalism was the death of American verse."

He set the glass in the sink to a sound like footsteps crushing snow as his hearing attended to the fire in the stove. Where had he been? He would have to tame this material into the confines of Roethke for sure. The rule of women over Roethke wasn't so apparent until he married in his late fifties. . . . Another thought plummeted like a hawk, opening an empty space in his consciousness like an ache.

He went to the table, to his file folder under the bulb swaying from its wooden bowl, and found he had six new pages; one more than he remembered. A flapping something distracted him, and he turned and saw a hole, like half a saucer, black as night, in the plastic facing south. A loose piece fluttered under the sieges and withdrawals of the waves of sleet. A bird? A bat?

Then he saw the plastic had been sliced into, in block letters he read at first as "big" until the half-circle flap flopped back in his direction: PIG.

He dropped his folder and jerked the chain on the bulb,

the nearest switch. The gold candle lights beside the windows still glowed. He leaped past the range and switched them off. It could be Beau. He unlatched the door and stood inside the porch, an icebox, his breath billowing in pearl blooms. He unlocked the door and stepped out, shocked by the cold and the grainy drilling beads of sleet, and walked in shirtsleeves, one hand up to shield his eyes, to the end of the dining wing, where he and Beau had stood, and checked the woods and nearest trees at hand. Faint footprints.

"Beau?" Not even an echo in the muffling sleet. "Beau, this would be a hell of a joke!"

He grabbed the sheet of plastic and ripped it down, an explosion that crackled and wound across him as he gathered it in a bundle over his stomach. He carried this inside, kicking doors shut, numb from the cold, and lifted the lid of the cookstove and stuffed the bundle into its firebox.

He could refill the glass, dim glint in the sink, but didn't want any lights on. Afraid, or stupidly unafraid, after the work he'd imagined? He stepped to the sink and rinsed the glass in the dark, a blind man waiting to be struck from behind. He jerked down a towel, dried the glass, and set it on its shelf. A surge of heat from the plastic in the cookstove warmed him so suddenly he was transported to the upper edge of a realm related to an undeserved visit from Ellen shortly after they met, when she appeared in his room in an outfit entirely of yellow, far removed from the logs and boards of the place where he now stood, and brought him into the world of the waking, a golden morning bound by bars of morning light, with a radiance about her of one arrived from such a great distance she was otherworldly.

The schnapps delivered a slight jolt, and he started to float down an angled line, shedding his clothes like a history of the years since that visit, until he lay enwrapped in her and her heat in bed.

7

In the morning he tore down the rest of the plastic and sat at the table staring out at nature unallayed. The cabin was extending to the limits of his vision, it felt, as if he'd cleared the additional space by his speculations late last night. He shook his head. The sleet was melting, and a wind off the lake agitated the limbs of trees so that he noticed their outlying twigs taking on color. He grabbed his file folder. It was the time of day when she sat at the cookstove and worked also, on whatever she was recording there.

The engine of the drilling rig remained a distraction that hindered their talk and angered her; but it stimulated his ability to concentrate, and his thoughts came in such a rush his only difficulty was deciphering them, once down. So when the three women in Roethke's greenhouse—

There was clack and slam in the porch above the rig's noise, and Beau walked in, his hair bound with a patterned headband like Tonto's, brushing the shoulders of his shirt. "God!" he said, overcome, his eyes glazed, and Ivan hurried behind, out of sight, and dropped at the stove.

"Give me a cigarette," he said in an aside, then again, "God!" He raised his head and gripped his hands as if in prayer. "It's happening! When I went to take my morning leak, a pair of kestrels, these beautiful, lovely birds, were doing aerial acrobatics above my hill. Then I spotted another fluttering way up, holding its place in the wind, and I thought, That's her! The woman. It's spring, man, spring!"

Chris handed him a cigarette, and Beau had it lit and going without a letup in his smile. "You've got to get those noisy dolts out of here before they ruin it for you."

"You're telling me!" Ellen exclaimed, and stepped up to him, displaced by Ivan at the stove, then slammed her notebook against her hip and stalked through the curtain.

"What's with her?" Beau asked. "That pair of jerks are scaring away the wildlife for miles."

"That's what. Plus she's working, like me. Remember?"

Beau waved this away like a fly, an irritant.

"How else are we supposed to get water?" Chris asked.

"Like me, like this." Beau worked the handle of a pump, then pulled up a chair to the end of the table, grinning, and sat. "There's a whole lake out there!"

"Would you drink from it?"

"Not after whitey's poop has polluted it so bad half its fish are dead."

"I bet there's a pipe your pump is hooked to."

"I didn't put it in, and it's been in for maybe fifty years and hasn't caused a problem."

"What if the lift rod breaks? You'll have to knock a hole in the roof to get at it."

"Mine's outside." Beau rapped on the wood tabletop.

"You won't see any sign of this, once they're done. It's a submersible. No more pipes in the ground from the pump house all the way to the cabin, either. Clean."

"But they're ruining the forest floor out there, man, did you see that!"

"Beau, I tend to live here."

"What's that yellow gunk running into the woods?"

"Mud, they call it. They put it down with water from their tank truck—for drilling, I guess. They hit rock."

"You better keep an eye on them. Get your butt outside. Dig the changes! You can't sit here!" Chris expected a request from this, and then Beau leaned forward in a sudden intimacy, and his hair, recently trimmed and reeking of shampoo, swung forward as he whispered, "This weather reminds me I got no woman. I'm horny."

"I'm Ole."

"Ole?"

"You know, the cowboys are out on the range, doing what cowboys do when they're not killing Indians, and one of them swears as how he's got to have some, so the boss tells him there's always Ole, the cook. 'Hey, I don't go for that stuff!' the cowboy says. 'I can understand that,' the boss says, 'because Ole, he don't go for that stuff, either.' "

Beau sucked on the cigarette so hard it seemed he'd suck it into his mouth, then said through the exhaled smoke, "Enough of the bullshit. Can you help today?"

"Beau, I told you I—"

"This winter's been such a bitch I got more orders than I can keep up with. I'll give you a cut."

"No cut," Chris said, and sadly shoved the pile of pages into his file folder, an Indian again. "I'll go."

SHE OPENED the drawer and slid aside her socks. It was still there, the dull green buttons nubbled like the skin of a chicken's neck behind the plastic. It would be an

escape from that engine and the rest of the noisy confu-
sion—Chris yelling, "We're going to cut wood!" then
the slam of the door. The first time, though, didn't you
need a guide? She'd heard people got sick, and what
would happen if she did, or if she had a bad trip, as it
was put? So far she'd been able to finish her seven
pages, not that these were a memorial to her lost son or
for the ages—sometimes it read like babble—but they
were down.

She heard a gnawing trill mingled with the racket of
drilling, and then the engine quit, and she realized it was
the phone. She shoved the drawer shut with her hip as if
she'd nearly been caught and ran into the other room and
grabbed the receiver. "Yes?"

"Ahh," the voice at her ear, like a young man's,
said with such satisfaction she nearly slammed the receiver down.

"Who is this?"

"You weren't there Thursday."

"Oh." The face of the musky woman with the mussed
mouth appeared as if she'd swung into sight in the
mirror.

"Won't he let you come?"

"I've been busy," Ellen said.

"What at?"

None of your business, she started to say, and realized
she was staring through the windows at a young man's
butt in jeans as he bent over a weld wearing a black boxy
mask that the jumping electrical lightning transformed
into the mask of a Hopi in action. "I'm sorry," she said,
and turned to the wall. "What?"

"Let's hope you're not too busy tonight, honey," the
mellow alto said. "Okay?"

"Look, I think it would—"
But the woman had hung up.

BEAU TOOK the shortcut past their orchard, driving so
slow he stayed in granny gear, as if savoring the scarlets
and moss-greens visible in the brush, his fine-boned hand
on the knob of the vibrating floor shift getting powdered
with ash from his cigarette. He blew the ash off, then
turned beside Orin's hay field, the triangle Chris had once
worked, and to their right the uncut grasses lying in swells
across the doctor's hill, bent double from prevailing winds,
swiveled and trembled in a breeze that was invisible.

"You got a road now," Beau said. "A whole new world
to the south, the direction of innocence and trust."

"What's that?" Chris asked. "Is that a dog?"

Beau hit the brakes and glanced through the back window toward the box where Ivan rode. "What?"

"Up the hill there, to your right. It looks crouched."

Beau shut off the engine, and they got out. "Stay," he
said to Ivan, his eyes on the shape in the grass, and Ivan
dropped between their chain saws, muzzle over his paws.
"I hope I'm not seeing what I think," Beau whispered.

"It's a fox!" Chris hissed.

"Hush!"

"What's wrong with it?"

"Oh, Jesus," Beau said.

They went across the road, the dry grass chattering at
their pants, and Chris saw that it was indeed a fox, its
bushy tail back like a plume, a front foot up and cocked.
Then he saw a forked branch supporting the foot, a stake
at the neck to hold its head upright, another stake at its
hindquarters, driven through them, the way it looked, and

tiny branches set in a line to display its tail. He gagged. The stake at its head was driven straight in, stained black, the neck fur not quite covering the hammered split end, and the animal's teeth were bared in a grimace, eyes wide.

"Good God," Chris said. "Is this somebody's idea of a sick joke on hunters?"

"Joke!" Beau said, and swung on him, hair flying, the same look on his face as when he straightened beside the birch. "Are you that stupid, brother? It's bad medicine! It's a fetish, a curse. Stay back!"

He stalked to his truck, and when Chris got in, he spun away. He wouldn't explain or talk, but went jolting over the last part of the road, eyes set ahead, at a speed that sent Ivan scrambling around to keep his feet. They entered the trees at the Indian settlement, and their poles of shadow kept crossing the cab in a process that felt endless. The dark shacks, like deeper shadow, were smoking faintly from their stovepipes but looked deserted. Chris noticed the neatness—a few old cars, but none up on blocks—as if a community were at work. Once past, he craned around, and the unobtrusive buildings appeared to straighten, caught watching. A man stepped from the nearest, and Ivan, who was panting with excitement on his haunches, rose and blocked the man off, looking in at Chris, his tongue out and chest heaving as if he were laughing so hard he couldn't stop.

"IS THIS the librarian?" Ellen asked, staring down her nose into the receiver.

"Well, I guess I am. That's what they tell me, yes."

Ellen nearly reversed direction and asked if a book she'd wanted was available, but then said, "Is there some sort of meeting at the library tonight?"

"Well, this group gets together, and we have coffee and cookies and some great talk, yes. If you haven't been in, do, you're missing something—is that what you meant?"

"Is everybody welcome?"

"Well, aren't you a dear, so polite. I doubt most men are, but sure you're welcome! You come along and join in! Don't say who you are and we'll keep this just between us."

ON THE blacktop Beau sped past his own place.

"Hey," Chris said. "I believe that was your house."

"I tend to live here," Beau said.

So Beau did hear everything (Chris had wondered about that) and remembered every shred of it. Now was the time to ask about last night, as they were batting along this highway, but Chris knew Beau wouldn't appreciate the insinuation of guilt, and then realized that last night's prank wasn't Beau's style, as the fox was not. Beau braked and swung so sharply onto a sand road the chain saws slid across the box and banged a fender well. He headed toward the lake a ways ahead, then suddenly eased onto the shoulder and shut the Power Wagon off, and Chris felt a give and sway as Ivan leaped from its box. "What?" Chris asked.

"Did that yellow car turn down this way?"

Chris turned, as he had when the saws had collided, to check on Ivan, and now was surprised that Ivan was nowhere in sight. "I didn't notice a yellow car."

"Some help."

"What is this?"

"I got all the deadwood off my place and I'm saving the good trees for timbering, when the title's clear." He pointed out the windshield. "That's for today."

Past the ditch, at the edge of a cedar swamp extending

into darkness, old logs and gnarled stumps were piled in a ten-foot heap, their outer edges alight with a skin of ice.

"Get out and leave the door open," Beau instructed him.

Chris walked around the Power Wagon, to pull his saw out on Beau's side, and couldn't locate any marks where Ivan had hit down when he'd leaped.

"God," Beau said, on his haunches at the woodpile, his saw balanced on a knee, bar to one side. "Look at this."

Chris stepped over and saw Beau chipping with a fingernail at the sleet covering a layer of soaked leaves. A red-tipped tendril, like the feeler of a creature underground, rose in a curve from a depression at Beau's foot, shedding crystals of ice from its trembling horn with its exertions to unfurl. When Beau touched it with a fingertip, the veined twistings of its green-red leaves sprang free.

"Look," Beau said, and in a crosshatch of sun ahead Chris could see dozens of the wormlike horns quivering above the leaves, probing through craters of sleet.

"Leeks," Beau whispered. "Visit here for leek soup."

There was a sound of shattering ice from the cedar swamp, and Beau cried, "*Ivan!* Leave those damn beaver alone!" He grabbed the handle on his starting rope. "We'll work the offside, away from the road," he said, and flung the saw away with his wrist and had it screaming at high speed. He stepped to that side, the cedars amplifying the saw's racket with a woody density, and the ends of protruding logs started dropping in stove lengths. Chris carried his idling saw to a downed tree at Beau's back, throttled it into the pitch of Beau's, and stepped down the tree, knocking off limbs but leaving enough to keep its trunk off the ground.

He crouched and took off the tree's tip, then set the bar in at stove length, dry wood streaming over his boots like ground bone and then, in a sudden brown-red rush, spraying the sleety leaves like blood as his bar hit heartwood. He gasped, and his stomach seized as it had at the sight of the fox. Had it been staked in place alive? Forgive me, he thought, to calm himself, and set his blade into the tree in a deafened numbness made worse by the pair of saws in chorus. He was nearly against Beau when he felt a tap on his back, Beau signaling him to stop. He killed his saw, and its last sounds went through the woods like a plane plowing in, gone.

"That's all the time we got," Beau said, out of breath. "Load it up." He pitched a length of wood over, as he must have been doing for a while, and it boomed into the pickup box.

"What's wrong?"

"Whitey's on his way."

Chris heard only a sudden trilling of birds, a chorus of warning, then a crash in the woods that might be Ivan.

"Come on, come on," Beau said, "toss it this way." He was at the pickup box, his saw inside.

Chris started tossing lengths from the tree he'd cut, and Beau, catching them, cried, "Where'd you learn that?"

"What?"

"Running the limbs off a tree like that?"

"Philip Nagonawba."

Beau almost fumbled the piece that arrived at his chest. "You worked with *Philip?*"

"He gave me a demonstration."

"That expertise from all those years on Fox?"

"I guess."

"I bet you heard the whole history."

"Not much."

Beau dropped in the last piece and then ran over and

started kicking leaves and sleet over the streamers of saw-dust. "Hurry. I'll get this. Put your saw in the place I left, down low."

The box was nearly filled to its sides, but there was space for his saw at the wheel well; then he hopped in the cab and slammed his door. Beau drove down to an approach, leaning over the wheel in anxiousness, swung aside on it, backed onto the road, and headed out the way they'd come. There was a clunk and a sway, and Chris glanced back and saw Ivan on his haunches on the logs, his legs and the graying fur of his underbelly soaked, tongue unfurled in the wind.

"Some dog," he said.

"He's never missed," Beau replied, then pulled his torso against the wheel, angling his head. "Do you get the drift of him now?"

"What?"

"Dick White."

They climbed a rise in the road, and a dusty pickup came barreling toward them, its driver jolting past a series of potholes and gripping the wheel with both hands to keep from hitting the roof. "Ron Naaden," Beau murmured. "His land." Beau continued at his speed, both of them sitting with the upright, unblinking innocence of crooks, and as the trucks passed, Beau raised a finger from the wheel in greeting and said under his breath, "Didn't catch me, yah! yah! yah! You got to catch me at it to make it stick, Dick White!"

THEY DROVE on to Beau's farm, past the house, releasing Ivan in a leap. At the far end of the curved drive, a barn, weathered gray-red, was set into the hillside. Its foundation was of stone, a six-foot bulwark that triangulated, as the hill rose, to a single row, so a farmer could drive his team or tractor into the second-story haymow from the hillside. Beau pulled around that way, to a pair of doors, drawn shut, that rolled back on rails.

"Would you get those?" he asked. Chris hopped out and rolled the doors back far enough to admit the Power Wagon, and a rush of birds, pigeons, he saw as he turned, came spilling past in startled flight. Beau pulled even with him, his elbow out the open window, and said, "Those buggers must be imported from England, like starlings."

"Pigeons?"

"The bastards splatter out about a cup of goopy chalk every time they eat a bug. No native bird does that."

Loose planks rumbled through the barn below like bridge planking as Beau drove in. Chris's vision was thrown by the shafts of light from parted boards crisscrossing in the dimness, and then brake lights flared red over a mound of logs piled as high as the hay in most barns, up to the beams spanning the roof, filling one-half of the mow.

"Good God!" Chris cried, and the rose conglomeration of stove-length wood went out like a vision.

A Power Wagon door tinnily clumped, echoing through the mow, and Beau said, "What's that?"

"You've got enough wood to outfit Alaska for a winter!"

"Half of it's from here." Beau stepped to the rear of the Power Wagon, into the faint light reflected from the rise of the hill, and set a hand on the tailgate, staring at his miniature mountain. "I make it a practice not to haul any out until I've hauled in at least a part load."

"Beau, what are you going to do with all this?"

"Burn it. Sell it to Dick to burn. Today I have to split a lot, so I need you."

"Split this? This'll take months!"

"Just some," Beau said, subdued.

"I could use some."

"It's twenty-five a pickup load."

"Twenty-five bucks!"

"I'll toss some off at your place someday. Meanwhile I'm thinking about whether to tell you about that fox."

This sounded like blackmail, and Beau slinked to a beam that formed the frame to the sliding doors. "I got all this." He gave a toss, and a pair of axes clipped into the floor next to Chris and trembled, hafts erect. Beau threw over a thumping maul that sent dust fountaining and, then, in a clatter, half a dozen metal and plastic wedges.

"Gee," Chris said, "don't you have a tomahawk?"

"All right!" Beau cried, and spun him by a shoulder, his hair swinging from the headband, giving him the look of an avenging Apache. "That's enough! It's no joke to me! Maybe to teenage punks, but not me! Are you that insensitive to a brother so beaten down by half-wits and whites he has to split wood to eat?"

"Beau." Chris wanted to hit him. Then he realized Beau had probably handed him the key to last night: the kids. "Do you really think the two of us can even make a dent in this with those"—he started to say *primitive*—"old hand tools? Don't you have a splitter?"

Beau walked to a chopping block beside his mountain and stood with his back to Chris, hands loosely at his hips. "Either I take you home or you help. I have to split enough for a half-dozen truckloads. I'm broke."

Chris picked up the tools and carried them over and let them clatter behind Beau's heels. No response. He rolled some of the pieces from the pile into better light, picked up an ax next to Beau's boot, raised it overhead, and slammed it through the biggest chunk in one stroke.

THAT WAS IT. She'd kept his dinner warmed and waiting, and now it was six. She threw her notebook on the floor, then picked it up, took it to the closet, and laid it on its shelf. Through parting clothes she could see the rifle, leaning in the corner, and was sure he and Beau had gone to town on a toot. At the cookstove she took the cover off the tuna casserole—baked to dry strings. All right, she'd eat. Then she'd get in the bus and drive to town and find out for herself what the meeting at the library was about.

THEY SAT on upended pieces of wood near the open doors having a smoke. Chris wanted to tell Beau about Johnny Jones but felt himself sink deeper into the depression he was sure by now he'd shed. "How much fits in your Power Wagon?" he asked.

"Mounded a bit, half a cord."

"How much do you figure we've split?"

"A cord and a half, maybe." Beau drew back strands of cold hair stuck to sweat on his cheekbones.

"So we're about half-done."

"Right."

"It's my turn to lay something on you."

"Shoot," Beau said, and they glanced at each other in alarm, then laughed.

"I don't have this all worked out, but I figure our problems began even before Columbus—Chrissy Number One—arrived."

Beau shook his head as if aggrieved.

"I mean with women."

"You're telling me!"

"It's not their fault. I don't blame them. It's the fault of the tribes, letting women take over."

"None did, not in main matters, anyway. Not war."

"No, the descendants of women were the members of Iroquois lodges, and women chose the representatives they wanted. They ran it."

"You're corked."

"It goes back further than that, to Eve."

"Now you're talking myth! A white one besides."

"It's pre color or race, I believe."

"Ain't Eve white?"

"I don't think that's mentioned."

"Who else would talk to a snake?"

THE LIBRARY did look like a Lutheran church from across the street, where she'd parked to check out the crowd. Or a fancy parsonage, if you viewed contemporary architecture as you should, cynically. Walls of pale brick, with redwood-stained eaves that overhung walks on each side, and a pair of slender windows in this gable end. A light went on, and through the windows she could see the polished hardwood planks of its cathedral ceiling. So somebody was inside.

"TAKE IT as a myth, then, if you want, but after the years I've spent looking everywhere else, it's the myth that has things straightest."

"We got better ones."

"With wily women often taking over, like Eve. It's the

quintessential story. Eve wanted a straight shot of power to the enth. Equality with God. Maybe even one up on Him. Adam jumped in after her, and when he got caught, he tried to pass the buck. Men have been passing the buck ever since."

"You're like a woman yourself—a frigid biddy with only one out—always flying all over the place. You sit there right now scared pale as whitey's poop, and it's not about that little bit of wood we got back from him. Have you been watching what you eat? Those buttons, I mean. Did you get taken so far away it's hard to get back?"

"Is the retreat into the wild all you've got? Is that all it means to you to be Indian?"

"When you worry about your blood, like you, you're not Indian. It's when you're worried you're white that you know you're one. The rest is just words."

"I've spent my whole life worrying about being white."

"Yeah, but your *whole* life—that don't count."

"Good God."

"Our myths and stories are better."

"I wasn't invoking Him. I'm sorry, Beau, I don't trust verbal transmission over so many years. And what about the myth of a universal flood, with only a few Indians saved? How do you square that with what's recorded in the Old Testament?"

"I've heard it. It only exists in a couple tribes and is probably about an overflow of the Mississippi, which Father Jesuit Dick White got written down wrong."

"I don't have anything to convert you to, Beau. I'm saying real Indian is a religion like any other."

"Amen. I know what I do from instinct. I don't need my head fooled with for university types to feel good."

"What if your instincts told you Genesis was right?"

"Wake up, I'd say to them, it's morning! Buddy, your intellectuality's got you fluttering off to the edges. You're making snow!"

Whether Beau drew this from the actual or not, it was snowing again, in lazy tumbling flakes that disappeared once they entered the dark of the barn. The two sat back on their stumps and stared out the parted doors at the powdery curtain drifting over the grasses of the hillside, both sunk in silence as silent as the snow itself.

THE DOOR was locked, Ellen found, and it was snowing. She started back to the bus, rubbing her hands, when she heard, "Oh, you!" It was the librarian, a plump woman with peroxided hair who always complained about her diet but had the look of one who could eat a horse, leaning her head outside the entry door, her legs smoky behind its tinted glass. "Are you the one to whom this is just between— You know what I mean. Come in! We use the back door to divert outside interest there, as Peggy put it to us once."

Ellen was delighted by the warmth of the entry, and through its glass walls she could see the heads of women bent over something in a distant, brightly lit room.

"Evie's brought her new piece," the librarian explained.

Ellen followed her through the dim building past tables that reminded her of a birthing room. All the women, a dozen or so, looked up as Ellen walked in, then withdrew from the object of interest—an elderly woman with frizzy hair in a folding chair with a quilt over her knees. "Then here," she said, continuing where she'd left off, "you use the same cross-stitch to tie these two together, see."

Ellen gave the group a quick look, but the bulky woman who'd spoken to her in the mirror wasn't there.

"It's a traditional craft!" a tall brunette exclaimed to a dumpy adolescent in a hippie shift, grainy with pimples, who had a hand over her mouth to conceal a smile.

"It's getting quite a bit past eight," the librarian announced, "so we better take our seats and get started on this." She herself sank down, spine upright and hands gliding down her skirt to her knees, beside the elderly woman. Ellen took the chair next to her.

"Oh!" the librarian cried, craning around, "don't anybody forget the refreshments when we're done, back in the corner by the table." A percolator thumped from there in emphasis. "Okay, Peggy," she said. "Start in."

The woman who had chided the hippie, in a black top that looked like a leotard and a long black skirt trimmed with fringe that swept the floor, hurried to a dictionary stand in front of the chairs, an arm's length from Ellen, and opened a file folder over its top—her podium. She glanced at Ellen, as though to place her, and Ellen sensed herself so drab she put a hand to her hair.

"All right," Peggy said. "So far we've talked about women in American society and women in the workplace." She threw out her chest. "Where you get all the grabs."

"Right on!" somebody said. "Tell it to me!"

"So tonight we're going to get down to the nitty-gritty of the matter, the chauvinist pig at home, as the beast that he really is—usually trying to make the two-backed one."

Now there was a chorus: "You said it! Right on! Hey!"

Peggy hooked a drooping strand of her Indian-black hair, done up in a French roll, behind one ear—all shapely whorls without jewelry setting it off—and paused to stare at Ellen again, directly now, and Ellen noticed a wormlike scar, raised red-pink, under her left eye, and felt her heart trip and strike like knuckles at her chest.

Peggy was talking, but Ellen hardly heard as she tried to recapture the stir of sympathy she'd felt at the sight of that scar.

CHRIS FOLLOWED the sounds of Beau in the barn below, searching for a kerosene lamp. He stretched out a leg from the stump, rested his weight on it, and sighed. He pictured snow falling over the pelt of the fox on the hill and was overrun by such a sudden premonition that he whispered, *"Ellen!"*

ELLEN KNEW the coconut cookies wouldn't do it for her; she needed a drink. The bus roof was frostily white, a foot thick, and she wanted to walk in the snow that fell heavier every second, dimming even the street lamps. Their muffled violet coronas swayed with the wind, and the hurried flakes across her face as she walked, like miniature wings brushing too near, were annihilated by her everywhere they touched.

"NO, I'M sure she had to drive to town for something," Chris said, but the moment the blurry probes of Beau's taillights sank below the hill, he strapped on the closest pair of skis and started skating off for town.

THERE WERE so many men in the bar that Ellen would have tried the snooty place across the street if a dozen eyes hadn't gone over her so thoroughly this might seem a retreat. She had no idea what occasion might have drawn

miners and lumberjacks here, as it looked, smoking up
the place and making noise. Then she stepped to the bar,
and the bulky fellow at her elbow, whose idea of winter
hygiene suggested a church-basement fish fry that had
gone on too long, said to his stoolside buddy, "Boy, this
bowling tourney's made the winter for me. What a week!"

Farther down the bar an old man with a varicose nose,
wearing a big gray Stetson with gray hair that seemed to
grow from the hat down over his collar, yelled, "Bartender! Get that pretty little thing down there a drink
that'll set her heart a-laughing!"

"When did old Rio roll in?" Fish Market asked.

The buddy, who'd exposed a mouth of gapped teeth for
Ellen's approbation, said, "I just noticed him myself."

"You come on down by daddy, gal," the cowboy said,
"and I'll save you from those bozos. A drink, Bud!"

"Take it easy, Rio," the bartender said, his whole head
flushed and sweating as he bent to a sink and plunged
soapy glasses over an upright brush.

Ellen gave the faded cowboy a faint smile.

"See! I knew you could! You come on over here now!"

She walked to him, and he said softly, nodding at the
aromatic pair, "Now, me, I've always appreciated a sense
of humor in a fella, nay? Why, I recall back in the thirties,
when Bud Welker—no skin off this Bud here"—he
nudged her with a knee, and she glanced down and saw
a pair of polished black boots on the chrome ring of the
bar stool—"Bud Welker and me was traveling in a fine
rig over the back acres of Wyoming and Idaho when it
was raw country yet." He winked, and a shot glass came
down in front of her, smelling of the world's worst whiskey, and then another for him. He tipped the hat back
from his forehead, picked up his glass and held it even

with his nose, so that his right eye looked like a marble at its bottom, then threw it back.

Ellen lifted hers and sipped, and the cowboy, in a voice clawed by the liquor, got out, "Air you go, gal!"

Then he pulled out a bandanna and blew his nose as if about to begin a sentimental cowboy crying jag.

THE BUS was parked at the library, to throw him off, he thought, though he wasn't sure what from. He knew she was in the bar. He tried the sliding door of the bus—unlocked—and threw in his skis. One banged off a window and came back at him, and he caught it on the fly and threw it again, like a spear, and saw it pierce the perforated headcloth. "Hell with it!" he cried.

"I WAS working the Boulder Dam down in Arizona, and all day sightseers kept driving up, so I said to Charley Groat, my buddy then, I said, 'Charley, ain't there some way a fairly intelligent cowhand can make a little change off these tourist folk?' We was working for Uncle Sam, you see: coolie wages, a ya! So me and Charley concocted a scheme whereby we would gather a bunch of rocks and pack them down the road a ways to where our work foreman wouldn't see and paint with plain old ordinary house paint on every dang one of them rocks 'Boulder Dam, 1935.' We called them genuine souvenirs of our nation's late wonder, and those tourists bought 'em for ten to twenty-five cents apiece, depending on the size. Two-bits was good money then, and it wasn't long before we quit our jobs and commenced to peddle rock full-time!" He slapped the bar like Moses gone mad, his head ringed in the cloud of his hat. "Yes, I've wrangled and panhandled, and I've prospected and gambled; I've been a plumber, a carpenter, a millionaire, and a bum. I've trick rode for the Ringling Circus, I've trick rode for Mr. Tom Mix, but the best trick riding I did was on a beauty—"

CHRIS SWUNG the door in and through smoky mist saw Ellen's yellow hair, and then, back at the same table, the woman with the football shoulders and smeared mouth. He went straight for her, and Ellen was in front of him, a hand to his chest, smiling with such pleasure he had to stop.

"How'd you get in?" she asked.

"I skied, you shit."

"That's my line! I was going to come in one night after you took off, and when you asked how I got here, I was going to say, 'I skied, you shit.' " She held up a glass of ice with a finger of whiskey at its bottom—rotgut, from the stink—and rattled it at his face, laughing.

"What, are you getting drunk?"

"Can't I?" She asked this over the glass, raising a shoulder against her cheek like a tease.

He went to the bar. He'd finished a measure of Beau's bourbon, once they were done with the wood, and hadn't taken time to pee on the way in, so he felt ready to go up on his toes and dance. He ordered a bourbon, and Ellen stepped beside him and pressed a knee into his leg.

"Uptight, big boy?"

"Ellen, what are you *doing?*"

"How demanding of you! Demeaning? I was invited to a meeting at the library. By the librarian!"

"You mean the moose?" For a moment Ellen looked

puzzled, off course, and then glanced over her shoulder, then back at him. "I didn't know she was here. She wasn't when I came in. How creepy."

The bourbon arrived, and he downed it and went toward the "Chiefs," noticing the woman pull away as he passed, as if she had a shopping bag to protect. Somebody who had to bow his head to keep it from hitting the ceiling was at the urinal, and when he saw Chris, he did a take, then a clownish stumble backward till he hit the wall. "You!" he cried.

Chris wasn't sure how to take this.

"Just kidding!" A toothy smile parted the beard of the sailor, who had the glazed look of a drinker far gone. He stepped up to the urinal again. "Safe in port!" he said. "What a night! I can't believe the stuff this woman did. I'm so ashamed I can't even think of it!" He covered his face with both hands, still draining himself.

"The way I hear it, nothing is shameful nowadays."

"That's what I thought, too, but this *was.* Boy, is God mad or what? He doesn't go for this!"

It wasn't a topic to pursue now, and by the time the fellow finished up, twenty miles down the line, Chris was beginning to dribble and spurt as he got it free. Ah, God, the relief that this at least always worked! Thank God for that.

Out in the hall he saw that Ellen wasn't where he'd left her. The woman at his back whispered, "Jealous, buddy boy?" or, "bloody boy," as if she'd heard on the underground telegraph about the teenagers beating up Johnny, and Chris would have turned if he hadn't then seen, rising from a stool beside Ellen, a gangly, silken-looking son who seemed to be stepping into a spotlight wearing the biggest cowboy hat manufactured, and then this cowboy draped his arm around Ellen.

Chris was hardly aware he'd moved, he had hold of the cowboy and was spinning him so fast. And was barely able to keep from uncocking his punch when he saw it was an old man, with an appalled old man's face dribbling Copenhagen out his open mouth. Chris slapped the man's chest with both hands and sent him staggering back, banging into the bar stool, one arm flying up, then caught him by the shirtfront, holding him on his feet, and again slapped his chest—the worst insult, not even fit to punch. By now there was the rumble like thunder of a barroom fight and shouts: "Hey, that's Rio! *Lay off!*"

Chris's arms were pinned from behind by some stalwarts solid as wrestlers, one reeking of clam soup, and he heard the bartender yell, "Get out of here!" along with Ellen's voice insisting, "Wait! Wait!" He was marched off by the citizens, and somebody hopped over a table to get the door. "And don't come back!" the bartender yelled.

Chris felt the group draw back to give him the heave (while the bartender added from a distance, to cover his odds, "Not till you learn some manners!") and then went sliding into the dark, trying to get his balance in his surprise at the snow, and heard a voice at his back whisper barely loud enough to carry, "Damn Indians!"

ELLEN SAID a woman named Peggy O'Regan organized the meeting but claimed it was the librarian who asked her to attend, and from her look he figured this was half true. Was his first impulse to destroy every man who assumed the patriarchal aspect of his father? Was this the case with Roethke? He was unable to continue the dissertation for fear of exposing his inner workings and sat at the table, stalled, watching snow sink below exposed tree roots. Bare ground.

"If it bothers you so much," Ellen said, "why don't you go see the bartender or that old guy, Rio, and apologize?"

He put his arms on the table and laid his head on them. He must have been asleep, because he rose to the thought of the carving in plastic. He called to Ellen, then in the closet grabbed the rifle, wondering when he'd last eaten. He went across the drive into the woods and leaned against a tree, feeling cogged bark against his spine, and realized he didn't have on a jacket. Trunks and boles of trees, bearing mottled rust, staggered off down the hill like a herd of long-legs in flight.

He saw a concavity in the woods below, half-drifted in, and something brown and circular, like the brim of a hat, protruding from the snow there. He walked closer, the rifle ready, and eased to a knee to study the half curve better. During their first summer here, in the heat of that extended honeymoon, he'd risen from her one night to the sound of tapping in the woods and had gone out in the dark, feeling his way to the noise, and found an old barrel rusted thin, holes eroded in it, resting near a sapling whose limbs were springing in the wind and striking the barrel in regular taps.

This must be an end of that barrel, now feathery as old felt. Had he expected a body dumped here, snowed on, buried overnight, the decaying vest of an old cowboy? Then he was inside the summer before, crawling to a spring-fed pool beside the beach to escape a rain, into a cave of cedar boughs overhanging the pool, and with a whir, a goldfinch was beside him, its claws like trembling vines as it released its watery song and was suddenly in the pool bathing, flinging showers of drops across the pebbles and his hands, and then it flew off, across a day so far removed from this one he saw the way in which seasons were used to preserve particular events, under grass or leaves or ice, so they were available to be released across any present state like the beginning of another season, a new time.

"Chris."

He sensed her hovering in the distance and then heard the forest floor crush under her weight.

"Chris, what are you doing?"

He didn't know how to answer her.

"Don't," she said. "Please come in."

8

HE WOKE THINKING he had to talk to Rio and felt well enough to work. But as he sat at the table, a radio went on—the portable Ellen sometimes used in the bedroom. "And if you will come forward now," a southern voice was saying, "and acknowledge in public, before this gathered throng, your decision for Christ, how the angels would rejoice!"

"Do you have to do that now?" he yelled.

"I'm looking!"

But the station didn't change or the volume diminish, and a choir began singing as Billy Graham urged people in his audience to make a decision for Christ—not the sort of thing a Catholic could put up with for long or the Puritans put up with at all. There was a knock at the door, and the radio went off. "What was that?" Ellen asked from her room.

"Somebody and his dog, I suspect."

But when Chris unlocked the doors and pulled the last open, a tall figure stood on the cement beyond the screen in a coat of shining black of the kind Chris had seen only once, on his grandfather, tailored from the hide of a riding horse. It must have taken a team of Belgians to supply the material for this one, because it hung from the man's square shoulders as he stood slightly stooped, smiling, to the toes of his gray-felt boots—his headgear as incongruous; a kind of baseball cap with a net-weave front, canary yellow. "Ya," Orin said, "a-ha-ha, I thought I'd try them skis, you know." He turned to the tree across the drive, with the light bulb nailed above, where he had propped a pair of wide wooden skis, the gold in his front teeth glistening with his tentative smile. "I got me them by Petoskey when I was a kid. Good skis, too, I'll say! They hie me over these few spots of white still left! No, ho"— he shook his head as if in amusement—"the partner, she thought I should come and see if you got wood!" He raised a wicker basket like Chris used to receive at Easter and seemed to consider its heft below the curved handle; it was packed to brimming with apples. "Ya, these Spys! I had to sort through the bin to find this many, and Spys are the ones the county agent says keeps the best!" He went into his low, breathy laughter. "No, I don't know! Maybe the Strohe girl can make you some applesauce."

"Why don't you come in and warm up?"

"Some got a good crunch to them yet, I tell you! I tried one coming up—always best in fresh air, ah-ya-ha!"

Chris suspected there was wisdom behind this as surely as Orin wore the camouflage of a dunce cap to cover his slyness. He swung out the screen door, and Orin set the apples on a workbench in the porch, then looked around. For wood?

"Grandma Strohe doesn't want us to keep it here," Chris said, entering Orin's world of non sequitur.

"No," Orin said, and gave a disillusioned shake of his head. "For apples, now, they say a cold porch is best."

"I meant—" It was foolhardy, if not impossible, to attempt to get things straight.

"Is that Orin?" Ellen called from the bedroom.

"Yes. Could I get your coat?" To Orin, who stood at his favorite place, inside the door, blocking it, one elbow on top of the copper-painted Kelvinator.

"No, ho-ho," he said, and gripped the side of his voluminous baggy tent and held it up as if to examine its hair. "No, I don't know about this bugger, if he keeps you warm as he could. Horse, they used to say, that's the best for cutting wind!"

"Is it windy?" Chris asked, coming unscrewed yet relieved by every farmer's favorite topic, weather.

"Well, you know, the Lord's day," Orin said. "You can't work today!" He stared at the sink as if it were about to work. "Them apples, well, I was thinking the Strohe girl might like to see some red this winter." He reached into a capacious pocket and pulled out a black book he placed on the refrigerator top. The Bible. "I thought I'd bring this, too. Good book! That new preacher now, though, he—"

Ellen walked in, to Chris's relief, dressed in jeans and a black sweater, but barefoot. "Oh, Orin," she said, "how kind!" Then looked around and saw only the Bible.

"In the porch," Chris said, "where the wood isn't."

"What?" she asked.

It's catching, he wanted to say, but asked Orin if he wanted something to drink.

Orin stared at Ellen's feet as if zeroing in on her vulnerable avenue, then squinted at Chris. "Not boose?"

"Oh, no."

"No, I guess I had my fill down to the house—that

coffee, you know." His smile twitched back his lips as he studied Ellen's feet. "Ya, ha-ha," he said, "no, I don't guess you go to church in those!"

"Oh, is it *Sunday?*" Ellen asked in the tone in which Chris had said, "Is it windy?"

"Ya, the partner, she was—" Orin laid his hand, still in a farmer's fuzzy orange glove, over the Bible. "Them apples," he said. "They'll keep."

"Sit down!" Ellen said, so self-conscious of her feet she seemed rooted, toes curling under. Chris pulled out a chair at the head of the table and got over to the other side, his place, and sat in a numb daze, thinking he must be humoring Orin to compensate for Rio. Then Orin said they should go to church with him.

"Would we have to come forward?" Chris asked.

Orin studied him as if he were a bunny.

"You know," Chris said, "make a decision for Christ."

"Oh, ho," Orin said, "no, I don't know about that now. Our church, you see, it's Lutran. We baptize 'em."

"You mean if I'm baptized I'm okay?"

"Well, now, not if you been baptized Catlick," Orin said, as if he'd read Chris's mind, because Chris was about to say he'd been baptized—but in the Catholic church, of course. "Den you're confirmed," Orin said with the weight of a Scandinavian winter conclusion. "You're *Loot*ran."

"I thought Luther's primary argument, or the one he's noted for, is justification by faith. Isn't his commentary on that point the real beginning of the Reformation?"

"Ya, ha-ha, that Martin Luther, he's a sly one, that one!" Orin said, as if Luther lived next door. "By fate you're saved tru grace!"

Behind Orin's back Ellen slipped into the closet and

stepped out in a pair of socks, then disappeared and came back out with slippers over these. "Tea?" she asked.

"No," Orin said, and gave his head a shake. "I guess we got one neighbor less. Old Doc Steele up the hill there, he went down in Detroit this week. Heart failure, I hear."

When? Chris wanted to ask, but was unable to get out the question for fear he might hear what he didn't want to hear at the moment.

Orin, however, had reached his conclusion; he rose, brushing his gloves in two swipes, and in a movement in which he managed to duck under the overhead light above the range, he was at the refrigerator. He picked up the Bible, shoved it into his pocket, and went out the door. Chris pushed back and stood, staring at Ellen, who was staring at him, and before either had a chance to speak, there was a dark movement, and Chris turned to see Orin under the drape of his full-length coat go past the dining-wing windows in the easy glide he had perfected on skis over his sixty-some winters of negotiating this local countryside.

CHRIS HAD packed a pint of Calvados when they left the city, hoping to celebrate with Ellen once their work was done, and now he tucked it into his topcoat pocket and slid out of the bus. He went into the General Store, nearly empty this afternoon, and stood beside the soda machine ("pop cooler," people called it), where Indians congregated, and noticed that the fee for soda had more than doubled in a few years.

Art rang through the only customer at the register and, when the woman was gone, looked Chris up and down. "I seeyur celebrating Easter Sunday! Where's the little lady?"

"Do you know where an older guy named Rio lives?"

"Stuart Borrup?" Art's eyes widened and appeared to tremble, as if he'd heard about the other night.

"He wears a big cowboy hat." Chris described its circumference. "People call him Rio."

"Stuart Borrup. I bet ee'satta Grand Hotel. Homeboy."

"You mean the other bar that—"

"No, ho-ho!" Art said, sounding as Scandinavian as Orin. "No, our Grandotel'sat old building kittercorner across the street." Art pointed and walked off as if he wanted nothing to do with this. Then he paused and said over a shoulder, "Stuart's kindalike our celeb. Ener in back."

The building had an overhang above the walk, supported by gray posts, and its big windows were grimy, secured by stove bolts at their worst breaks, with tape radiating from the boltheads. Chris walked down one side of the building, following a path where bootheels had plunged, to a back door. He knocked and somebody yelled, "Yo, in!"

He opened it and was shocked to see through to the tape at the front. In the grainy light, piles of junk—steel cabinets, screw jacks, farm tools—stood in heaps. He saw a stairway in the corner and headed for that.

"Hey, buddy, here," a voice said, and Chris wondered if it was the saddle that gave cowboys high tenors. He skirted a disassembled wringer washing machine and found Rio on the floor, lying under a quilt, his boots and hat at hand, his head propped not on a saddle but the elbow of a stovepipe.

"So," he said, and remained where he was, then rose on an elbow. "The Turk. Going to clean house on me today?"

Chris cringed at the idea of slapping Rio's chest, then

said past his adhering tongue, "I wanted to say I'm sorry."

"Apology accepted in the spirit given." At the slight slide of Rio's eyes, Chris figured he had a pistol handy. "Your pretty lady gave not one clue she was attached."

"I brought this." Chris held out the Calvados, and Rio shoved himself into a sitting position so fast that the quilt dropped to his waist; an undershirt with straps. He held the bottle at arm's length to read its label.

"I see the spirit that moves is more generous than usual. Accepted." He broke open the seal and had a shot. "Ah! That'll put feathers in your dresser! Have some."

Chris shook his head.

"Sit a minute, young fella."

Chris found a five-gallon bucket and lowered himself over its top, slipping a bit inside.

"It'd be more comfortable flipped, youngun."

Chris shrugged and watched the sparse white hairs over Rio's head, bald on top, turn gold as Rio shifted into a shaft of sun to recap the bottle.

"I'm sorry," Chris said.

"I believe you mentioned that. I've been trying to think where I tasted brandy of this quality, and if memory serves right, it was Santa Fe. There's a statue in Santa Fe of a priest, outside a cathedral I could see from my hotel. Old fella, I thought, you are about as useful as that bronze bozo baking in that Mexico sun. I don't envy this latter end I've reached. I like to talk, son, and that's about the extent of it. There's no retirement home for old cowboys."

Chris shied like an animal from this last word.

"I was coming out of Nevada with a string of ponies once, headed for some lovely buttes across in Utah, when I saw two Injuns on horseback. I'd hate to say how long ago this was—pre–World War One. I rode on over. I never come across anybody in such a bare spot, and I was too full of myself to think mischief. Civilization had arrived, in my book, and at my age the more the better! They had nothing on those horses but little rawhide hacka-mores you wouldn't think'd throw a flea, and they was sittin' on skins, as I recall, about as naked as the day Mother Nature made them. It took about a minute to see they didn't speak a word of English. I never packed firearms. Oh, a carbine now and then to keep the coy-otes honest, but not that day. These fellas each had a Springfield in the paw not holding that curl of rawhide. They got me to understand real quick I should dis-mount. Springfields look about the size of this stovepipe at the business end.

"They stripped my horse. One of them took the saddle, though I can't say he put it to proper use. He tied the skirting thongs about his waist where he sat on his horse— a heavy old cavalry saddle with that camel hump at the front. Then this other fella, well, it about floored me. He wanted my hat. I held out my hands, begging, you know, but he was dead set. It must have been a hundred degrees. My mount followed when they rode off with the string like he'd fallen in love, and they went over the next hill neat as nails. I later found out I was fifty-five miles from the nearest civilization, as I would term it then. It was three days before I saw a human face. I beat those boys blue with my tongue the first day out, but after that shut up. I never saw such countryside so close up, and never will. It's not there now. I never held a grudge against them two. I guess they took what they thought was owed. I rode that same trail twice more and never saw them again and don't know to this day what ground they rose from. I didn't hold it against them, son, and I won't hold that other night against you, either."

He handed the Calvados back. "Now you take this home to your missus and treat her to some."

"Oh, no," Chris said, starting to rise, and the bucket, clinging to his butt, dropped with a thump. "I couldn't. She wouldn't understand." Why he'd opened it, he meant.

"Maybe, but in this matter, well, you're the boss. Okay," Rio said, and laid the bottle at his side and stretched out as he'd been before. "I need some beauty sleep. You go on home and tell that lady we patched things up."

NOW THE heat opposed him as he worked—in the high seventies, though it felt ninety, and the slowed molasses of his winter rate now seemed a sparkling spring. The roof was shaded by birches, but the swelter of heat thickened his thought. He looked up from the table onto arid countryside, Manitou a shimmering beast in the distance—Rio's landscape.

Ellen was nowhere in sight. She didn't answer his call. He saw the bus at the head of the drive, where they parked it now, and shut his file folder and jotted, "I've gone to Beau's, Love," and left the scrap on the burned-out range.

He took the back way, slowing for the doctor's hill and a glimpse of the fox, noting how its pelt was peeling from the stakes, muzzle shriveling, its eyes pecked-out burrows. A sawing trestle stood in the Indian settlement near the road, with stove-length sticks below, their bark and a patch of ground powdered with sawdust. He cranked his window open on the resinous scent, and a scolding bluejay

set the trees ringing. Then, in the rearview mirror, he saw
a man step to the trestle with a hand up and gunned the
bus away.

Ivan didn't come to the window, up on his hind legs, paws
smearing the glass, as usual, when Chris stepped onto the
porch. No claws clattered as Chris swung the door in.

"Beau? Hey, Beau!" The silence held overtones of his
own voice. Beau used only the back rooms, so he said,
and such a lustrous patina lay over the table it looked
wiped minutes ago with a wet cloth. Chris glanced into
Ivan's room: a maroon-colored milk separator bolted to
the floor, rust stains around its legs, a chill of winter present in the midst of the heat. Dark paw marks marred the
white walls. Shelves to the right, white as the rest of the
room, were piled with pieces of worked flint, attempts at
axes and arrowheads, and higher up were cartons of
canned dog food.

Past the cookstove, tepidly warm, he caught himself on
his tiptoes. The summery set of the sun sent pure radiance
through the eggshell room, and Chris stood over Beau's
cot, where a red Hudson Bay blanket, tucked in at the
foot, was peeled back as if he'd left in haste. Shelves here
were stocked with food, books stacked haphazardly, and,
near the head of the cot, Beau's bottle. Chris gingerly
removed it from the shelf, as if he might disturb a network
in the house, unscrewed the cap and sniffed, then sat on
the edge of the bed. Where are you, Beau?

The pillow was homemade, dark green, embroidered in
Potawatomi geometry. He touched the sheet, cotton flannel, and brought up a long black hair. Why was hair connected with witchery? Scalping? He held it to the light
and saw a red core, bright as neon, down its center like
blood. Then he heard a vehicle come over the hill from

the other way and was on his feet, trying to set the bottle in the outline of dust on the shelf and leave at the same time and had to dive to catch the bottle as it tipped. He set it where it should be, too late to get out of the house, and hurried into the kitchen, wiping his hands on his jacket just as Marty's Buick went flying past in the direction of the curve.

Chris stepped on the porch, out of breath, feeling he should wipe the doorknob—my God!—and saw paw prints over the porch boards. The prints circled in front of the door, and an outer ring of them looked fresh.

ELLEN WAS at the far side of the cabin, near the well rig, abandoned again today, in the tree she warned him never to come near with the chain saw—an ironwood that grew a few feet straight up, then bent in a perfect right angle and ran parallel to the ground a ways, and in another right angle rose again above the cabin. She sat on the horizontal trunk, an arm around the upright, her cheek against bark.

"Did you see my note?" he asked.

"No." She chipped at the bark beside her face with a fingernail. "I was thinking of going down to the beach."

He eased himself beside her. "El, what is it?"

The ironwood stood near the fireplace chimney, which was built of hundred-pound stones, each a different hue but all furred with moss—like weighted layers of this wordlessness that often overtook her in the city.

"The same thing," she said.

A baby, he tried to say, but felt his lips tremble.

"How are we bound without one?" she asked.

He shrugged. "By marriage."

"That isn't quite the gravitational equivalent of one's own flesh, is it? What happened to the— You know, the one who didn't make it? The one who's *dead.*"

"I don't know."

"Don't you have anything hopeful to say? You don't even ever say anything definite! How can I live with this!"

"The one thing worse than depression is being dead."

"How would you know?"

"I suspect."

"For you everything's up for grabs or simply another figment of philosophy to diddle with. I keep looking!"

"You could become a churchgoer."

"Nice," she said, and stood as if she'd walk off.

"I mean, the Bible deals with death and its aftermath."

"I tried that. As you know. Then I met you, and you took that, the one thing I had, apart. I have nothing!"

"I'm sorry."

"Really? Why? Let's try that stuff Beau gave you."

"We should give it back."

"Don't you dare!"

"It's peyote!"

"Is it more sensible to study the Bible and try to make some kind of religious leap of faith from it?"

"That's a faulty analogy, I think—Kierkegaard, or some Lutheran, wasn't it? The Bible has every shade of belief and unbelief down in dozens of ways in explicit language. My experience of life is it's a mystery that complex."

"Sure, you're an Indian."

She might as well have slapped him, he thought. "In the same way I could say, 'You're a woman' if I wanted to dismiss an idea of yours I didn't find congenial."

"Oh, shut up. How can anybody believe the Bible!"

"Take it for what it says, I assume."

"I don't want that kind of safety net."

"If you believed it, I doubt if it's a safety net—more like being up against the one who can fry you for good."

"That's your perverse Catholic upbringing. Mary Baker Eddy doesn't even mention hell!"

"I suspect that's because the one who mentions it most is Jesus. Mary has trouble with him."

"Why are you saying this?"

"I had to read it!"

"All that chauvinistic paternalism!" She turned toward the woods to test these sharply articulated words.

"Me, you mean?"

"Just now I meant it. IT!"

He heard a knobby trilling communicated to this end of the long cabin by the largest logs and felt he'd just awakened. "The phone! Grandma, surely."

"Why don't you talk to her for a change?"

He took off for the back door and, as he rounded the corner, heard her call, "Be nice!" and almost turned to say, as if in a continuing dialectic, According to whose standard?

There was nobody there when he picked the phone up, and he was almost out the door when it started again. This time he got it on the second ring: "Yes?"

There was a rough wash past the connection of somebody on the line, then, "Me."

"Beau."

"Get over here. Two guys need to talk." He hung up.

So, Chris thought, as he set the receiver back, he knows I trespassed.

"DID YOU have to snoop?" Ellen asked.

She had asked to come along, for the drive, she said,

her mood dissipated by the time he got back to her at the tree. So as he took the back road in the bus, he had told her he'd been in Beau's house.

"Really!" she said. "I sometimes wonder if you realize what you're turning into. I feel I hardly know you."

"Is that so bad?"

She looked out the window, her profile skimming over grays and tans but no expanse of green, and then the pegged fox, sinking half-hidden in the weeds, went by without notice, a relief. Then the poles of shadow, more netlike now in the sun, passed over his arm out the open window, and he saw somebody heading at an angle to the road in a rush. "Who's that?" he asked. "I think he's been greeting me."

"I should know, he's so familiar. He works for Orin, I think, or used to. I saw him once or twice on our road."

The man's tack drew him closer, past the trestle, his expression turning merry, and Chris waved and was about to say hello, since they were nearly on a collision course, when Ellen cried, "Chris! he wants you to stop!"

Chris went for both pedals and the gearshift, confused about misinterpreting the man, who now paused with a look like Carlyle's, in a denim jacket and jeans with the washed appearance of a costume, dark hair oiled back. The abashed resemblance, Chris noted as the man sidled closer, had more to do with a redneck from high school who dressed and had a do like this, and then the man said, "I seen you using this road."

"Is that okay?" Chris asked. "I mean—"

"Is it a private road?" Ellen called, leaning forward to see out Chris's window.

"Nobody owns nothin'," the man said, then glanced

behind to check on something. "There's one thing I got to ask," he said, and raised a finger as he came to the bus, head bowed, until he was at Chris's window, then looked up, grinning through an olive tinge that might signify a breed, and said, "Ain't you the sonofabitch shot at my wife?"

Chris felt Ellen draw back so quick he turned, then heard a clump at his side and saw the man had locked an elbow over his window ledge in a death grip.

"She said this bus is yours."

"Who are you?" Chris asked.

"Dick Henderson."

His hangdog attitude had disarmed Chris, but now he recognized it as the smiling menace of his high school enemy, the redneck who would walk up grinning, sock you in the face, and say, "How's that for a knuckle sammich?"

"She said you shot your damn twenty-two at her." Keeping his elbow hooked, Henderson grabbed the front of Chris's jacket with a slam and twisted.

"I didn't." Could he get going fast enough to shake him or stand a wallop before he did? he wondered, and saw that Henderson didn't have a scar on his face.

"He didn't!" Ellen cried, and her fervor threw the man.

"I have about five witnesses," Chris said.

"Witnesses, shit. This ain't court!"

"It will be!" Ellen yelled. "I'll tell Orin!"

This slowed Henderson a second, though Chris saw his unengaged hand, balled in a fist, start to draw back.

"You can talk to Philip and Carlyle," Chris said.

"Dumb, dicey goons!"

"All right, get in, we'll go to Beau's and have a drink and set you straight on this."

The surprise of this affected Henderson, whose grip on Chris's jacket gave. "Ha!" he said. "That fancy Dan, sober-as-a-judge old fruit wouldn't invite me in his back door!"

"Get in and I'll take you there. Let's settle this."

"This side," Ellen said, reaching back and popping open the sliding door, and in a glance Chris saw that she was furious.

"You try and pull off," Henderson said, still with his hold on Chris, "and I'll grab my shotgun behind this tree and blast you and this damn van west of Manitou."

As he jogged around to the other side, Ellen whispered, "I mean, did you have to do that? Ask him along?"

You opened the door, he was about to say, but it rolled back, and Henderson was inside, in the space where Chris had removed the center seat for hauling cream cans. Henderson dove at Chris and got a forearm over his throat in a choke. "How'd you like to live with a broken neck?" he asked. He levered down a tighter grip, driving a heaving cough through Chris that couldn't escape, then gave him a box on the ear, hard enough to hurt, and in the position Chris was twisted into, trying to get a breath, he saw a woman in front of the nearest shack—her round, flat face alight—giving him the finger.

CHRIS STEPPED down Beau's porch steps, crawled up into the bus, and said to Ellen, "How long ago was it he called?"

"I don't know. I had to get ready."

"We ain't good enough for him," Henderson said.

"But Beau—" Chris began, then raised a hand to his throat.

"Hurt?" Henderson asked. He was lolling in the rear seat like an exec in a limousine, Chris saw in the rearview mirror, one arm laid out in ease across its top.

"A bit," Chris said.

"I had to show her I wasn't letting you off easy," Henderson said. "Does she bitch!"

"Hey!" Ellen said. "After all that—I mean, *really.*"

"We could go to town and see if Beau's there and"— Chris glanced at Ellen and had to swallow hard past the dent in his throat—"maybe buy something."

IN THE GENERAL Store Chris got a gallon of wine, white, so they wouldn't be drinking rotgut, and was relieved to see the usual cashier, an elderly woman, running the till. Then Art came around a corner carrying a package of cookies he was sampling, waved, and said, "Having a party?"

"THIS ISN'T like Beau," Chris said at the door of the bus after another session of knocking. He walked down the curving drive to the barn, around to the earth ramp, and felt his breath go when he saw the open doors, but Beau was nowhere in sight: no accident with an ax. On his way back he heard their voices from the bus and wondered at the wisdom of leaving her with Henderson. He crawled behind the wheel, and Ellen stared out the windshield, red-faced.

Henderson tipped back the jug in a gurgling draft, then came forward in a squatting creep from the back, keeping his head below the ceiling, and held the bottle between them.

"No, thanks," Ellen said.

"What's the matter?" Henderson asked, grinning, already pungent from the wine. "Afraid you'll get trench mouth?"

"Not quite," Ellen said.

Chris wasn't much for passing a bottle but didn't want to offend Henderson, so he tipped it up, plugging its neck with his tongue; it wouldn't do to have too much.

Henderson waddled back and sat, an arm along the seat, the jug in his lap. "Let's go in," he said.

"I don't think we should," Chris said.

"Without asking teacher permission?" Henderson asked. "They say Beau's always got hard stuff in there."

"I'm hot," Ellen said.

In the mirror Chris saw Henderson wink, then drag his tongue over his lips. "It's not long till night now," he said.

How to get rid of him? Chris thought, and Ellen climbed out and went to the porch and leaned next to the door, her arms crossed. "Mama ain't happy," Henderson said.

Chris went and knocked again—stupid, after their wait.

"A waste," Ellen whispered. "We could be working."

The door of the bus slid back, and Henderson ambled up, a cigarette dangling, looking gallant in the fading light, the wooden steps giving under his swaggering weight as his eyes slitted like a lizard's with his intent. He poked Chris and said, "This is how Indians do it," and jerked open the door and was inside. When he wandered past the window, with its storm still on, as smokily dusky through the panes as a mirage, Chris realized he was checking Ivan's room and sensed Beau's outrage at the invasion.

He went inside, and Henderson stepped to the cookstove, tapping his fingers over its top, as Chris had.

"Where's the jug of wine?" Chris asked.

Henderson leaned against the stove, folding his arms across his chest, a chieftain, and a glint of winy emotion crossed his lizard's eyes. "You trying to run me out?"

"I don't think it'd be pleasant if Beau caught us."

"Are you afraid of everybody?" Henderson's body swung from the stove, then suddenly stilled. In the twilight filling the kitchen his face appeared blue while a misty silence, generated by his stillness, spread from him like light. He took a step up to Chris at the dim wafer of the table, then went past to the living-room door, hung with its tarp. He grabbed an edge and jerked it back as if to reveal somebody on the other side, and Chris came forward at the sight. Rough-sawn, bare open joists spanned the room, furry and hung with webs, with dank open spaces to the basement. A path of boards led to a wall to the left, where a door stood ajar, and through it Chris could see piles of hardwood flooring, some of which glowed in the faint light, as though recently refinished. Then he noticed another set of planks leading to a curved stairway whose hardwood steps seemed to lead, as the stair wound behind a wall up into darkness, toward open sky.

"Just like Beau," Henderson said. "All empty in the front room."

"I think it's Beau's pickup!" Ellen called from the porch, and then stepped inside, looking wary; she'd never been in the house. "I'm sure it is."

"Right on time." Henderson pretended to check a watch on his wrist, then flicked down his cigarette, sending up a shower of sparks, and ground it into the floor. They heard the rattle of the truck, and by the time its engine went off, Ivan was outside the screen, his eyes on Henderson, hackles up, rumbling with the growl Chris had heard only once.

"Can it!" Beau called, and Ivan was gone. "Hey, I'm sorry," he began, coming up the steps. "But those two guys are such—" He pulled open the screen door, and at the sight of Henderson his face shifted to the set of the Apache. "What are you doing here, Dick? What did I tell you?"

Henderson smiled so broadly dimples dug into his cheeks and a *hunh!* came from his throat. "How about if I squat in your living room," he said.

"You looked, you bastard!" Beau cried, his cry edging close to grief. "Leave my place alone!"

"Ain't it common property?"

"How could you bring this drag-ass in," Beau said to Chris. "I want you out!" He shoved Chris aside as if he meant him but was on his way to Henderson. "Your sneaky meanness gives Indians a bad name. You've blind-sided and clubbed so many brothers from behind, I don't think you can take a man straight on."

Henderson squared himself, and his right hand, balled in the fist, cocked back, but Beau stepped in close and jabbed the fingertips of both hands into his jacket. "Don't fake an attack against me, buddy! Not in my house!"

Henderson glanced at Chris, angry and perplexed, but with his tense fist ready.

"Try it," Beau said, "and it's your last."

Henderson uncoiled, rolling into his massive ease, and wiped a finger under his nose. "I wouldn't want to give this lady the pleasure," he said, and went out the door.

"Go on, get out," Beau said, turning his back on Chris and Ellen, then grabbed at the tarp. "You make me sick!"

"SEE," HENDERSON said, "he's too good for us." From his sprawled repose in the back, he glanced around the speeding bus as if he'd just bought it. "I like this color, red and white. Cops drive half-breeds, too." He hee-heed, and in the dimness Ellen saw him pick something from between his teeth with a fingernail. "Beau's a pussy."

Oh, aren't we brave in the taxi afterward, she thought, and said, "I don't appreciate that kind of talk. And I'd like to know what pleasure you think I'd get from a fight."

"Isn't that how society ladies get their kicks?"

She glanced at Chris, whose mouth was set so firm he looked more Indian than Henderson and Beau put together—the chauffeur or servant hurrying his master home, as per orders.

"I'll have to smooth this out with Beau," he said in general, going too fast. "The way he is about his house!"

"His house!" Henderson said. "That house is some family's down in Grosse Point. They're gonna bust Beau."

"You know the people?" Chris asked, alert.

"They was moneygrubbers here, so they'd be worse. Rich! If anybody from Grosse Point says they ain't interested in money, their main course is bull, and they're serving you snowballs for dessert. Nobody with money's going to let a dip like Beau tear their place apart!"

"What I can't understand," Chris said, leaning to see in the mirror, "is why he didn't leave the flooring down and use a sander like everybody else. Unless he figures he has to refinish both sides to remove Charley White."

Henderson ha-hawed and raised the wine bottle.

"Or maybe he's planning to peg it," Chris went on, caught up in this, "and figures this is the only way to get rid of the nails. Maybe he can't live with nails! Maybe—" He was staring so steadily into the mirror he neglected to see the road bending ninety degrees around the dome-shaped hill ahead, and she was about to tell him to pay attention when Henderson yelled, "Hey, that curve!"

"Chris!" she cried, and went forward at the same moment she was hit from behind and heard glass explode. The bus was skidding so badly she couldn't tell where they were but kept hearing an avalanche of glass.

"Good God!" Chris cried, grinding them at last to a halt, halfway down the opposite ditch. "Are you okay?"

"Why don't you watch where you're going!" she said, and saw Henderson's head hanging over Chris's shoulder.

"Hey," Chris said, turning, then whispered, "Oh, no."

Henderson said, *"Umf!"* and tried to rise, but sank back onto his knees, swaying. "What the—!" He shook his head, and her face was sprayed with wine, from the reek; she saw Chris's nose so splattered with it he had to wipe one eye clear. "He's hurt!" he cried, swinging in the seat.

Henderson sprang away, saying, "You bastard!" and struck the ceiling so hard he went down. He swung and hit the side door, denting it like foil. His face looked smeared with molasses, and he kept slipping on broken glass.

"Dick, Dick," Chris said from the wheel with a fervor she seldom heard. *"Please.* You'll hurt yourself."

"You hit me, you sonofabitch!" Henderson said. He swung from his kneeling position and hit the door again. "Uff!" he cried, and put a hand over his face. "My head!"

"Wait," Chris said, now between the seats.

Henderson swung, and they slipped back, stumbling. Then a pair of headlights started toward them down the road.

"I have to move this if I can," she cried. "Hang on!" She backed with spinning wheels to the right side of the road as the car swung past, horn blaring, and saw Chris heft Henderson onto the backseat. Fresh blood from Henderson's head was running over blood congealing there in strips, like varnish over leather. She put her fingers to her cheek and found that the spatters there were also blood. Chris's nose was smeared with it.

"Get us to the clinic," Chris said.

"No doctor!" Henderson kicked glass around trying to get to his feet again. "Oh, my head! *No!*"

"I thought you cut yourself on the jug, but I think you hit the back of my seat," Chris said. "Look at that."

"My head," Henderson wailed, and took it in both hands as if to keep it from cracking down the split that widened above one eye and poured fresh blood past a liverish clot.

CHRIS HELPED Henderson through the glass doors and at a counter inside punched a bell that brought a handsome nurse with graying blond hair down the hall in a swift walk. She called the doctor, the town's only one, then said, "Dicky Bird, have you been a bad boy?"

Henderson tried to assume a swashbuckling look.

She put a finger to his eyebrow. "That's some blow."

"Ow!" he yelled. "It's sore as a bitch!"

Ellen sighed at this, and the nurse, taking note, said, "I see. Did you find him this way?"

Chris explained how it had happened, and then the doctor was there, a farmerish fellow who had put on so much recent weight he walked with his arms held away from his sides, stiff and barely swinging, to keep them from hitting his butt. He looked down at the wound, like lips parting, and said, "Well, Dick, this time I think the other guy—"

Chris explained again what had happened, and the doctor said, "I'm Slater. Let's go in the operating room."

"Not me!" Henderson bellowed, and started swinging his elbows as if he remembered half of how to run.

"Be nice," Slater said. "It'll take a few sutures—the same as I took on a little boy today. He did fine."

Slater helped Chris guide Henderson into a room whose only feature was a leather-covered table with tissue down its center. "Sit," Slater said, applying pressure until Henderson did, then switched on a spot that sent Henderson off in a dash, paper ripping, toward the far wall.

"Those're glass doors!" Slater yelled.

Henderson fumbled at the latch, and Chris took his arm, looking toward the bottom of the hill the hospital sat on to the lined-up lights and treetops parted into the squares of a town. The nurse came in carrying a draped tray, and Slater seated Henderson, drew a syringe from under the towel, keeping it concealed behind a hand at his hip, then inserted it at several angles around the edges of Henderson's wound.

"It hurts!" Henderson yelled.

"Slight prick," Slater said, working the needle.

"Oh, yeah?" Henderson said, looking ready to hit him.

"Pull down your pants, Dick."

"There's women here! The cut's on my head!"

"You need a tetanus."

"I got 'em both, wise guy."

Slater glanced at Chris, sighing, and put a hand on Henderson's shoulder. "Look, Dick, I own this town."

"I know, you rich sonofa—!"

"I've tricked you into revealing your bias, Dick. I'm a very humble man, actually, and I'm deeply in debt. Now, drop your pants or I'll jam this needle right through 'em."

The nurse unbuttoned the front of Henderson's shirt and ran a hand over his chest to his shoulder, stepping behind him. "Mmmm," she hummed. "You got sweet muscles, Dick." Henderson craned to see her, beaming, while she worked the jacket, then shirt, over his shoulder and in a quick pull pinned his arms as Slater got him in the biceps.

"That's enough!" Henderson cried, on his feet again.

"Oh, Dicky," the nurse said, wrapping her arms around him and pulling him back onto the table, her cheek against the nape of his neck. "Does it hurt so baddy-bad?"

"Let's get together after this," Henderson said to her.

Ellen, beside the door, pale and appalled, walked out.

"She can't abide a hospital atmosphere?" Slater asked.

"She's Christian Scientist," Chris said.

"That explains it." Slater set to work with a curved needle in stainless-steel pinchers, Henderson protesting and complaining while the nurse embraced him and whispered in his ear. He started raising a fist, looking ready to swing when Slater said, "One more," and turned for another threaded needle on the tray. Henderson was at the door so fast nobody could lay a hand on him and got it rolled back and outside and was down the first terrace of the hospital grounds on a run, his jacket ballooning behind in a hump.

"Let him go," Slater said. "That last one was mostly for looks—cosmetosis. I pumped enough Demerol in him to knock out a cow! It must be the mix. Why doesn't some famous medical team do a study on alcohol tolerance in the American Indian?"

The nurse, who was silently cleaning up, shrugged.

"How much do we owe you?" Chris asked.

"Well, since you're paying, only a hundred bucks."

A hundred bucks, Chris nearly cried, tucking his chin in for control. He got out their checkbook, and as he leaned over a counter (he'd write it to the hospital, not this guy, he thought), he saw a white-enameled reflection of his face darkened over its nose by the same caked blood that covered his right sleeve.

"All right," Slater said, and tapped his back. "Now that it's over, compadre, why don't you tell me what really happened?"

9

THEY DROVE UP the narrow clay road, the front tires taking their own erratic paths in the ruts eroded by spring storms, and came over the crest of the hill to see a light burning at the back door. They hadn't been able to find Henderson, and as Chris was climbing from the bus, where he'd parked it on the hilltop, Ellen said, "What's that?"

"We obviously left it on."

"I mean all over the cabin!"

He came around to her and in the dim ocher light saw streaks and palm-shaped imprints on the logs. "Damn," he whispered, walking closer, and realized that whoever had done this, had used the mud from the drilling rig. "Pure Indian," he said. "It means by this hand I touched you, choked a bear, killed Mr. X and X—"

"Good God!"

"An intentional fingerprint, or 'Kilroy was here.' It's not Beau's style. Could Henderson have made it back?"

"It's those damn kids! Would you please see if they're inside. Or *got* inside. I can't remember locking it."

Even the screen door was splotched with clayey goo,

the inner latch smeared, but the door was locked; he had to use his key. There were no footprints in the porch or kitchen (with his head poked in Chris pictured Beau in plaid earflaps saying, "Boo!"), and he went to the dining wing and grabbed his folder. The page he'd finished before Beau's call was on the tyrannical rule of Roethke's Prussian father, who was one of those sick drinkers, from the evidence, who got a bigger kick from a drunk by involving his children in it. Chris saw room for a final sentence and scribbled, "Could it be that early emigrants to America, mostly poor Europeans like the Roethkes, inherited their sense of inalienable property rights from the Indians?"

He went out and found Ellen nicking with a fingernail at a perfect handprint on a log. "This is going to be awful to get off," she said. "Could somebody take a cast of it?"

"The FBI? Let's go to town and keep looking."

"Chris," she said, and took his arm. "This is creepy."

HE WOULDN'T go near the bar, so she went in on the pretext of using its facilities, but Henderson hadn't been there, she said when she got back in the bus. "Rio's busy, though, carrying on like before. Was there something about him and you that you were supposed to tell me?"

"We patched things up." Chris started the bus and tapped the gas pedal a few times. "Go ahead, I'm waiting."

"He said, 'Greet The Turk.' "

He drove out of town, his neck stinging, to the only through highway in the area; it had to be taken south for thirty miles, off this peninsula, in order to head north, the direction of escape, unless you wanted to escape to

Detroit. He saw lights ahead at Johnny's and wondered if they should stop when silhouettes, as if rising from the road, appeared in the headlights and took on color and substance, walking with their backs to the bus.

"Philip and Carlyle," Chris said.

"Stop! They'll know where he is."

He pulled over, and Philip trotted up and slid the side door open, grinning up at him, his nose a skewed purple bulb in the light, and said, "I thought I seen our bus." Then he noticed the floor near his knees. "Did you have a fight?"

They hadn't cleaned it out.

"Take us on up to Johnny's, huh?" Philip asked, and with a sway of the bus he and Carlyle were in the backseat.

"Have you seen Dick Henderson?" Ellen asked.

"Oh, yeah," Philip said, nodding, solemn, and then he and Carlyle started giggling and elbowing one another.

"What's that?" Chris asked.

"We was down by the harbor where the phone booth is and saw a guy was on the ground by it, like maybe hurt, so we went over. It's Henderson. 'Go away!' he said. 'Can't you see I'm here!'—like he was hiding. He had this big caterpillarlike thing over his eye. 'Hey, Dick,' I said, 'you playing Indian?' 'Get away!' "—said in Henderson's exact gruff voice—" 'I'm waiting!' "

" 'Are you waiting for a bus?' " Carlyle said with the mincing mockery he must have used on Henderson.

" 'We're waiting, too,' " Philip said. "We stood us a ways back where he couldn't grab us, see. Then Betty pulls up in her big black Buick she drives, and Dick's in—*wheep!*—both of them yelling, and they're gone."

Chris glanced at Ellen as they pulled up to Johnny's place. It was half the size of a railroad car, painted white,

with a high peaked roof, a little gable over the door, and
green flower planters under every window. The Nagonawbas piled out, and then Philip stuck his head back in.
"Hey, come on," he said. "Johnny wants to see you."

Chris hesitated, thinking, Didn't he say, "Come see
me"? Ellen was already sliding out in excitement.

A dozen men were in the only room, on cots and stools,
and Johnny presided at the far end, on a chrome kitchen
chair beside a potbellied stove. Two men rose from their
places and went to a cot in a back corner, next to Denny
Wing, who grinned toothlessly, then pointed at Chris and
cried, *"You!"* Philip and Carlyle took the lower tier of a
bunk to the left, Philip crouching under the springs above
and Carlyle leaning forward on his knees. At least one
man, with his back to the room, was lying on the cot
above them. Johnny gestured at the vacant chairs, and
Chris and Ellen sat. "You been nice," Johnny said.

Ellen felt the smoky eyes single her out with a formal
curiosity rather than a drilling challenge, though every
time she looked at someone, they were studying the linoleum. She opened her coat. It was stifling, but Johnny sat
next to the stove in a plaid shirt buttoned to his neck, with
the gray of long underwear extending past his cuffs. He
smiled from his benign cheerfulness and opened his
hands to them. A jug of wine was passed to her. She
looked down its mouth, into the liquid rocking below,
then held her breath and took a swig, so sweet she started
to gag, and sensed a ripple of response around the room.
She handed it to Chris.

"At a boat," Johnny said, "a big, ugly fellow, very busy,
going about making all the noise and mischief he can."

There was light laughter from the men, and she wondered if he was picking up a story in the middle.

"Once I's in a war," Johnny said. "I joined up, and the

sergeant says, 'What's your name?' I said, 'Sweet Bear.' He looks. 'Oh,' I say, 'it could be Bear-in-Honey, could be Honey Bear,' I say. 'Anybody call you another name?' he asks me. 'Sure,' I say. 'In town they do.' "

The men laughed.

" 'I mean, *baptized* name,' he says. 'A man in town, he calls me "Johnny," ' I told him. 'Ah-ah,' he says, 'I thought your name was Johnny Jones.' Now it is."

There was quieter laughter, and older men nodded approval. Philip, so malformed in the face, now looked entirely so, hunched under the bunk, lost to this, and Carlyle, so sleekly handsome he seemed to have shed ten years, kept staring at the stove, entranced.

Johnny opened his hands to them. "Johnny," he said.

"I'm Ellen."

"Chris."

"Hey," Philip said with his head, though still hunched, emerging. "We was down by the harbor, to see if anybody was fishing yet, down where the phone booth is. Somebody's on the ground by it, maybe hurt, we think, so we go see. Dick Henderson. 'Go away, you damn dumb Indian!' he says. 'Can't you see I'm here!' Like he was hiding! He had this big cut like a caterpillar here. So I figure somebody clipped him!"

Philip looked at Chris, who glanced at Johnny, who seemed to roll associations in a way that troubled Chris.

" 'What's up, Dick?' I say. 'You trying to play Indian again?' 'Go on, dope!' he yells. " 'I ain't no damn Indian!' "

The men laughed, and Philip kept repeating the last line and elbowing Carlyle till his bent nose bobbled, but Carlyle stared at the stove, sheared down to essence, pure sadness, and Chris felt sick with shame at the trouble he had caused.

"That's people," Johnny said. The index finger of the hand resting in his lap pointed up. "I thank Him all time for everything. Don't give to me, don't buy, don't sell. Thank Him all time for everything."

"Amen," Philip said, and doubled over with his giggling laughter. There was no response, and Carlyle, still staring at the stove with shining eyes, sighed as if he'd reached the concluding result of his grief.

"Philip," Johnny said, "he'd sell his mother."

"Ho yah! old man," Philip cried, turning on Johnny as if he'd go for him, but Chris could tell he was afraid.

The placid smile remained on Johnny's face as a log in the stove went off like a pistol shot. A sheen of oil lay over Carlyle's face, and in the stifling atmosphere Chris recalled a play he and Ellen had seen on Broadway, about the depredations of Cortés against Atawalpa, sun king of the Incas, God-on-Earth to them, and the sound that rose from the actor in the role of Atawalpa when he was bound to a post in a trial of his deity—"Atta-wahahh-ahl-pa!" he cried. In the hush of the New York theater his cry rose again, plaintive and searing, "Atta*waahhl-paa!*" and you could sense the city theatergoers poised for a miracle.

Now Chris's throat ached as if he'd released the sound himself, and for a second he couldn't place himself as the cry, nearly extinguished, started to rise from Carlyle.

Johnny raised a finger as if he'd heard. Then his application came: "All the time I was hit by them boys, I'm thinking, I thank Him all time for everything."

Chris felt heat on his thigh and looked down to see one of the prints from the cabin resting there, white. It was Ellen's hand. Time to go.

*   *   *

BEAU, HE thought, every interfering intellectual has tried to interpret Indian life, like the missionaries giving tribes a Great Spirit. The Algonquins, maybe, had a Great Spirit. That was it. He sipped at his schnapps, done with three pages, a further three for the day after the guilt endured at Johnny's. Our generation interprets Indian life its own way, too: an ecological imperative fueled by drugs. Along with the tinge of a semi-Eastern mystical retreat into nature: the All. Some retreat when you had to worry whether you'd freeze in a tipi. The stoicism Cooper tried to pass off as Indian wasn't there, if you figured the raw time spent trying to exist. Communing with nature isn't possible when everything has a spirit, maybe an evil one, and the idea of communing itself came out of eighteenth-century pantheism and a belief in a creation controlled by a benevolent God. *Good.* Johnny was saying that.

Nature hikers aren't quite in the same class as naked natives in a forest, with panthers, bobcats, and—

The phone's knobby trill gnawed. Ellen wasn't going to answer, was apparently asleep, so finally he picked it up.

"Those two guys are back again."

"Beau!"

"You'd better come on over."

"But you just—"

"Get over here."

There was a silence as Beau remained on, dreamily listening, it seemed, to the tumble and tenor of each of their separate thoughts. "I don't know. Ellen and I—"

"Come over. We'll patch things up." He hung up.

CHRIS TOOK the long way around, and when he came over the rise of a hill, on a straightaway to Beau's, the kitchen lights gave the house the appearance of a fire-place, the porch spread out like a hearth. He pulled into the drive behind a vehicle like a Land Rover, and in the glare of his lights on its tailgate he saw an Oriental name that released a smell like cherry blossoms. Or were the cherry trees hung with blooms along their boughs?

Beau was on the porch, lit from behind, his face black, and he took Chris's hand in a sudden grip that Chris couldn't remember him using even when they met, then swung their arms upright so they were drawn against each another, palms up and thumbs hooked. "Let's drop it," Beau said. "Okay?" Then whispered, "Be cool with these goofs."

The two were sitting at the table with tumblers and Beau's bottle, and Chris had to blink to take them in. Both were wearing puffy vests of polished nylon—one hunter's orange and the other bright blue with a yellow collar (like the shocking pigments of civilization after a week in the woods)—and this threw Chris so much he didn't catch their names. They shook his hand as Beau had shaken it and sat, one overweight in the way adolescents get, all belly and big behind. He scooted his chair back from the table as if to assert his centrality and announced, "Beau says we should talk." He smiled, long teeth emerging from his blond Van Dyke, his hair macked down like a latter-day Caesar's past his ears to assume the shape of his beard over his balding crown, from a point so central he could be hung from it.

"We're with VISTA," the other said, an acronym Chris recognized as belonging to some government agency. "We're putting together a powwow and doing some organizing in the area." He held up a badly rolled, thick joint. "You hip?"

"Not right now. Thanks."

"I mean," this one said, and glanced at the fat blond, grinning and shaking his head. "Do you know what's up?"

"You're smoking dope."

The two laughed with the helplessness of people who've had only enough to be comfortably high, the fat one leaning back and throwing up both hands, and then the other, whose hair overflowed his shoulders and was bound by a bandanna, stroked the front of his vest with such subtlety it moaned. Ivan, Chris realized, and saw the door to his room closed.

"Back up," this one cried. "Rewind! It won't start yet! We're stuck where the projector light is commencing to burn through!" He had a ruddy complexion, with razor streaks down his neck, and whistled asthmatically under his cackling laugh as his face brimmed with blood. A stitched name was attached to a medallion on his vest, in French script Chris couldn't translate. The one in orange, whose vest bulged like a pillow over his belly, bore AGSCO above a pocket, and Chris noticed that this one was giving him the once-over, up and down. Chris had thought of throwing on his topcoat.

"So you're from New York," Plump Agsco stated, and rolled his cigarette between finger and thumb in front of his mouth in an appraising way. "You been in a fight?"

"Actually, we hardly started," Frenchie said, back to the time before the projector, in imitation of Chris, and tossed the joint beside his tumbler. "I'm a working man."

The two cackled, and the fat one sat back, placing a hand on his haunch and set his cigarette, raised at a jaunty angle, to his lips. He let uninhaled smoke drift past his eyes, smiling, his face spread so broad by his smile it looked flattened. Then he pulled himself forward and said, "We know about your tiff with Henderson."

Chris glanced at Beau, who leaned against the counter of the kitchen cabinets he had started to build, arms folded as he stared off, his hair in a ponytail bound its length with wrapped rawhide. "Serve him right," he said.

"Where'd you hear this?" Chris asked, moving the blood-caked sleeve behind his back. He was in a corner, or worse, with Johnny at the potbellied stove, wondering how much everybody knew.

"Underground telegraph," Frenchie told him.

"Beau, don't be so glum," Agsco said. "Let's do everything in our power to maintain this lovely roll. Tell him."

"They've organized a powwow for next week at Keewadin," Beau said. "On the other side of the bay."

"Well," Agsco said, bending over to examine the end of his cigarette as though to check whether it was out, giving Chris a glimpse of blue scalp through his brushed-forward hair. "We've been designing this a couple months. They'll be here from all over the state."

"We're organizing *organizing* now," Frenchie said, and gave Chris a wild look. "You ever hear of Means or Banks?"

Chris, who'd been edging toward Beau, suspected the two were professional baseball aficionados, the sort who never played, and asked, "Ernie Banks?"

Frenchie laid his head on the table and said from the echoing cavern his arms formed, "Oh, God, no. As Tonto's widow said to Tonto, 'You should be recruited to do an imitation of yourself for eternity.' " Then he sat upright and asked, "Have you heard of AIM?"

"Fire."

"Forget it," he said to Agsco.

"Look around, read a newspaper," Agsco said, unpacking a pleased smile. "Tribes are getting *dang*erously organized."

"Under the government?" Chris asked.

Even Beau joined their laughter now, sending up rapping barks from Ivan in his room. "Quiet!" Beau commanded. "The Destroyer of Villages in D.C. ain't doing nothing for us. Nothing!" The two nodded in solemn agreement, and Beau said, "Do you have a cigarette?"

Plump Agsco sighed, as if he'd been supplying Beau for the day, then pulled a pack from the pouchlike pocket of his vest and tossed it in a flashy tumble across to Beau. He leaned back and evaluated Chris. "Do you dance?"

Chris studied him for the malice of the gay netherworld. He wore new, wear-softened jeans, the style even among fiftyish professors, and laced leather boots with Bean rubber soles. He put a foot on a knee, to model the boot reaching his calf. "Or chant," he added, as if to erase the double entendre. "Do you do crafts? I mean, for the powwow?"

"No."

The two looked at Beau, then at each another, and Frenchie said in a voice starting to erode into his cackle, "Can you be part of a giveaway?" He nodded at the table like a wooden pecking bird with his seizure of laughter and got out, "We asked Beau, and he won't!"

Beau took such a deep breath it drew him straight, then sighed and said, "You tell him."

Agsco flipped ash on the floor, scooted up to the table, and said, "We're organizing Neshnawe County. We need activists who aren't timid boogery kids, real *leadership*."

"Why did Peggy quit?" Beau asked.

"Peggy?" Chris said.

"Peggy O'something," Beau said. "You know her?"

"Regan," the one in blue said, clearing his throat.

"What do you know about her?" Chris asked.

"I thought things were okay with your wife," Beau said.

"You go for the ficky-fick?" Plump Agsco asked.

"You won't get close enough to Peggy to even put an arrow in her," Beau informed him.

"You should know," Frenchie said.

"Who is she?" Chris asked again.

"Some disaffected artsy fart from the city," Beau said. "She opened the sixty-fifth tourist shop in Leland a year ago. Is she from Chicago? Detroit?" He looked at the two, but they were now glum, staring into their glasses.

"Does she say beeick for back?" Chris asked.

"What do you mean?" Beau said.

"That would be Sha-*kag*-go."

"You trying to talk Indian?" Frenchie asked.

"That's the way they talk in Chicago."

"Because that's a hell of a job of it," he said. "That's one area where he's definitely excluded," he directed to Agsco, as if Chris weren't.

"Peggy used to work for them," Beau said, as if the other two weren't.

"It seems they're working both sides," Chris said.

"Three," Agsco intoned.

"How can you if you're paid by the government?"

The unworldliness of this obviously called upon Agsco's entire tolerant patience. "Uncle Sam gives us the entrée," he said. "We take it and run." He yawned wide, revealing molars capped with gold, and cried, "Hoo-whee! Tired!"

"Let's hit the sack," the other said.

"What did you want to see me about?" Chris asked.

"Come to the powwow," Agsco said. "Have Beau educate you enough by then so we can talk."

THE BUS wouldn't start. It ground away like an empty coffee mill, the gas gauge at three-quarters, and finally

Chris got out and removed the gas cap and smelled its tank. The vested duo had left, hitting the sack elsewhere, and after another session of the starter's shrill whinnying, Beau walked out. They opened the access hatch at the back of the bus but couldn't see the engine. "I don't have a flashlight," Beau confessed. "I'll drive you home."

Chris slammed the hatch. "Beau, what are you up to?"

"Neshnawe County's a warp where everybody's skin's being used. It's a symbiosis of real mystery, because it's still under Indian sway. No, more. More. Take Henderson, how he caught up with you and the rest that went on. It's much more."

Chris stared toward Beau, as if to gauge his reaction to Henderson and the accident, but could only make out a hard-bitten adamantine in the dark, a presence he might have missed if it hadn't been for a scattering of stars like pinpoints arrayed far off above the darkness of Beau. "The big wide past will get us by the neck," Beau said. "Me, you, those two, the— Wait a minute, what am I saying!" he cried, and struck his forehead with the heels of both hands. "The tribes! Has our past caught up with us?"

BEAU TOOK the back way with his headlights off. "Those two can help," he said. "They got money and some power."

"I've been around universities enough to recognize a crook when I see one. The bigger they blow themselves up, the more surface they notice and figure, Hey, I'm something!"

"So maybe dumb enough to use. When you didn't show, they wanted to see Gaylin. Then his grandad, and it got to be a tour. We ended up at an orchard owner's abandoned house—McCormick's. They're getting kids to squat there."

"What kids? *Who?*"

"A couple. She's knocked up, so they figure it'll take a court case to kick her out."

"Who's they?"

"Those two! Why are you getting so hot?"

Chris told him what had happened at the cabin, studying him in the greasy dashlight for any telltale expression, but Beau only nodded, his mouth set, while his ponytail, wrapped with the rawhide so that only a wisp of hair curled from its end, trembled. "When I finally got loose from those two and got back to see if you were waiting, you had Henderson in!"

"I was actually trying to get him out."

"That backstabber wouldn't come close on his own."

Chris remembered Henderson saying, "This is how Indians do it," before he opened the door, and now, as they idled through the settlement in the dark, he watched for Betty's Buick or Henderson with a shotgun, though Beau claimed Betty wouldn't let him touch one. Near the doctor's hill, Beau turned his headlights on, and Chris said, "So who's Peggy?"

"Stick with your wife."

"I've never even seen the woman!"

"So what's your interest?"

"She supposedly organized some kind of meeting."

"Peggy's always organizing something. Stay clear."

"Beau, what's this about? What's up?"

"We're being used, man. We're part of— Heads up!"

He braked so hard Chris had to hold himself from the dash, and once Chris recovered he saw that they had stopped short of the pump house, at the edge of the meadow where the three brush piles once stood, and he was sure he'd seen somebody in the woods ahead.

"Your hill, man!" Beau cried. "Your hillside! Look!"

Chris started to ask who it was, but Beau was already out of the pickup, running toward the trees, his back suddenly brilliant in the headlights, through the ditch and up the side of the slope that the road to the cabin climbed. Then Beau went down in the center of the headlight beams, leaves spraying up, and rolled on his back, arms wide. Chris jumped out and crouched beside a tire, listening, keeping him in sight. Beau tossed up leaves and cried, "This is it!"

"Beau, what's wrong?"

Beau rolled over in a self-embrace. "Oh, my buddy, all this is trillium! We made it! Spring is here! They can't hold it back now!" He turned on his side and touched one of the blossoms Chris now saw scattered in dotted profusion over the hillside. "Oh, my beauties!" Beau said, and leaned forward and cupped a blossom in his hand and then bent his lips to it and kissed it.

BUT WAS somber parked at the cabin, where the clayey marks glowed over the logs in his headlights. "Call me when they show up," he said. "I'll come over, and we'll teach them a lesson. It's part of that symbiosis, the fox and the rest. Here." He reached up and flipped on the dome light and pulled a piece of paper out of his breast pocket. "I've been getting back to it. Spring."

"I see," Chris said, though he didn't.

Beau smoothed the paper over the steering wheel and cleared his throat, and read:

> *Weeds leaning into shadows*
> *Weighed by the day's blow*
> *On Doc's hill, a fox on sticks*
> *Above his weedy shadowland,*
> *Red dog froze in stride,*
> *Branches poking through,*
> *Hide drying on green sticks.*
> *Good pinning, Philip says*
> *When he talks, but he's sly,*
> *Shuffling dance and gone.*
> *Who did it? Done this way.*
> *Old Doc is going to die.*
> *And did, this moon, fox he*
> *Never saw set, who said once,*
> *"See that peninsula beach?*
> *I'm going to see homes and*
> *Boats and lots all along it*
> *One day. You wait and see."*

"Hey, that's good," Chris said. "I don't know if I understand it all, but it's wonderful! Can I see it?"

Beau tucked it into his pocket. "It'll do for starters. Maybe I'll say it for you when it's closer to finished." He shut off the dome light and stared ahead. "As Olaf says—"

"Ole?"

"There is some s. I will not eat," Beau continued in a Scandinavian accent. "*Olaf*, as in 'I sing of Olaf glad and big whose warmest heart recoiled at war.' Cummings. I been to school, too. What does that kind of learning get you?"

"If you can get your hands on an original document

nobody's seen, you're close to *something*. The rest is educated hearsay. It's passed from one uninformed prof to the next. The system exploits consensus."

"There's things I know."

"I know," Chris said. Such as about the fox, which you won't tell me. "How about Roethke's final phase? Or the Puritans—a sermon from Jonathan Edwards? Or would you like to hear about James the First, or Cromwell, Lord Protector."

"Trash."

"Almost you persuade me, Beau."

"Are you quoting one of your fetid British destroyers?"

"Think of this twist. After the Roundhead faith faded, Indians kept right on practicing their native religion and were banished to alien country for it, or to inner alien places, by the forces that be—persecuted by our emperor of Rome, the director of the Bureau of Indian Affairs. The Destroyer! They're the separatist Christians now!"

"Any minute it's going to snow."

"I'm going to tell you something, Beau."

"You said that."

"Those two are the ones that supply you with dope."

Beau took hold of the steering wheel before he turned. "Where'd you get that? I haven't even been smoking."

Chris hopped out as if to avoid being hit and said, in the second before he slammed the door, *"I know."*

A THIMBLE OF schnapps was sitting in his glass where he'd left it. He picked it up and leaned against the stove, dead cold, and said, Beau, the attitudes of that pair are revised versions that are used not only on the public but on Indians, too. When Indians become activists, what do they look to? White histories. You can get glimpses of the real world, maybe, as it's strained through a European head, but only from the outside. There's no hint of the life at the center running it. So researchers go for our graves.

He downed the drink. If you believe in a resurrection of the body, maybe it isn't so criminal to stir up a few bones to get at artifacts. But if you're fooling with a person's standing in the spirit world by that, you better not. Jehovah of the Jews and Christians won't abide any other God. He's authoritative, autocratic. He doesn't permit equal spirits in His kingdom, being the originator and maker of it, as He claims. Other gods exist only to turn people's hearts against Him, He says, so there's no excuse for His judgment when it falls—a way of making sure there are no automatons or neutral, free-floating spirits.

It's all impossible to trace historically now, Beau, but some of the fear might have led to counting coup—an act of bravery if you only touched the enemy with feathers or a stick in the middle of a battle otherwise to the death. You let him live. Was the spirit world the reason for no suicide—or not till whites arrived—as if to say, Who am I to send you to that eternity of spirits, or send myself?

At a clack of sound Chris killed the lights and went into the dining wing to the south window and stood staring out, as he had the night Beau— If there's a benevolent God and his judgments are just, it's different. You tend to suspect He's on your side, as the Pilgrims did. Even if you aren't quite sure, everything will come out okay in the end, when He separates the sheep from the goats. Your life, in fact, is meant to lead to that otherworld, eternity. That was the Puritan's goal, though a Puritan wasn't supposed to send himself there—all-controlling, jealous Jehovah didn't go for that.

These stars, the terror of a night when you're alone and

know schemes are rigged behind your back. I'm sure you didn't cut my plastic, Beau. How our cry of attack was interpreted from the first, by trappers and traders, hardened criminals with their eye out for the bullion of pelts in francs and pounds, is maybe instructive. Every one describes it in that cliché they really seemed to experience—hair-raising. Was it because the ancients knew what was waiting on the other side and were screaming that out as they ran into a moment that might send them there?

They'd scared up panthers and bears and birds and heard them roar or drum out the terror of their end. Legends were a way of coping with that, and the one of twins, one evil, one good, involved in a creation sequence, was meant to explain away the duality they saw dividing the world. The earth, our Mother, is generous to overflowing, teeming at times—bison rumbling toward you over the prairie in a stampede caused by a wolf pack—but the same quality can swallow you up.

Where are the accumulated generations of wisdom about the workings of that world, commented on at every point of contact, and what do we do, now that that wisdom is lost? You can see even Roethke trying to get back to what his trio of women had taught, and that was the tradition of Europe. You troubled the graves, disturbed the bones, as Shakespeare begged sextons not to do and ended up, as he probably feared, being the most picked over corpse in history. You build your work in any intellectual endeavor on dead men's bones. One of the most dreaded of all evil spirits, the disembodied head, was a prophecy of the white man's intellect about to arrive.

Is that why you don't want me in school, he thought, and turned from the window, in the direction of Ellen, feeling cold radiate over his back from the panes. You're connected to the earth in ways I'm not, you and Beau, and ways I'll never be. Especially here. I'm turned around backward inside my own skin. The Indian world is the world of a woman, no surprise. If you haven't got an actual family, your attachments pull things lopsided; you love others more than your own, or dogs more than people. Dogs can be wonderful, don't get me wrong, and wise as Ivan, but not human. No substitute for a son.

Roethke the mystic God talker and guru was terrified of God in his last years. He hated Eliot, the Christian. A pious ass, false humble, he called him. A cliché even among Indians is that the Sioux are crazy, and Ogalala are Sioux. *Ogalala?* Roethke's real fear was insanity.

He lived in and out of it enough to need a settled world: his young wife, the confederacy of the East, the lodges of the Iroquois. A true Michiganite, only as western as Detroit. Pilgrims and natives, Beau, in the kingdom of God, are synonymous beings. The divisions between them have been blasted away by a force infinitely more powerful than all of the false stars and cerebral drift of any poor intellectual's perpetual snow.

IT WAS the distributor cap. Moisture had condensed in it, Chris discovered, and he dried it with a match as Beau stood watching, looking forlorn. They jump-started it, and Chris rolled down his window and said, "Thanks! Runs great!"

"That peyote I laid on you," Beau said.

"What?"

"I need it back."

"You said I should keep it."

"I want it back."

"All right, Beau, here's what. I'll make a *gift* of it to you." Chris got the bus in gear and started cranking up his window as he pulled away in a jerking hurry while Beau ran to catch up and yelled, before Chris could get himself completely sealed off, "Keep it, white man!"

CHRIS FELT bad enough by evening to skip his glass of schnapps. He pulled the Bible from his bookshelf, looking for a verse he believed Roethke was echoing, and ended up reading the whole Epistle to the Ephesians. Something struck so deep in him he thought he heard a gunshot and was sure he'd been hit in the heart. He closed the Bible with a thump. Was that it? There was such substantiality and space to the dining wing he had to close his eyes. Was this the Spirit? He lifted his face and felt his features bathed until he was sure they were shining like the bulb overhead, but was afraid to look. His face was taut with drying salt, and he could hear tears scattering over the papers of his dissertation lying as distant as all the silent generations far below.

10

"HI, HONEY," the dusky alto said. "Sorry I wasn't at the meeting. Baby troubles. Life, you know."

"Oh," Ellen said, taking "baby troubles" as an affront, since she had seen the woman the same night in the bar.

"Peggy said others have problems making it Thursday, so is Friday better? Can you come then? Same time."

"I won't be here."

"You're *leaving*?"

The woman's shift in tone was so surprising that Ellen said, "We'll be at a powwow."

"How's that? I mean, where?"

"Keewadin, I think he said." She checked the hall into the kitchen in a quick glance.

"Can I go?"

"I"m not sure it's for the public."

"Hell, they all are. I mean, can I go with?"

Ellen stepped around, unraveling the telephone cord, to the end of the hall, where she could see Chris at the table in the dining wing, with newspaper spread out, sorting through the peyote she'd persuaded him to unpack.

"I'll be a nice girl," the voice said, ironic.

"I'm sure I don't know. I'll have to ask my husband."

"I'm sure I knew you'd have to. I'll call back."

The presumption, Ellen thought, at the disconnection, and then the countryified razz of the dial tone; but taking her would at least be an excuse to ask Chris to replace the seat in the bus. She had cleaned out the interior with Lysol, but Nana would still sniff out the wine. Keeping her ear to the receiver, she studied Chris, who was leaning into sunlight, and decided she should keep up the pretense of being on the phone until she had decided how to explain the call.

"I see," she said, turning to the wall opposite the closet. There the black-ivory horns of a longhorn steer, bound across their center with green baize, were mounted on a varnished plaque, and below, on the same plaque, a pair of milk-cow horns, a fifth the size of the others, protruded, with BELLE carved below in the wood, as if some Clausen had recognized the worth of a good milker, a woman.

"All right," she said, and hung up.

She let him wait before she went to the wing. He had the peyote stumps set on the newspaper in rows, and the sun sent squat shadows over the print. What had looked so bulky in the bag seemed meager now—shriveled miniature things with their spines plucked. She counted nineteen. He'd turned one of his notepads over, cardboard side up, and was leaning over a chunk of the stuff, holding it endwise as he used a razor blade to shave fine slices free; he'd tried peyote the summer he was in California, which was her wedge.

"The bitch," she said.

He looked up. "Nana again?"

"The fat lady, that one I met in the bar."

"The dark lady."

"She wants to go to the powwow with us."

"How'd she hear about that?"

"I let it slip."

He shrugged. "Maybe we'll find out what she's up to." He put everything down and sat back, as if they had days for this, when it was only because the well drillers had left for casing that they'd decided to try it. "We should slice a few up like this and let it dry well," he said. "Less suspicious looking. You can get awfully sick on it, and a whole button might be too much. I wish I could remember that time in California better. I got pretty twisted. This way you can measure out a dose until you're where you want to be. I think it's the strychnine in it that makes you sick. I wish I could find a book on it."

"Just cut one in half. I don't care if I puke."

HE WAS still in his chair, looking up at the roof of the wing as if to locate a leak. "There."

"What?" She was across from him, feeling unwell from watching him pack everything so carefully away.

"It's starting."

"What?"

"Whatever it was the other night."

She stared up. A deer head hung from the gable, with cobwebs spanning both antlers, and its lifeless eyes, which had always bothered her, now shed pained surprise, as if the head were being birthed through the gable. She laughed.

"What's that?" he asked. He rose, a rustling benevolence filled by a wash of air, and went toward the living room, his shoes implanting sound into the boards.

The drilling rig started up.

"Look," he said, and she was enwrapped by the word as she studied the attachment of the shining chips of bone to her fingers, a cuticle clipped to each, growing. She didn't want to turn, then wasn't sure she could, but once the chair was back, her body moved as it never had beneath a socketing center of travel she realized was her eyes. He stood in the hall, radiant under his clothes, staring at the plaque, her earlier pretense discovered at its source. She was afraid, the carved name BELLE harsh as on a gravestone, the corners of her mouth drawing down at the way everything tended toward death.

"It never occurred to me," he said. "Belle we know, but who's the big guy here at the top of the picture?"

She was so grateful to be able to laugh she put her arms around him in a complicated business that meant his somehow had to get out of the way, but they did, and his heat entered her to her inner folds.

"Wait till it really hits," he said, and the prospect of that turned her legs so hollow he had to hold her up.

SHE SAW how the heater where she lay had a wrapped and heated core, the cone of strangling wires she had once tried to pluck, and then a thunder deeper than the rig came traveling through her bones as he thumped up in a crawl with a sample of the kitchen counter Nana wanted to install, then set it on the boards that were the coolest she could find for her face, and she saw the gold flecks below its white surface start to flow in streams that set branches coiling in motion in a liquid continuum.

"Some swarm," he said.

*   *   *

"KITCHEN OR bebroom," he said, or so she heard it, and then she was rising, his face swelling at his mouth like a baboon's. It would burst. She could see his blood, pulsing through the eye trained on her, increase in speed and heard her own faint cry of "Oh," already off.

IN AN HOUR she felt enough relief to want to try a smaller slice, and he said if they were going to travel they should travel now. "Let's go to Sleepy Bear Dunes," he said, and she pictured the park forty miles down the lake, asleep on the beach, the pleasant place she'd visited with her parents when she was a child. "*I*" was a child, she thought. Her legs shook. "*Sleeping* Bear," she corrected.

"That, too."

He was right to counsel her not to have a slice. Currents of air came at her in the roar of the rig, men there, worse than walking naked under water, poured in at every seam, the bus a barn echoing this noise. They got in, a parade of color pulling the woods inside, and didn't remember how to drive, frozen under the pouring detail, yet he drove. Even the dashboard looked unstable, unreeling past her knees until she had to pee. He eased to the side of a foreign road, and she got out and was so pegged by the event, connected to the earth in an electrical fountaining, she knew she was gone.

There was a clunk, and he stood propped against the bus, his face an olive. "Shall I carry you?" the pimento said.

DRIVERS DROVE for a tourist's tour of Sleeping Bear, a mercy to Chris. He checked over the fleet of specially built 1956 Oldsmobile convertibles, with portholes in the front fenders and chrome strips like check marks down each side. But the driver they got was crazed, and they rolled through sanctified huddles of sand, a desert minus the camel, doing sixty, the oversize tires whining like a semi's beneath the remnants of Chris's memory. The man steered with a finger, elbow on the door ledge, or with a knee, and was smoking, swigging a Coke, talking into a microphone that amplified his voice, and measuring their response through mirror shades in a rearview mirror the size of a medicine chest as he gunned over a dune and cried, "This is how you bury one of these Oldsmababies!"

Ellen covered her face with her hands, hair streaming back, but Chris kept eyeing the center of the reflecting shades in the mirror, feeling himself grow gigantic, not about to relent, not even if the man's hair resembled, as now, rivers of porridge. Then, in a sudden crosswind off the lake, Chris's stocking cap lifted off, the top of his mind gone, brain briss drying in a high wind, free. The driver, aiming a dribble of Coke into a jaw he extended beyond his face like a drawer—fingers gripping a cigarette—didn't notice the difference when he checked the mirror again.

"That's Lake Michigan, a few miles below our flight pattern," he said over the microphone. "You okay, lady?" A smile cracked his tanned face in the medicine-chest mirror.

Ellen nodded, both hands covering her face, her hair like feathers straight back.

I'll have to get him for this, Chris thought.

"These dunes have been here since the Plasticene," the driver announced. "Before the Anthraneacite, or whatever. That's about 800 billion years, according to the scientists. They also say these dunes move a quarter mile a year, but if that's right, I figure they would've wrapped the globe about a dozen times by now. The Indians named the place: Sleeping Bear. We figure they went out in a canoe to see if there was a way around this stuff—damn hard walking if we get stuck!—and had a few berries that made them think they saw a bear. This'd be, oh, hell, about two million years ago. Lotta sand's moved since! Pardon this. I'm supposed to tell you I gotta speed up through this stretch since so many buddies buried their Oldsmababies up to the aerials here—it's a long walk on that bear!—so here goes!''

It was the steepest drop yet, and Chris wanted to stand and whistle, like a brave sailor on a roller coaster, but couldn't rise. There was a leveling length of flat after the dip where Chris felt his innards remained, the tires crooning in soprano, and then the highest climb, wrapped in beige, as the car began to slow in a way it hadn't since they'd left the town where they'd actually paid for this. The driver swung off the track toward the edge of the dune, past a sign that read WARNING, and braked.

"Here's where we bring the Detroit Tigers," he said into his mike, more subdued, as if by the view. They were at the crest of a dune falling sheer to the lake, hundreds of end-over-end somersaults below, and the wrinkles were waves under a mist that glowed gold in the distance. The sky. Around them was sand and combings of stunted cedar in a black-green straggle. The driver got out, reached under his seat and pulled out a beer—"When I'm not drivin'," he said—popped the can, and stood at the edge.

"Oh," Ellen whispered. "I don't think I can take it."

"Him?"

"This view." A balled tear struck down her cheek as if squeezed.

I could push him, Chris thought, shoving the front seat forward. He went toward the driver, slogging through the gravitational pull of the sand, and watched the man pour beer into his extended jaw, and then was astonished to feel the man take his hand. It was Ellen, at his back, tremulous.

"This is real deceptive, as they say," the driver murmured, surveying the vista through his mirrors. "A slide could start and the whole damn car be buried so deep we'd be apple cores before they got to us. We bring the ballplayers here, or anybody that acts tough, and tell them to throw a rock or whatever they damn well please down to the lake there. Simple, huh? Like it's a straight shot down and you could lob it over the edge and it'd plop? Nobody's done it. Not once in the history of this place."

"Where's a rock?" Chris asked.

"Did you hear what I said?"

"Here are some," Ellen told him. She gave one a toss, and it sailed out a ways and struck the side of the dune and rolled cockeyed, slowing. Her irises from the side were yellow-brown, the same color as the sand and her hair, a roasted gold in the light, and she was staring at the point he could reach with his rock, he was certain. He grabbed one the size of a walnut and gave a heave, and they watched it arch into a distance that reduced it to a pea and then hit below hers, dribbling down in a hurried route, kicking up sand like a one-legged flea.

"See?" the driver said. "I'm no dope."

Chris couldn't keep from laughing. Blood and molecules were flowing under his skin in a surge that implied the deed accomplished, and he felt that hundreds were watching, minions who could be counted on for support. The problem was a rock. All sand now, miring him, swirling weeds circling in its lees, angling sun into his eyes.

One lay farther off, sand splashed at its base as if it had just dropped. The size of a baseball. Better? He could picture the prints his feet would leave, a last one hollow from the force of his fling, and heard voices cheer. The rock, black and flat on two sides, was so hot he had to toss it up and down, and in the quartz-kiln day he felt his face go red. He started forward in a run that became the beginning of a dance, and the weaving cells through his body, joining the rhythm, gave off sound. This rose in volume like a rushing wind—voices mingling in at the edges—and then the wind hit him head-on, picking the air clear for his last step, and he was at the edge with blue below, gigantic, one of the original ones back to free his people. A howling urge from the wind brought his arm around, and then a shout returned from the dunes as he doubled on himself in a spin, pitying terrestrial life as the weight of the sky entered him. His cry became a scream that sent the driver staggering back. He saw Ellen shade her eyes to follow the rock, and her focus brought his eyes to it, spinning out past a gull rising in angles on stiff wings, and then its momentum gave out. They all gathered at the edge as it started down, a speeded-up plummet, then flinched at the socketing hole where a wisp of whitened spray of lake water rose—a plume above its burying contact.

"I'll be go to hell," the driver said. "What kind of stunt is that? What have you got, a slingshot?"

Chris pulled off his jacket and let it fall at his feet, grabbed one side of his shirt and jerked, buttons popping off, wrestled out of it, and dropped it, feeling Ellen's eyes covering him like the sun.

The driver backed away. "You crazy sonofabitch!" he cried. "What are you?"

*   *   *

CHRIS THOUGHT that if his head fell off, from the effort of holding it up to drive, the wheel would catch it in its basket, his solace. He cleared the crest of the hill, unable to look at the lake below, and drove in at the head of the drive, all the way down to the door of the cabin, to block the noise of the drillers and shield Ellen's exit into the porch. When he turned to her from his opened door, planted on the ground, he saw she needed help. She began to disentangle herself from the beams of looping colors over her whitened face and slid into the driver's seat, and then, as he gave a hand for support, she whispered, "Oh! Oh, God."

However this went, they had to be in bed soon, the key in the lock enough to engorge him like potatoes and corn on the cob. Somebody was yelling, so he pressed Ellen into the porch, feeling waterfalls of fatigue over his face as he turned. It was Kitchum, his grieving gullies gone and tinted molecules springing from his head to form the solution to the four-color problem.

"We did it!" Kitchum cried, and gave Chris's shoulder a thump. "Two hundred and eighty-five feet down, and we got us a gusher!" Copenhagen ran from his gaping mouth in the shape of Africa.

He swung an arm to indicate, and Chris saw his son, stripped to the waist, with soaked hair over his shoulders in strings, spinning around a five-foot standpipe between his legs while beige water bubbled from its top over his arms and jeans and the ground below in a soaking froth.

CHRIS WOKE from a peyote dream of a whiskered thing to the hard-edged actual, a bedroom packed like a sausage with heat, his brain scoured by steel wool. He tried to sit but couldn't, his thighs weak from the night, and rolled to Ellen. Scattered sparks went off above her hair, and he realized their explosive sounds were knocks.

He pulled on his pants and made it through a cabin he wasn't sure he could take, from the nausea its solidity started up in him, and got to the door.

"It was locked," Beau said, stepping in.

"We are."

"Up for the day? It's noon."

"Which day?" They had decided to have some of the finer slices to ease back down after the drillers left.

"I'll run this by you. Imagine you're a white mother."

"Beau, I can't take this."

"Listen, you're a mother, white, and you got a teenage daughter—sixteen, say. I deliver some wood and we talk, you seem interested in me, but I see your daughter is giving me the eye. You don't notice, of course. Wait a minute! This is it. I call you in a week or so and say I'm in a spot, the sitter for my kids is sick."

"You don't have kids!"

"I'll get some loaners if it gets to that. The sitter's sick, and I have to go away on business. I have a sob story about my wife I'll spare you. Would you let your daughter come over and sit my kids for the weekend?"

"Where's this woman from?"

"Uh, let's say Sutton's Bay."

"I hope she tells you to stuff it."

THEY PICKED the woman up at the edge of town, at her request, and every time Chris checked the rearview mirror, her hefty bulk in heavy makeup, held in the squared coat, loomed so close in the reinstalled seat she looked about to bite him. She stared with stalled eyes when he started to talk, affronted, and answered only in monosyllables—so bearish Chris knew they had been prudent to forgo even the tiniest slice to enhance the day. In the bayside town of Keewadin, partly a marsh, it seemed, he saw cardboard signs: POWWOW, and below each an arrow. These led to the public school.

They walked through the parking lot, the woman lagging behind in a hauteur that looked familiar, and Chris felt the heightened angle of warm spring sun. Then he noticed Beau's Power Wagon beside an Oriental Land Rover. In the gymnasium, somebody was speaking over a PA system with the noise of a waterfall run backward. A crowd milled through the gym, and Chris headed toward the far bleachers.

"How many cheeves?" a voice behind him asked.

"All cheeves, no braves," another said.

"Nobody brave, no?"

Somebody tapped his shoulder, and he turned to a dancer, bare-chested, with black and yellow bars over his cheeks. "See you soon," the apparition said.

"What?" Chris asked, glancing at Ellen, off balance.

The painted fellow put both hands to his chest, and bells attached to bands around his wrists chattered into ringing. "Hey," he said. "Gaylin!"

"Right," Chris said.

"I'll be over."

"Wood season's done."

"This thing Beau told me." Gaylin was off quick into a corner where others were donning feathers and costumes, and an elderly man, in graying double braids, stood applying body paint to a giggling teenager that looked like Marty.

"You have to have the real motion inside it," some-body said, and a set of dancing bells burst into shaking rhythm.

"We're running things as *live*-ly as we can!" came over the loudspeakers, suddenly intelligible, and Chris saw Agsco of the orange vest at a stand mike near the bleach-ers. "We got Pontiac here, Michimillamac, Escanaba, Pshawbetown"—there were shouts and whistles—"and Vilhalla, and that's just starters, folks. We're going to have some authentic dancing soon, some name giving, and a giveaway. You name it, we give it! Make your way to the bleachers—okay?—and we'll get giving! Are the boys from Mackinac here yet?"

"They went off the road!" a man yelled.

"What was that?" Agsco asked, not quite getting his plump hand over the mike in time.

"Pabst Blue Ribbon!" the man yelled, and everybody in hearing distance laughed. It was Henderson. Chris edged Ellen to the other end of the bleachers, far from Hender-son (they hadn't talked to him since that night), toward a row of women in traditional dress with shawls over their shoulders. A few rows below them he saw Philip and Car-lyle, and he sat beside Philip, in the front row. "Excit-ing?" he asked.

Philip looked at Carlyle, who craned his head in the other direction, and then Philip cupped a hand below his nose, directing his voice sideways at Chris without turning his head, and whispered, "Better move up a row, huh?"

"What's this?"

"Paiu! Henderson."

Chris stepped up onto the next bleacher, and Ellen set-tled beside him. "What was that about?" she asked.

He shrugged and saw their dark lady, still in her black coat, talking to a dancer built like Henderson, but with a swag of belly bowing his dancing trousers down.

"My money's on Sugar Bear," Philip said into a hand curved back toward Chris. "Him with Loudmouth Woman in Black."

"That's her name?" Chris asked, studying her again.

"Ha! No, she mouthed us at the bar once the other night." Philip put his hands to his knees and rubbed them, done with this.

Then Chris saw Beau going from group to group in the gym, greeting people with the arms-up handshake.

"Enjoying yourself?" It was Frenchie, the one wearing a blue vest the other night, now in a checked wool shirt.

"Watching."

"What a scene! Half these guys are potted. Their women, too. What can you expect?" He walked off.

An elderly man with a Hudson Bay blanket tied at his waist and a single eagle feather at the back of his head, sat on the floor and began shaking something that looked like a turtle shell. "Lame Wolf," Philip whispered. A group of men seated to one side of him started thumping a thin drum trimmed with feathers, and Agsco announced, "Young guys first, okay!" A group gathered at the middle of the floor, and people still wandering headed toward the bleachers. The young men were cavorting more than dancing, and then one of them with a small red shield at the side of his head, with a single feather dangling from its center, began weaving among them at a faster speed, as if passing on an urgent piece of news. It was Gaylin. He broke into a gliding run without bothering to set down his feet like the others, to activate the bells attached to bands at their ankles. His weaving grew so swift he looked about to fall or crash into somebody, and then he stopped dead still and cried, "Ho-ho!"—shaking his hands to stir up the bells on his wrists. "Ho-ho!"

"Cut it out, Gaylin!" Chris heard in Beau's voice, but didn't see Beau. The drummers had been speeding up and ended with a sudden thump. Gaylin shook a fist at them, bells chiming, before he ran off to the corner where the man with braids stood waiting. "Son," he seemed to say, and took Gaylin in his arms.

"Okay," Agsco cried. "Free for all!"

The drummers picked up at a firmer pace, and a bigger group moved onto the floor, mostly older men, though Gaylin pulled free and joined them, and then the brave with the belly, Sugar Bear, crouched and stomped a leg with a power that set the gymnasium shimmering. He had sets of bells attached to his biceps, and now he clenched his fists below his waist and shook his arms in a shivery clamor as he flexed one foot in step, and with the action a tuned chorus of ringing rose up. He took a step and suddenly was moving nimbly with the beat, a subdued clamor from his arms doing double time, hardly a sound now at his light step from the rows of bells laced around his lower trousers. He was moodily attentive to keeping quiet now, it looked, or as quiet as he could with all his hardware. He came down the side of the gym, along the bleachers, knees lightly flexed with his weight, now and then executing a turn, with a tapping jig or two at the end, and young women stood and wailed in acknowledgment of a star. He grinned, he waved, but when he came chiming past the Nagonawbas, he was set again in his trance, and Chris could hear him crooning to himself, eyes half closed.

Then he leaped up, shaking both arms, and came down

in three hard steps he fashioned into a spinning turn, setting off a carillon whose effect was like a scream. The drums stopped. "Hooo!" the men on the floor cried, and Sugar Bear stepped to the bleachers and gave a stout woman a hug and a peck on the cheek. "Hey!" Philip cried. "Some more, hey!"

"Anybody for a fancy dance?" the voice over the mike said, and Chris saw pudgy Agsco grin in his direction. The drummers and the fellow with the rattle couldn't agree; they started several beats, each going his own direction, it seemed, and finally settled on a song similar to the first. Sugar Bear, shaking the circular bustle fastened to his back with thongs around his chest, walked off the floor and stood aloof, arms crossed, studying the big woman in black.

"Okay, that's it for now!" Agsco yelled into the mike, before the drums had hardly stopped. "Let's pick an overall winner and give him fifty bucks!" People applauded, and Philip gave a piercing whistle. The old man with the rattle rose and went to the mike. "Lay-tuh," Lone Wolf said. "We naming now." He began shaking his rattle and chanting a song one drummer echoed, and then two women in nineteenth-century dresses, long and proper, walked to him carrying infants.

"Where's fellas?" he asked, and two men sheepishly came over to hoots. He started chanting and then stopped and stepped over to a mother and whispered in her ear. She bowed her head, and he returned to the mike. "Little-Rabbit-in-East," he said, and everybody cheered.

Again he chanted, for a longer stretch, his voice going high with difficulty, and then he swung to the other mother and laid a hand on her child's head. He was still chanting, bending as if to smell the infant's hair, until such a loud wail shivered up the mother drew back, ashamed. Lone Wolf returned to the mike. "He-Who-Speaks-Well," he announced, and the crowd applauded.

"One more," he said, and held up a feather. "Him." He pointed the feather at Agsco, and Agsco placed spread hands over his vest. Lone Wolf nodded and began chanting, trying to signal Agsco to stand facing him, and finally a bystander led him to the proper spot. Agsco bowed his head, as if to bury his pride, and the chanting stopped. Lone Wolf held up what looked like a knobbed stick, which Chris hadn't seen till then, and handed Agsco the feather. "Big Turtle Head," he announced. Some people cheered, but as many were laughing, holding their mouths, and Chris could see Agsco's big ears turn pink, and then he noticed the curve of his skull, where his plump neck appeared to press up his yellow hair, forming a fold like the curve of a plastron. Lone Wolf spread his arms, rattle in one hand and knobbed stick in the other, and cried, "Winnuh! Shugah Beah!"

There were whistles and shouts along with the applause, and Chris saw Gaylin tear off his red shield and throw it on the floor. Sugar Bear was nearly across the gym, his bells ringing in response to every step, when Agsco, back at the mike, said, "Before I present this award, I want to say how honored I am to be inducted into this tribe. Thanks, guys."

Sugar Bear, in a jingling flurry, took an envelope from him and started back and then paused as if pinned in the air, silent; then his left foot, bare now, struck down hard. His fists and arms were clenched down low, one fist out ahead as if he'd drive it through a door, his head now down too, and then he broke into sudden motion, trying several directions from his crouch in a heel-to-toe faster than a tap, the gym filling with the chirring of cicadas on a summer night as his body appeared to grow greased with sudden sweat. People rose up in the bleachers, clapping, and Sugar Bear did a variation on the action of his legs, one crossing the other as steadily as the drummers at their fastest beat, and Chris saw through to the grass beneath him on an open plain, with the sky spread above, clouds at one side in gray swells, a picture of the land as it once was, pared down to this ancient golden deadening of no words, and then Sugar Bear spun and hit down, arms wide, one shoulder shaking to keep some smaller bells in chorus with a foot that hadn't yet stopped, and cried, "Hi-yah!" and spun and then was going across the gym, *jing, jing, jing, jing*, as if he hadn't interrupted his walk and the crowd had imagined the dance.

Philip, up on his feet, was smacking his hands so hard his big nose jarred from the force of it, and he turned and called to Chris, "He about made us some rain, huh!"

Beau stepped up the bleachers in the noise and said close to Chris's ear, "I got a message."

"Gaylin?"

"Gaylin?" Beau's lips firmed, paling, and he stared at Chris in frowning puzzlement. "What about him?"

"His coming over."

"Oh." Beau waved this aside and, now that the crowd was quieting, leaned and whispered, "These guys,"—he nodded toward Turtle Head—"they got business for us. Tonight."

BEAU WAS at his table, a kerosene lamp burning in the center of its circular top. "The white establishment shut my juice off," he said. Ivan was on the floor in front of him, his head in Beau's lap, eyes closed, meditating on Beau's method of fondling his ears. "He's been ranging," he said. "That's the trouble with these. They're bred to run deer. I don't know where he goes." He gripped Ivan's head in both hands and raised it to stare him in the eye. "Get us some venison?" he asked. "You better, if we're going to eat." Beau sighed with dismissal, and Ivan drew against the wall near the door, revolving his head to examine Chris—one ear raised and his tongue emerging in a friendly pant.

"You like me?" Chris asked.

Ivan barked once.

"Good dog," Beau said. "It's just that ranging."

"If dogs run free, why not me?" Chris said to Ivan.

"You still looking for strange?" Beau asked.

"I didn't know I was."

"There's a powwow party we'll go to."

"I told Ellen she should call here if that carload of kids shows up. I figure they're about due."

"They'll be at the party. You'll see some real Indian life, not that hotdogging hogwash for the whites."

"I liked Sugar Bear."

"Sugar Bear wore more bells. That's about it. He's hotdogging himself. You should have seen the purity of that brother when he came out of the woods after his vision."

Chris pulled up a chair and sat, drawn into the corona of light, where a single moth, the first of the season, was wobbling in a stumbling orbit around the glass chimney. It edged too near the top and with a crackle dropped beside the wick, fanning the light dim with a last pump of its wings.

"You've been inside too much peyote," Beau said.

"What do you mean?"

"Involved in details. Did you have a vision?"

"Getting free from an Oldsmobile driver at Sleeping Bear Dunes State Park."

"That's good!"

"I sailed a rock out past the dunes into the lake."

"The original strength coming back!"

"It scared me."

"Everything does." Beau set his elbows on the table, and his hair swung forward as he studied a hand, opening and closing it in a fist. "What they've taken from us!"

"I like Tweedledee and Dum less than before. Isn't that what they're up to, taking from us?"

"A development company is planning a 'recreation community,' they call it, out by Indian Shores. They have dozers and scrapers in already. It's virgin land, the cedar swamps so thick nobody's been in 'em for years, and we figure there were burial mounds back in there. They want the machinery stopped."

"Those two?"

He shrugged. "They got some power, I said."

"If they can get enough Indians as lackeys. What do they mean—TNT, sugar in the gas tanks? What?"

"According to our evil imaginations."

"Ours?"

"Generic."

"Yours and Gaylin's?"

Again Beau was taken aback, neutralized in the light. "You're onto a lot," he said.

"You can't do it, Beau."

"Do I let an anonymous Detroitie ruin my land?"

"Now you own the land?"

"Nobody does. It's mother to us."

"Those are your words, Beau."

"Give me a cigarette, would you? I'm in a spot."

Chris slid an unopened pack across the table, and it dropped into Beau's lap. "So," Chris said, "government-financed crooks make enough to hire you to do their dirty work, right?"

THE PARTY was partly a celebration of the move-in to the McCormick place—a two-story, high-ceilinged house with forest-green walls, every room bare. The crowd was mostly in the kitchen, but some had gathered in corners or at the edges of empty rooms, one couple along the baseboard, and Chris walked from room to room looking for Marty and his cohorts. Out a huge front window, the lights of an ore boat moved like a procession of vigil lights toward the north, and he could see the red-starred radio masts on Manitou. He felt like a housebreaker.

"Old Manitou, he's so pretty tonight," Philip said, stepping beside him, "I think I'll ship me back to Fox."

Beau came up and led Chris away, to a side room where a table lamp, plugged into a corner, rested on the swept and stained floor. A teenage couple sat next to it, leaning back against the wall. They were holding hands and staring as if absent, giving off the same strain of sadness Chris had sensed from Carlyle—not stoned, as he'd thought. At Beau's introduction, they said, "Hi," politely, hardly glancing up, and Beau explained, "This is the couple moving in."

To the side of the woman was a dresser drawer that appeared to contain a jumble of clothes, but now Chris saw the profile of an infant in it, with black swirls of hair over its skull, blankets stuffed around it for packing. At a clout of sound in the kitchen, like a two-by-four struck, the infant stirred, opening and closing the fingers of a hand that had seemed a design in a blanket, and the young mother said, "Ooo, I hope he don't want me again."

"You're taking a real step," Beau said to them. "This county is going to change. Think of the brothers who won't be the same after tonight, right here in your house now."

Chris was left with the couple, both still staring straight ahead. "Is there anything I can do?" he asked.

"Get me some of that new formula in the blue can," the young woman said. "My boy"—she looked at her husband—"he ain't happy with this nursing."

Did she mean formula in the house? He started for the kitchen and turned into one room to see Rio jogging on his bootheels to remain upright, saying, "I've been a plumber, a carpenter, a millionaire, and a bum. I've trick rode for the Ringling Circus, I've trick rode for Mr. Tom Mix . . ." It was enough to make you swear off, Chris thought, but at the thought wanted a drink. He knocked back a whiskey in the kitchen, just as the organizers arrived, looking pumped up in their puffy vests, their eyes bloodshot, highflying.

"You want it stopped?" Chris whispered to Turtle Head above the noisy greetings all around.

"Use your imagination." He pulled out one of his long cigarettes and lit it, then handed it to Beau, bristling with magnanimity, and lit another. "Any way. Get it?"

A smiling, toothless Denny Wing slapped the shoulder of Agsco's orange vest and cried, "Hey, Big Turtle!"

A blush appeared in red scoops under his eyes, but he said, "Accepted. Isn't it the great turtle that bears the earth?" He beamed his smile around, a benign watchtower.

So that was how he'd reconciled it to himself.

"And get this," he said, turning to Chris as if this were solely for him. "I've been named by six nations now. I'm Indian six ways, but I'm white. How does that grab you?"

"Like a rubber muff."

Beau nudged Chris to the edge of the room, side-stepping people passing through, and stopped at a shipping crate for fruit lugs, with the name of the canning company stenciled upside down across the front and empty bottles heaped inside. "Pretend you're friends with him for me," Beau said. "Don't stir up strife, okay?"

"You're getting double pay for the two of us?"

Beau hiked himself into his offended posture, staring down one side of his nose from a frightened eye, and walked off. Somebody tapped Chris's shoulder, and he turned, set to swing, but Gaylin was there, faint stripes of color still on his cheeks. He was with an older fellow whose wrinkles had so wizened his face he looked Oriental. They both wore black armbands with AIM scratched on them in chalk. "You like my dancing?" Gaylin asked.

"Why not?"

"I should of won the prize. I danced 'em all."

"You've got time to win. You're young."

"Who says?" Gaylin glanced around, angry, then leaned and whispered, "You got some business."

"What do you mean?"

"Upstairs, take a right." Gaylin started off, then

turned and nodded solemnly, affirming the gravity of this.

Chris went up a set of wooden box stairs, with a single bulb burning at the top, and stood in a hallway with several doors leading off it. One door was ajar, and in the dim light outside it he could see the prints of bare feet in a film of linty dust.

"Here," a faint voice said.

The room smelled of aging corncobs, as if it had been used as a bin, and a bed was set up under a bulb that hung on twisted cords from the ceiling. A girl who looked like a kid sister to the one who wanted formula sat against the wall at the head of the bed, holding a sheet at her neck, her hair massed against the green wall and spilling over the sheet in such dark luxuriance it reminded him of how hair like this fell over his arms from a stocking cap in the struggle with Michelle.

"Are you the one, your name's Chris?"

She spoke so rapidly he might not have been able to put the sentence together if his name hadn't been attached. He looked around the room for anyone in shadow and saw only a wooden chair, with clothes scattered on the floor beside it.

He nodded.

"You ready to jump me?"

"Jump you?"

"Them boys said you like jumping a little squaw."

"Gaylin?"

"You don't wanna jump me? I'm sweet."

He had to sit to relieve his sudden sick weakness, and the whiskey from the kitchen hit, sending his mind sailing off to a gold afternoon barred with golden light. "I suspect so, but no. No, I won't."

"Too much wine and tea?"

"Huh?"

"I had some, too. They give me some to jump you."

"You'd need it to?"

"I like your eyes. You read?"

"Yes."

"They're real deep."

"I wake to sleep and take my waking slow."

"That's Indian stuff. You don't talk smut."

"I try not to."

"Talk to me awhile, huh?"

"What about?"

"Tell me something neat, maybe about your first piece."

"That might be smutty."

She laughed the full-throated laugh of a ten-year-old and dropped the sheet, wearing only a man's undershirt, a ribbed white tank top, small-breasted and skinny as a whip.

Beau hurried in, haughty and rocklike, as if he'd had too much to smoke, and stared at her, then at Chris, then at her with a growing difficulty of unsticking his stare. "What's going on?" he asked, out of breath.

"Oh, my big brave Beau," she cried, and clapped her hands. "You blew it again!"

"Come on, Allie, can't you keep your pants on?"

"Every time I see Beauchamp Nagoosa."

"That's about your limit, huh?"

"They said this nice guy wanted to jump me."

"Who?"

"Them boys."

"Gaylin wouldn't have anything to do with this!" Beau exclaimed.

"He told me to come up," Chris told him.

"No, it was Marty and um older guys," Allie said.

"Good God," Chris said, and was up out of his chair, setting the bulb above swaying. "They're at our place right now. Ellen's there alone. Beau! Give me a ride back!"

11

W<small>HEN</small> B<small>EAU</small> <small>STARTED</small> slowing for his farmhouse and the bus, Chris cried, "Go! Kick it or I'll figure you're in on this, too!" So as Beau floored it past his place, Chris craned to see the bus and noticed a dim pygmy at the porch window, hands on the glass—Ivan on his hind legs, surely—and then they were over the hump of the hill, gone. Beau rattled though the Indian settlement, and as he started into the curve around Orin's field, Chris yelled, "Straight across! Head for the light!"

The pickup jolted over the ruts of cultivation, tossing them against each other, and in his efforts to find a place to hold to, Chris noticed a knife at Beau's hip, in a black leather sheath. He tried to read the printing stamped into the leather, below the head of an antlered deer, but Beau punched off the lights and picked up speed. Beau's mouth was crimped in pain at the pounding the Power Wagon was taking, and then he crashed through the hedge of the pump house, lifting into the air over its brushy stems, and landed with a wallop that sent Chris into the roof.

Marty's car was in the drive at the back door, and through the south window Chris could see bodies milling in the dining wing. Beau hit the brakes, sending the rear end slewing around, and before the Power Wagon stopped, they were out the doors and going on a run for the cabin.

Ellen was against the cookstove, looking pale but grim that she'd held the group—Marty and Fat Anfinson and Horse and Lonnie and two others—at bay until they were trapped.

"Home again!" Chris exclaimed, exhilarated.

"Beau," Marty said, leaning against the green cabinet, his face taking on its color. He tried to smile.

Chris stared around at each of them. "You know I asked you not to bother us at night, when I work."

"You're working?" Horse said. "Ha!"

"When did you get out of jail?" Beau asked, and before Horse could answer, he said, "Do you want to go back?"

"I can take the interruptions," Chris said. "But after all the times I've helped you out, it really gets to me that you'd sneak up when we're gone and rub this place with *mud.*"

"Mud?" somebody said. "What mud?"

"I didn't rub no mud."

"Bothers me?" Chris said, taking his library book, the report of the commissioner of Indian Affairs, from the top of the refrigerator. "It busts my ass!" He swung the book down on the range, and its brittle cover splintered as if detonated. He looked up, appalled, and everybody stepped back as if he'd shattered a skull. He threw the remains to the floor and went to the closet and grabbed the rifle, then back in the hall saw Marty trying to ease out the door while Beau, with a hand on his knife, grabbed Horse.

"Hey!" Chris called to Marty. "Stop! I want you to know something important."

Beau swung to Chris, startled, then backed into the porch, shaking his head, and the others followed him.

"See," Chris said, and held up the rifle. "I've got this thirty-thirty"—surprised at his own obvious lie—"and I want you to know the first time I hear anybody driving up or sneaking in the woods I'm going to get it out and let fly!"

"A thirty-thirty?" Marty said, still attempting to smile, but yellow as amber. "It looks like a twenty-two to me."

"Is that right?" Chris said. "Well, you go on outside with the rest." Marty hurried out the porch, glancing back, and when he got out the door, he swung around, wary, keeping an eye on Chris. Beau stood behind the group on a rise across the drive, frowning and shaking his head *No.*

Chris jabbed the screen door open with the butt and stepped out, a few feet from them, holding the rifle at port arms. "So this looks like a twenty-two?"

He fired it from its position to his left, and the shot echoed off the cabin through the woods, and then, in the thwarted whine of a ricochet, sent a plume of sparks spraying from the top of the drilling rig, sending lightning through the sprouting trees, and before anyone could react, he said in a shaky voice, shocked himself, "That's the kind of rifle it is, see. And I'm that kind of a shot."

ELLEN SHOOK him awake. "Beau's here," she said. "Did you order all this wood?"

By the time he got outside, Beau was flinging off the last of a load of stove-length wood on the rise across from the back door, where he'd stood last night. He hopped out of the Power Wagon box, brushing his hands, and said, "I think that was pretty stupid, what you did."

"You mean running them off?"

"The rifle."

This gouged Chris with further guilt; he shoved both hands in his pockets.

"I need twenty bucks for this," Beau said.

"You said you'd bring some for helping you out."

"Another load. Later. I'm strapped for cash."

Chris went into the cabin and came out with a pack of cigarettes and a twenty-dollar bill.

HE'D HARDLY been able to work from the time Henderson was hurt, feeling they were about to be broken in upon, while Ellen retreated as if to draw him in her direction. He sat down to catch up and just after twilight heard a soft knock at the door. It was Gaylin, washed pale in evening light. "Beau said you got peyote," he explained. "He said you'd be my guide. He don't want to."

Chris let him into the porch, searching through the screen for a dozen others. Nothing could surprise him now, and he felt an undercutting desire to destroy the order of life, including his work, with dope. He shoved the bulky folder aside and had Gaylin sit in the chair he usually used. In the light from the salad-bowl reflector Gaylin's face looked boyish, engorged with fear, and Chris sensed himself at a decadent new low: this seamy and questionable initiation of youth.

"Are you sure you want to do this?" he asked.

Gaylin nodded, breathless, his mouth open, baring the steel incisors that looked like pinpoints of empty space.

"What about Beau?"

"He's going a different way."

"How about having him here?"

"He's not in on this."

His tone was so dismissive Chris went around to the

cookstove, which was nearly out, and stirred up enough coals to brew a pot of coffee.

"Do you have to heat water for it?" Gaylin asked.

"For coffee, is that okay?" Then Chris thought of the schnapps—deadener and soporific. He went into the main room, looking for Ellen, then to the door of their bedroom, and drew the muslin curtain aside. She was on her back on the bed, uncovered, in her teddy undergarment, her arms at her sides, staring at the ceiling.

"Is that right?" he whispered.

"Right?" she whispered.

"Lying there like that. We have a guest."

"Is that right?"

"What?"

"Having a guest."

Then he saw the plastic bag, open, on the dresser top.

"I just had some," she said. "Join me."

He drew out two buttons, like nuts in his hand, and said, "I have to get rid of him or do this quick."

"Me, too," she said, too loud, and the ambiguity of this hovered between them as she continued to stare upward. He glanced at the ceiling, as if to see what she was seeing, bare boards, and then backed through the curtain and went to the hall and stopped beside the bathroom door. "Gaylin," he said, "maybe tonight's not the night."

"No, sir!" Gaylin replied, and raked back his chair as he stood. "Beau said you owed him this!"

CHRIS SIPPED his second cup of coffee, studying Gaylin from across the table, in Ellen's place.

"Can't I have more'n a shittin' slice at a time?" Gaylin asked, and Chris heard a change in his voice.

"You'll take too much and get ahead of yourself."

"I ain't feelin' nothin'! I got to meet my grandpa in Cedar by nine. I got something to tell him. Come on!"

Do you expect everything to run on your schedule, Chris thought, annoyed that he'd probably have to drive Gaylin thirty miles. He got the Formica counter sample from the refrigerator top and came back and stood at Gaylin's side, then held the sample in front of him under the light. "What do you see?" he asked.

"Fire ants!" Gaylin said. "How'd you get 'em in a box?"

Chris sighed—just as he'd thought—and set the Formica on the range, then dropped a few peyote slivers into his cup of coffee. He sat across from Gaylin and sipped, sucking several down. He could feel an energy from Gaylin enter his skin, and with a swoop again he was gigantic, with minions in service, sure that he would soon be asked to aid his nation as its Wovoka. A jagged, angular force traveled down Gaylin's face, following the lines painted on him at the powwow, and a flicker of response tugged over his features as if to alert him to this.

"I have to meet Grandpa by nine!" he cried.

"I'll drive. It's just past six."

"Are you Grandpa?" Gaylin asked, staring at Chris with the ferocity of terrible fear.

"No."

"You look like him. *Now!*"

Chris felt his features bend under the force of Gaylin's fear and knew he shouldn't have had any peyote himself.

"I have to hump," Gaylin said. "I'm hungry!"

Chris wasn't sure he'd heard right, since a catch from the slivers had drawn him into contemplating his inner state, and then Gaylin grabbed the leftover slices and gobbled them up. "See what I mean! What do you think of that? You think I can't do it, huh? How about this?" He grabbed the button that wasn't cut into and swallowed it whole. "See. I do it!"

Chris looked into his cup, where silver microbes were circling, and probed his interior for the proper response.

"Don't act like Grandpa when I know you ain't!"

Gaylin's features were pulled in all directions, his face raining in patterns no face should undergo. Then his jaw narrowed, black eyeteeth appearing as his nose enlarged, Ivan's face emerging from his, and Chris, clinging to the table, felt so far from words he was only able to lean closer and go "Woof!"

"Arrgh!" Gaylin cried, eyes wide, choking on the sound.

"Let it go," Chris whispered.

"I have to!" Gaylin said, standing bolt upright. "I have to at nine!" With a sway he sat, drool sparkling down his chin. "My legs won't hold me! What'd you *do*?"

"You had too much." Chris was a badger clinging to the table with fingerlike claws he didn't dare examine and wasn't sure this came out in words.

"Help!" Gaylin cried, barking and backing from Chris at the sound. "Help me! Rarf!"

WHEN CHRIS imagined Gaylin was as huge as Henderson and supported him, Gaylin could walk, and finally they got to the bus. But after Chris started it up and then, at the top of the drive, switched on the headlights, Gaylin cried, "It's too high! We'll fall down the hill!"

Chris could sense how he felt, perched in the bus with no hood, and said, "Good brakes." He touched them.

"Don't!" Gaylin yelled. "We'll fall off!"

Chris found Gaylin's seat belt and fastened him in.

238 • L a r r y   W o i w o d e

"It's all moving! We can't move, too. The front here's turning into a roller coaster! Stop!"

"How can we get there if we don't drive?"

"Not so fast!"

"We're hardly out of the yard yet. Here's low."

Both were silent so long that Chris sensed they were on a surreptitious mission and was conscious of moving even the gearshift with stealth. The dash clock gave them an hour and a half, but a ways down the road they entered fog, in clinging, bloated clouds in valleys, with streaks skimming in *whops* across the windshield on each hilltop.

"Big chief smokes," Gaylin said.

We should have, Chris wanted to say, and felt his skin bulge from the inflating force of inner pressure. A car, passing them through thick fog, became Beau's truck.

"It's too fast!" Gaylin cried.

"Thirty-five. We're crawling."

"I can't do it anymore!"

"We have to get there," Chris said, but slowed.

"*Mama!*" Gaylin screamed in a new register of alarm. "They're all inside! Get them out!"

Chris slowed more and put a hand on Gaylin's arm.

"Oooo!" Gaylin said, eyes closed. "It all steams!"

It was past nine when Chris saw the lights of Cedar. "There," he said, to calm Gaylin, who was shouting at him again to quit this. "Where should I stop?"

"Anyplace!"

"Where will your grandpa be?"

"Anyplace!"

At the edge of the village Chris pulled to the side of the road, his back rocklike with tension, and saw that he was parked beside an implement dealer. He pulled

into the lot, among bright-painted farm machinery turning purple under a streetlamp, and shut off the engine,
then the lights. Lit squares, windows of houses, enclosed
two sides of the lot.

"Grandpa!" Gaylin cried. He started struggling with
the door, and Chris reached across and undid his seat
belt.

"We're here," he said.

"How can we? It doesn't stop!"

Chris started opening his door, meaning to go around
and help Gaylin down, but Gaylin had his wide and was
out with a leap. "Grandpa!" he yelled. He started in
the four directions Sugar Bear had demonstrated in his
dance, etching them in the air, then ran off but stopped
as if against a wall, so that Chris felt suspended, too,
falling into further responsibility for Gaylin if they were
caught. Gaylin sidestepped to a new cultivator and
called for his grandpa, and Chris saw the machinery as
Gaylin must: green mandibles, cultivating beaver teeth,
shields racked in storage down a disk. He heard a sound
like Beau's pickup. No, Beau's voice warning: *Gaylin.*
Chris slid from the bus, and reflected sparks flared over
the windshield of a combine. Gaylin was gone. No, farther off, at a corn picker, bending over as he vomited,
and beside him, with a hand on his shoulder, was the
elderly man with braided hair who'd painted him at the
powwow.

Chris heard a voice say, "You're fine, son," and then
the old man lifted his face, blank black from a streetlamp behind, and turned to Chris and gave a nod. Chris
scrambled into the bus, the cockpit of a plane in flight,
and at the house ahead a porch light went on, setting a
door into a yellow frame. This opened, and Beau

stepped onto the porch. Chris craned around to see if Gaylin was witness to this, but Gaylin and the old man were gone. A woman with florid good looks appeared in the doorway, and then a lovely twin in a work shirt and jeans—her daughter!—pushed by, Beau seeming to inhale the aroma of her hair as she passed and hurried down the porch steps into the line of the combine hopper. A slam of Beau's Power Wagon door. Beau started backing from the woman, who suddenly placed a hand on his sleeve and then, smiling, held a finger up: One A.M.? Once? One weekend?

She closed the door and the light went out.

HE AWOKE naked on the couch. Had he? No, Ellen had elbowed him from bed, since he wasn't there when she wanted him. He pictured the girl gliding down the steps into the line of the combine, and his gills filled thick. He pulled on last night's clothes and ran out to the bus, then took the long way around, sensitive to Henderson, and on the drive noticed pink clumps and mounds in rows on hillsides—orchards in bloom. Was it April? Late April? He'd lost track. He wasn't sure how to handle this, but as he pulled into Beau's drive, he decided that whatever was going on couldn't continue.

He had the door open before he was aware he hadn't knocked. The kitchen was empty, the table a glassy circle in the sun. He wasn't sure he'd seen the Power Wagon and was backing out the door, closing it on himself, when a noise came from Beau's room. Caught, he registered, and then Gaylin stepped from the room into the kitchen.

"What's this?" Chris asked, sensing the currents from last night stir under his skin to reunite them.

"I don't want you," Gaylin said, the dark points of his eyeteeth emerging in fear.

"Where's Beau's truck?"

"The barn."

"What are you doing?" Chris was out of breath.

"What are *you?*"

"I mean here."

"With Beau." Gaylin stepped to the cookstove, with a hand out to steady himself, and touched its top, then jerked the hand to his mouth, sucking his fingertips.

"How'd you get back?"

"Grandpa. I told him I'm with Beau now." He sucked.

It was always easier for Chris to say he was sorry than admit he was wrong, but before he got to either, Gaylin said, "I was in your bus, huh? It wasn't too bad with Grandpa. Then I started going through the wall here, and Beau talked me back." He gave a sickly smile. "I'm with him now."

Sensing he had Gaylin, Chris leaned against the door. "You said Beau's going another way."

"This girl. I answer if somebody calls. I'm his kid, see. He's going to adopt me." Gaylin's wan smile trembled.

"But this is—"

The tarp over the door to the living room jerked back, revealing a sheet of plywood on the joists beyond, with a blanket over it, and Beau stepped into the kitchen, his hair a tangle, in a loincloth. No, a towel around his waist.

"This is an outrage," Chris said.

"Come on, I just got up." Beau reached up to pass a hand over his hair and discovered its bushman's disarray.

"I saw you pick a kid up last night, and I don't think I was seeing things. A girl."

"Is that what's got you so hot?" Beau asked, and in a sudden shift of perfect poise, he grinned.

"What's going on?"

"Did you tell Gaylin what was going on when you were running him all over hell?"

"Right," Gaylin said, and nodded vigorously at this.

"I drove him where he asked me to."

"You took off!" Gaylin said.

"Gaylin!" Beau said in the tone of command he used with Ivan. Gaylin returned to the eggshell room, and Beau, grinning wider, nudged Chris. "Is she a lusty wench!"

"Spare me, okay? This is sick! How do you figure it isn't getting back to others? Her mother, I mean."

Beau leaned and whispered, "To tell you true, I think the old lady's behind it. I think she wants a mature stud to straighten out this kid's sexual kinks."

"Beau! I refuse to support you if—"

"Support me!"

"I mean, I'm going to have to—"

Gaylin was back in the kitchen in a stance of readiness as the tarp behind Beau popped aside and a girl with a plump and rosy Swedish face, with a blanket over her shoulders parting on bare skin, stood blinking into the morning light, then across at Gaylin, now beaming and flexing his arms, then at Chris, and then she turned to Beau, raising her hands inside the blanket to grip him, and said, "Who is this dip?"

ELLEN DIDN'T like this turn in Chris. He had unpacked his recording of Indian chants and played it nonstop on the hi-fi in the main room. When she went birding with the binoculars, always alone now, she could hear, far off in the woods, the urgent voices chanting from the cabin.

And now when Chris worked, he sat at the table in her old stocking cap and the ratty jacket he'd found in the bus, a derelict. Once, as she returned from a walk, she saw him, through the main-room windows, trying to dance. He had his own style, with feints she hadn't seen at the powwow, but held his head wrong, too upright, as if his thoughts could spill over his face.

He barely ate and wouldn't talk. The schnapps sat sealed on its shelf, and she had to keep the fire up. The drillers were interring an underground tank, so the cabin would soon have running water and plumbing, but she'd already had to haul water once herself, furnishing material for Orin's gossip. Chris often wandered off, across the meadow into the woods at Doc Steele's or into the woods north, or he got in the bus and drove off. She or the peyote or a combination of them kept him in this state, she was sure, and when he was gone, she pulled out a notebook and continued her commentary on his behavior, a new project, now that her book on the loss of their child was done.

CHRIS WAS AT Beau's table, in the chair he always took, staring out the window to understand why he was here. The built-in cabinets in the kitchen were finished, of solid birch, oiled to a luster, and now Beau was nailing plywood over the open joists. Underlayment. The floor squeaked, Beau said, and he wanted to replace a few joists and shore some others up, which was why he'd removed the flooring. The tarp was drawn back, the girl secreted in the upstairs bedroom she had claimed and occupied on weekends. She was allergic to Ivan, she said, so Ivan, when he wasn't riding in the box of Beau's Power Wagon, lived in the haymow, in a burrow under the heap of wood. Beau disapproved of *Black Elk Speaks*, but Gaylin was always reading it, or studying it to learn to read, and kept asking Chris or the girl, Glynn, how to pronounce words and what they meant.

Now Gaylin stepped from Beau's former room (Beau had moved to an upstairs bedroom) and stood beside the stove, where a stew pot was simmering, and said, "I hate this place!" He threw down his book, and Chris, in the depression that was driving him deeper into the past, saw Gaylin throwing down his headpiece at the powwow, crying "Fire ants!" and pouring out exclamations over their trip. "I hate it the way he hangs around her all the time! He even drives past her place during the week—to have a beer, he says!"

"Are you talking about me, Gaylin?" Beau's voice came from the living room; the hammering there had stopped.

"I say I hate this place! I wish I had a tipi!"

"So?" Beau said, and the hammering picked up.

"Bastard!" Gaylin whispered. "I hate him, too!"

"Don't, Gaylin," Chris said. "Make yourself a tipi."

"Sure."

"What do you think the people did?"

"They knew things I don't. Everybody does!"

This adolescent petulance. "Here," Chris said, and went out the door, past the bus and down the drive to the barn, then along its stone foundation, to the mow. Ivan gave a rapping bark, and Chris said, "Hey," and saw Ivan, in the dimness of his burrow, drop his head, setting his muzzle on the floor; then he raised it up, ears alert, confused. Chris knelt and drew Ivan's head up on a thigh. "See," he said, "I like you." Ivan blinked from upturned eyes and nudged Chris with his nose, ashamed.

"So we're jacking the dog?" Gaylin stood black as spades in the open space between the sliding doors.

Chris took an ax from the floor and gave it a toss, sending it into a looping circle high in the mow, and Gaylin caught it by the haft on the downswing.

"Watch it!" he cried.

Chris grabbed another and went up the hill behind the barn into the woods, to a growth of young pine, and found a spindly, dying specimen, bolt upright, with little wefts of limbs, less than four inches at its base, and brought it down in two strokes. He stepped off sixteen feet, lopped off its top at an angle, then stepped down it with the strokes Philip had illustrated with a saw, more suited to an ax, rolled it, and lopped off the branches left. In the shade of oaks and maples leafing out, in a swale farther up the hillside, he found another, took it down and trimmed it, then heard *thocks* from a spot below the swale he couldn't see. He dragged his skinned poles from the woods, the ax in one hand, into a bright-lit meadow. Patches of alfalfa and vetch spread spiky tentacles below the unmowed grass, and he walked in a scent of crushed fernery to the top of the hill. The buildings of the farm below looked plaintive—boxes strung along a line. Behind was the bay; ahead Lake Michigan and Manitou under mist. Gaylin emerged from a stand of saplings overgrown with vines, and Chris yelled, "Is this where you want it? Name the spot!"

As Gaylin got closer, looking out of breath, he said, "I name it . . ." and muttered some melange in Indian that sounded obscene. "No, go on up, out that ridge," he said. On the ridge, Gaylin dropped his pole and paced the area, his eyes closed and one hand out, as if he'd read Castaneda. He stepped onto a flat bench of land below the crown of the hill, looking down at the buildings, and said, "Here."

Chris trotted to the saplings and hacked down some of the entangling vines, came and laid the poles lengthwise beside one another, and then laced their tops together five feet down with a snaking vine he tied in a knot. He stepped to the butt ends and took hold of the center pole and started back, drawing the tops of the outside pair with him, and said to Gaylin, "Spread them a bit at the bottom and hold them there." He stepped farther back, pulling as he went, and the vines held, all three poles rising toward the upright, and then their shadow struck his face, and he felt himself leaning from thongs under his chest muscles, his eyes widening in a bronze rain of sun, and began to rotate, both arms back, and then the end of the pole pawed the meadow at his feet and dug in from the weight of the other poles jamming against it. He went over and took a pole from Gaylin, dragging its end out to one side, then skidded the butt of the other in the opposite direction, forming a tripod above them.

"Jeez," Gaylin said. "Where'd you learn that?"

"My grandpa."

Chris saw from Gaylin's faltering expression that he wasn't sure whether Chris was poking fun at him and his grandfather, so Chris frowned. "Now cut about thirteen more this long and stack their ends in the forks up there. You make the circle of the tipi with their butt ends."

"Thirteen!"

"You'll need a dozen more for the tipi and two for the smoke flaps."

"Fourteen!"

"Make it fifteen," Chris said. "Tell me when you're done." He walked off down the hill dragging his ax and had hardly got home, he felt, with barely a wobble in time, before it was another moon, May.

HE STOOD ABOVE Gaylin, who sat with canvas heaped in his lap in the heat. Chris had been drawn to the shelf on the hill by the pole tips against the sky and found that Gaylin had arranged nearly twenty in a perfect circle from the original tripod. "I'm impressed," he said.

"I'm going all the way," Gaylin told him, and passed a hand over his head. His hair was shaved off, down to a bumpy skull, except for a hank in back where a single feather was tied, dangling onto his bare shoulder.

"Where'd you get those?"

Gaylin raised the canvas in his lap. "Some pieces in Beau's barn. Some other places. I got plenty um."

He was talking more like Philip, the true native among the locals—maybe from his sojourn on Fox. Chris looked at the sky as if the gold heat falling over them were the cause of all the misunderstanding in their talk, these disjunctions.

"I meant the poles."

"All over. Woods all over. Some five miles."

"Beau hauled them?"

"Who'd ask? He's with her. I drug um."

"Can I help you?"

"No," Gaylin said. "I'm alone in it. Grandpa says a half circle, ten to eighteen skins, so I figured ..." He shrugged, still bent over, and shoved a thick needle held in a plier's jaws into the canvas and punched its tip through farther on. Chris noticed the substantial flesh over his ribs and shoulders, so he must be well fed, and wondered if he was bare under the canvas. Then had to cough to cover a sudden realization. He was taking on Gaylin as the son he'd lost, or had never had, and now might not ever have. He tried to sigh at this and the absurdities the loss had driven him to (that dissertation!), already halfway out of his depression.

"Did you just lose your best friend?" Gaylin asked.

"It's possible."

"ISN'T IT exciting!" Glynn said.

Another sun-drenched day with Chris and Gaylin sitting in the shadow of the tipi after installing its covering. Beau stared at the smoke hole, his hair down and a belt with his knife nipping the waist of a multicolored shirt hanging outside his jeans. He paced back and forth, checking the tipi from every angle, hands on his hips, a cigarette in his teeth, beaming approval and moving with a swagger that seemed partially enacted and the derivation of "hipster." Indeed this was so, Chris understood; Beau was a hippie, his culture's child, as much as an Indian.

Glynn stood with feet planted and head back, plumply pretty with her somber eyes and swollen, pouting lower lip, streamers of yellow hair lifting from the headband she'd taken to wearing with jeans and work shirts. "It's so beautiful!" she said, clasping her hands above her ample breasts. "I just want to run and dance and sing for you!"

Chris stood and sighed, ready to leave.

Gaylin sat with his head bowed and arms out, bare except for denim cutoffs, and Glynn walked up and nudged the sole of one of his feet with her boot. "You," she said. "I'm damn proud of you. Hey, you did this whole dealie with your own two hands, man."

Beau, who was standing behind her, suddenly made pop eyes and dropped his jaw, tongue hanging out like a goon's and knees giving, then waggled both hands at the sides of his head and broke into his hearty *hooga hoos*.

"Sometimes, you know, Beau?" the girl said without glancing at him but giving Chris a quick up-and-down assessment. "Sometimes when you laugh like that it sounds like some old guy blowing his cookies."

CHRIS WAS wandering along the end of Beau's barn, touching its sun-warmed stones as if to recall his task— the bone in his hand—when he heard something and looked up. Gaylin was above him at the corner, wearing what looked like a canvas breechcloth, holding a shotgun. It rested over an arm at his waist, not aimed, but the double barrels angled downhill at Chris. The same thought, a trigger jerk, occurred to them at the same instant, from Gaylin's shocked recognition, and Chris couldn't remember if Gaylin was present when his shot from the rifle hit the drilling rig. No, he thought, and felt safe. "Well?" he asked.

"What are you doing here?"

Chris glanced at the soup bone and let it drop. "For Ivan. I have to tell Beau something."

"You remembered?"

There was obviously a household joke about Chris's absentmindedness. He stared up the hill, conscious that the barrels hadn't shifted, and saw the pole ends above the tipi as the upper half of an hourglass. There were blue handprints now across the canvas. He turned to Gaylin. "Does Beau know you have his twelve-gauge?"

Gaylin's mouth came open, the spots of steel teeth dark

sockets. Chris walked up and grabbed the barrels, and Gaylin practically threw the gun into his hands.

"Is it loaded?"

"Beau wants them birds shot!" Gaylin exclaimed, backing away in alarm. "He won't do it himself!"

Chris broke the action, only a sliver, onto the brassy ends of two shells whose center beads were still pristine and figured he wouldn't have heard a thing, only numbly sensed the impact sending scraps of him scattering. "Scare some up," he commanded.

"What?"

"Rattle that barn so some leave."

"Those pigeons flocked up and flew off."

"Do it!" From beside the barn Chris was at a level with the upstairs bedroom, and he saw a body there draw out of sight.

Gaylin backed to the sliding door, keeping an eye on Chris, and banged it with a fist. A dozen starlings came around the corner in a peppery cackle of upset, and Chris, setting his feet, swung on the lead and fired, sending it in a nosedive, then leveled on the last of the swirl, where a pair wove so close together he didn't have time to choose before he squeezed off the second, and from a central explosion of feathers both twirled into a raglike tumbling.

"Jeez!" Gaylin cried, and ran up the hill to the spot where they'd struck and came running back with both in one hand, suspended by their legs. "Two in one shot! Look!" He raised them with a youthful glee of accomplishment, heads bobbing between unhinged wings, bodies oozing drops like grease; but projected over them like an afterimage was the orange handprint Chris had seen on the butt of Gaylin's breechcloth. "Boy," Gaylin said, "we'll have to hire you!"

"Just lead them a bit and squeeze the trigger."

"I mean when we take over."

"Take over?"

"You can execute the whites and dumb Indians that don't do what we say when we take over."

"Who's this?"

"Me and Beau. Maybe Grandpa. Maybe you. We'll see."

CHRIS WAITED until Wednesday, in the evening, when he was positive the girl wouldn't be there, but as he and Beau sat at the table where a kerosene lamp was burning he heard laughter overhead, then a sound like hurried footsteps.

"She's here?" he asked.

Beau leaned back and took the elbow of his smoking arm in his other hand, keeping the cigarette near his lips, although he wasn't drawing on it; he studied Chris from lowered lids. "They're listening to music."

Chris considered a comment on Beau's growing family but swallowed it back; he had to enter this gently, down the lines of an earlier talk. "You know, the more I work this thing out, the more I think you're right."

"Good," Beau said. No more, not even whether the "thing" was his dissertation. Only this sleepy study.

"Say the Puritan arrival, or invasion, as you call it, was wrong, and their scriptural ideals were crap, but—"

"Are you going to be bouncing these intellectualities off me the rest of my life?"

"Okay." He could drop it. He held up his cigarette like a candle. "But think of this. There had to be some impetus behind what they believed that was valid, or they couldn't have—"

There was a knocking noise, and Beau was on his feet so fast Chris thought, *Unstrung*. Both their eyes went to the ceiling, and Chris rose so carefully he felt he wasn't displacing air. "Beau, what's going on?"

"I believe that's the fifty-eighth time you asked that, dammit!" Beau's eyes rolled at him like a horse's in anger, shining at their centers with an image of the lamp. "You can't hear what you're talking about, you're so tied up in yourself. You can't get out. You're stuck! You're saying it's great those slick white suckers burned my land bare." He stepped up to Chris, lips trembling, and yelled, "Do you hear? Can you hear me in there? You're a traitor!"

"Okay, now let me tell you what Gaylin—"

"I don't want to hear!" Beau cried, and gave Chris a version of the pushing slap he'd used on Henderson.

"You know, when you think of—"

"Out!" Beau said, one arm flying up, a finger indicating the door. "Out of my house!"

"I've tried to help you when I could, Beau. There are times when I've felt like the Bureau of Indian Affairs."

"Can't you *hear?*" Beau grabbed the back of his neck, pinching so hard Chris saw black, and got him out the door.

Chris staggered on the porch for balance, then turned and set his feet. "I work hard at what I do, which supports me, ultimately, me and my wife both, and half the time, lately, Beau, you. So when—"

Chris was spun so fast he wasn't sure how it happened and received such an angered version of the bum's rush from the bar that he went off the porch pawing air and barely touched down, missing the bus and Power Wagon, before he saw he'd have to dive for the lawn. He did, hitting with an impact that went through his bones. He waited, he tried to roll, he looked up at a tall gabled house with its lights out. He groaned, then listened for a response. He whimpered, adding, "Beau," and heard a door slam inside. He could fall asleep, he thought with a jerk, and got up and crawled into the bus. He waited for half an hour, by the clock on the dash, and then he started up the bus and took the long way back home.

HE HELD THE rifle in his lap as he sat and stared at the red-tipped masts across the lake on Manitou. No, Beau, there was something to them. It wasn't all crap, though most of it might seem so now. They possessed a power that hasn't been seen in this country since, or anywhere else in the world. Only dozens arrived to begin with, and the force of their commitment to set a city on a hill was like uranium. Nothing could stand in its way, and it moved in waves across the continent, unstoppable, to the California coast. An entire country civilized, however you took that, with cities as stunning as any in Europe linked in networks of thousands of miles, in the space of two hundred years, when Canterbury Cathedral took four hundred just to build! It's staggering. It's a phenomenon no single mind can encompass. Much as I hate the depredations, I can't dismiss that.

The phone rang, and he stepped into the bathroom and locked the door. No, Beau, it wasn't crap— The ringing ground into the other side of the shower stall at his back. He looked at the mirror above the sink and saw the shower curtain, draped in folds, bearing gold flecks down its length, and felt his legs start through the floor. His face in the mirror assumed the snouty aspect of the other night, at the center of shaggy aluminum hair.

Ellen grabbed the phone, but all he could hear was garble. He sat on the closed toilet seat, with his head in his hands, and it seemed another morning when Ellen knocked.

"Are you okay in there? Chris, what's wrong with you?"

Excruciating depression, he wanted to say, but was afraid it would come out in a baby voice.

"It was Nana. She figures since the well is in and the tank and pump installed, we should have water tomorrow. She's been in touch with Kitchum."

"Okay." He sounded in a well himself.

"Sort of. She's coming up next weekend, since they couldn't make it for Easter, when the water will be in."

"Easter!"

"I see I forgot that. She was waiting on the amenities— her words. It'll take Jonesy and her to get Grandpa here."

"Grandpa!" He stepped out of the bathroom and couldn't understand why she kept backing from him until he realized he had the rifle. He shook it at her. "No!" he said. "Start packing. We're leaving Monday. We're getting out!"

HE BLINKED against the sun, like a bleaching element over his face as he walked in Ellen's wake into the General Store. A dim fort stocked with riches, through Indian eyes. In the dull light he could see only Ellen's outline against the sparkle of the shopping cart she trundled away.

"By golly!" a voice exclaimed, and Art was in front of her, blocking the aisle. Chris stepped up to face whatever Art might have in mind, and at the end of the aisle he saw one half of Johnny Jones, in the light from the street-side back door, a display of cans partly blocking him. Art glanced toward Johnny, turning solemn, and whispered, "Jouheardabout our fire in Pocahontas-town? Terrible. Whole house clean gone. Couldn't gitourpumper in. It couldabin his stove or smoking in bed. Heckofawinter forum." He winked and added, "*Wood*burners," as if summing up a class rather than a source of heat, from the way he wrinkled his nose.

"*They* tried to put it out by throwing bucketsawater at it, but there wasn't a chance"—lower whisper—"and mostum prolly drunk, Friday night—not a chance in hell. It was over butfurroursoakin' the coals." He took hold of the front of the cart and drew it to the end of the aisle, drawing Ellen along, then looked from her to Chris to Johnny. "Johnny's brother was caught in it, wan't he, Johnny?"

Art performed doleful nods at Johnny, and Johnny studied Chris with a plaintive crinkling to his eyes.

"Johnny's *older* brother, Jimmy's place. We found him ona mattress. Han't moved, maybe from the smoke, right, Johnny? I doughknow how long since we gotr new pumper somebody's been lost. He was a good Indian." Art went to Johnny and put a hand on his shoulder, then an arm around him, standing at his side, and Chris blinked, seeing Art with his slicked-back hair, pouchy cheeks, and shining eyes, like a manikin awaiting its master. "He dintdrinkmuch, worked hard like Johnny, kept his place up, went to church on Sunday. He was a decorated veteran of the U.S. Army too, wan't he, Johnny?"

Johnny looked down, as if studying his placement on the indentations from the potbellied stove, and then his hands slowly rose, palms out, in speechlessness.

"They'll prolly put a write-up inna newspapers," Art

said, "because Jimmy won alotta ribbons, a hero, a real one, not like some Indians, huh? Say, I didn't mean you, Johnny." He tapped Johnny's mackinaw, giving Chris a concluding nod, then hurried to the display of cans he had started setting up.

Chris stepped to Johnny like a prodigal son. "I'm sorry," he said. "It's terrible." He glanced at Art, whose back was to them, the feather duster in his rear pocket, poised, and wanted to say, And even worse to hear about it again like this, but was aware Art was listening.

Johnny shrugged and studied Chris with his same slight smile and a new softened consideration. "You two," he said. "You come. The funeral, it's Saturday."

"Saturday, Johnny?" Art said. "That's almost a week."

"Saturday," he said again at Chris. "You come."

Art was beside Chris in a dash. "Dija hear that?" he said, and now took hold of Chris's shoulder. "It's prolally going to be something special—I mean, different, being Jimmy was a hero, Johnny, huh?"

"Jimmy just talked Indian on a radio," Johnny said, as general information, so the truth was known, and Art said, "Did you and Ellen know Jimmy, Chris?" The possibility of their knowing any Indians other than the regulars who appeared in his store seemed troubling to Art.

Chris adopted a semblance of Johnny's silence.

"Because I didn't think Injuns astus to their buryings," Art said, glancing at Johnny to confirm this, and Chris wondered what Art actually knew about Indians, since he was always isolating them from others.

"Oh," Johnny said, and raised his right hand, index finger up. "These are People-on-Bluff-Where-One-Arm-Built. They drive red-white Nishnabe bus."

"Omigosh," Art said, and pulled out his feather duster

to have something to hold to. "You don't expect them to drive for you at Jimmy's funeral, Johnny, do you?" And then the appalling potential of it seemed to strike him, and he stepped back for a better view, and said, "My golly, Christofer, you're not *Indian*, are you?"

12

Fog over the lake and woods and a prison atmosphere in the cabin with no sun, a smell of damp and milt
rising from the log walls, invading Chris with the cloudy
edge of mental illness. He kept working all night, into the
morning, and finished ten days late by his schedule, but
done. At dinner he placed the file folder beside Ellen's
plate. "Great!" she said. "I have something for you." She
got up and returned with a folder somewhat thicker. "It's
the journal you told me to make a book of. I have."

He opened it and started reading a fictionalized account
of the night they arrived. She had him drunk, sprawled
on his back with the skis on, wailing.

"What's this?" he asked.

"It used to open with a statement about our—about him
dying, but that seemed too abrupt. So I thought I'd show
some of the effects of it in the present first."

"You mean, you think I was loaded?" he asked. He
leaned out of the light and entered the blizzarding flakes
falling so fast they formed clots he flinched at, the grocery
bag rattling; then, on a second trip, the weight of the pack,
as a ski slipped, dragging him onto his back. His wish to

remain in the snow as it sang in changing levels above his eyes, then a schuss and the dark bulk of her above, waiting.

"You think this is fair?" he asked.

"You mention Roethke's divagations, no?"

"But that's history. Roethke's dead."

And then he saw it; that was worse. Then the entire manipulation of history by people called scholars, but each with his or her own agenda, started tumbling into place, and he understood there was no end to it.

"And you know," she said, "the crazy thing is—" She studied her hands on the table. "Here I am working on this, about *that*—" She drew her hands into her lap and then, with her head bowed, shook the thought off. He was so sure she was about to say she was pregnant that he had to stand and stare out the window to steady his emotions. Then he saw that the pile of firewood across the drive was double the size it had been last night.

HE DIALED the university, asked for the dean's extension, and said, "Have I got something for you!"

"Isn't it about time, dear?"

"That is, the dissertation. I mean it's done—the whole thing! I think I've really got something here."

"How I hope. Hopefully, you've remembered to keep it, ah—remember our hopeful goal of two hundred."

"Oh, yes, I've taken your injunction seriously."

"Injunction? Size is size, you know. It's content."

He wasn't sure he'd heard this correctly over the rural static but said, "Right!"

"Just one thing. Indent."

"Pardon?"

"You know, your paragraphs. A thesis I have now is all big blocks with white spaces between, no indentation. That is *not* proper style. I think he even used the university's mainframe. This printing is too uniform. Are you listening, boobie?"

"Yes I am."

"Indent."

FULL MOON, a howling moon, as he hurried past the bar he had vowed he would never enter, and across the street to the hotel, able to see through its porch window into an area now a restaurant. Empty. The new owner had slyly put up a partition inside the entry, so you had to step around it to see to the bar, and Chris opened the door on a smell of stale beer soaked into pine. Past the partition, a half-dozen patrons sat in dimness at a horseshoe bar; then one turned on the corner stool and said, "Well! Look who's here." It was Marty.

"It's time we settled this," Fat Anfinson said.

"Get him a beer!" somebody called.

"Yeah!" Horse said, leaning from behind his brother. "Then I'll punch him so it squirts out his nose."

Everybody in the Indian bunch laughed, and Chris saw the owner standing against the cash register at the back bar, stout and balding, his face nearly as red as his wiggly-looking fringe of pink-red hair, cowed and fearful.

"You guys must've had your birthdays," Chris said.

"Yup," Marty answered. "Alla um this week."

"Oh, be quiet," the bartender said.

"Hey," Horse said, "I heard that, you queer!"

"I meant him," the bartender said, indicating Chris.

"I figured," Marty said. "You been so nice."

They laughed, and Horse slammed his bottle on the bar. "More!" he cried. "Give that pimp his last one!"

The bartender hopped to the cooler and grabbed three bottles in each hand, popping their caps off at an opener and smartly setting them around. When he got to Chris, Chris said, "No, thanks, I'm going."

"Drink or die!" Horse bellowed, perhaps a new slogan.

"Don't you dare leave," the bartender whispered. "They got me backed against the wall. Help!"

"It's the least I can do for you," Marty said to Chris, and tossed a ten on the bar. "You been so nice."

"Look, Marty," he said, and took the sleeve of Marty's shirt, grabbing at his only hope. "You said to me once, 'I won't hold it against you, brother.' Did you mean that?"

Marty turned, a hesitating fear in his lively eyes under the horn-rims, then looked away, his mouth fixed.

"I told you real history and read you a lot of it."

"Don't bover us wif dump!" Lonnie cried.

"Your history is dump? Did any of you read *Black Elk Speaks* before this? Did you even hear of him? Or Vine Deloria, or *Bury My Heart at Wounded Knee*, or *Tough Trip Through Paradise*, or any of those other books I read you?"

"I lived it," Marty said, turning to him. "I lived it, and I live it every day, right here, see. How about you?"

"Wasn't Siouxs the ones we chased to South Dakota?" Fat Anfinson said.

"Let me!" Horse yelled. "I'll kick him down Main Street!"

Chris started around the bar as though to take Horse up on this, and the bartender cried, "Not in here! Not in my place, you don't, by God!"

This slowed everybody enough so that Chris continued

toward the rest room and found the phone, beside a ciga-rette machine in a hall, and got a dime in with trembling fingers and dialed Beau's. He heard somebody at the bar say, "Beau kicked him out, Gaylin said. Beau's got a girl now." They laughed. The phone rang as Marty said, "He's telling his old lady good-bye," and then came off the hook. "Hey," Chris said, and whoever was at the other end hung up. He couldn't find another dime and stuck in a quarter, and when the phone came off the hook in lis-tening silence, he whispered, "Beau, I'm at the hotel in town. You have to come help. Please."

"Help?"

"The kids. They've taken over the place, literally. Come *on*, it's only a couple miles. They want to do me in."

"That damn rifle," Beau said, and hung up.

Chris dialed agin, but it rang on and on, and finally, leaving the receiver dangling, he went into the rest room and heard, "Can he get out of there?"

No, a cell with no window. He splashed water over his face at the sink and heard Horse crowing, "I'd just kick it out of him!" Maybe he should emerge and make his way to his stool, then sprint for the outside. But Horse was there, along the wall with his brother; they'd get him at the door.

He stepped out, and everybody turned; and the second he started down the bar, Horse slid off his stool, between the bar and wall, waiting. "Ready?" he asked.

"That," Chris said and pointed, then muscled past him, expecting a blow from behind, and went to his beer.

"Marty," he whispered.

"I got nothing to say to you."

"You're bright. I like you. I quit buying to keep you out of trouble. A guy who knows your dad said—"

"Listen at him *beg*," Fat Anfinson said, and tipped his bottle up, eyes wide, smiling on both sides of his guzzle.

"Come on!" Horse called. "Let's get out there and go!"

"All right," Chris said, figuring it was his only out. "One more first." He meant a beer, for anesthetic, and with a jolt pictured the needle entering Henderson.

"You're kind of half a pecker length as brave without your rifle, ain't you?" Marty said. "A thirty-thirty, huh? Shit."

"Just make sure he don't run off crying," Fat Anfinson said. "I want sloppy seconds." Everybody laughed.

Chris breathed out, trying to relax, trying to call on the strength he could summon in emergencies, hoping Horse got so stumbly he could be outrun, if nothing else, and then the door behind banged in. Rio came around the partition, saw it all in one look, and was gone.

"We shoulda cleaned his clock, too," Lonnie said. "It's allus that cowboy dump wif him."

Chris decided to nurse his beer, the first one, half-done (the bartender was now ignoring him), and then dash into the restaurant side, cover his face with an arm, and leap through the window. "You know," he said to the bartender, "you could do something about this."

"You could've, too," the man said, and crossed his pink-fuzzy arms. "Earlier. I'm serving customers now."

"You're—?" Chris swallowed, knowing he should keep quiet. "You'd do anything for business, wouldn't you? No," he realized, taking the man in, "you're a coward, aren't you? A true-blue coward from Detroit."

"Throw him out!" the bartender yelled at the young men. "Get him out of here and beat him up! Get him!"

There was such a commotion of stools Chris wasn't sure
what caused Marty to sit back down until he saw Beau at
the partition in a black T-shirt so tight it looked like skin,
his hair down, hands at his hips. Beau slapped the knife
at his side and went to Marty and spun him by a shoulder.
"You should know better," he said. "Since you're so
scared you duck when you see me, you fool!"

"And you, Bobby," Beau said at the next stool, "I
know your big mouth and the way you keep flapping it
when Horse is here to back you." Beau grabbed his
shirt. "Now what?"

Horse was off his stool as if to swing, and in the act
of shoving Bobby down Beau gave Horse a backhand
across the chest that sent him wallowing for balance.
Beau beckoned with both palms up, fingers jerking
back. "Come on!" he said, "I'm ready!" Beau shoved
him aside and poked a finger into Lonnie. "You're too
numb above to be bad," he said as Horse began a
windup from behind. Beau spun, clouting him on the
shoulder, knees flexed, then slowly straightened. "You
just backed down again, Horse," he said. "Bob! Bill!"
He shook the two at the far end of the bar. "Wake up!
Don't you see you're jailbait!" He stepped back around,
tapping each one hard as he passed, and stopped at
Chris. "Get home."

The owner finally spoke: "He was the one they—"

"Shut up, faggot brain!" Saliva blew from Beau's lips
at the blast of this. "You," he said to Chris. "Out!"

Chris was out and crawling into the bus when he
heard footsteps and turned to face whoever; Beau, out
of breath, eyes troubled, alone. "Straight home! Don't
try anything intellectual or invent some great comeback,
just get home!"

"What about you?"

"I'm taking my advice." He went running off.

ELLEN WONDERED who had rearranged the ceiling to cause her queasiness and then remembered they were in the bed upstairs. An experiment, he had said, when he returned from town last night, carrying the rifle up—here under the slant of the roof. Or she was, she saw, turning; the quilt was folded away from the other side of the bed to doubly cover her, Chris gone. She heard a sound like Beau's truck at the same moment a metallic shrieking rose from the back porch. Then silence. A face seemed lifted to her, listening.

She was sure it was Beau, hearing Chris's voice from outside, followed by solid, hazy *whocks* of wood being split in morning mist. She was sick. She pulled on her nightgown and was down the halved and polished steps of logs, a hand over her mouth at the smell of coffee, when a sudden knock rattled the back-door latch. No bathroom, she thought, and remembered Chris had freed the weathered bolt of the front door. She went for it and had cleared the concrete steps outside when the upheaval came. She hit down on her knees at the base of a tree, bent at the waist, feeling the unnatural gathering of voices in the cabin forcing this up. She removed the remaining strings from her lips and wiped her fingers on grass damp with dew.

She picked up a twig as she rose, snapped it in pieces and dropped them over the clot below, such a small mouthful, after all that, and went in a daze over the wet lawn to the edge of the bluff, hoping it would be a girl.

The lake was bright blue, bordered by a lime-green

band where waves kept retracing the contours of the shore in collapsing lines. She couldn't tell Chris until she was positive; meanwhile they had to stay here. She ran around to the back porch and opened the door to the kitchen, almost ramming old man Kitchum in the butt, and he turned and said, "Morning, ma'am." He was in his denim jumpsuit, cap off, his pretty blond pride nowhere in sight, the weathered creases in his face merging into smooth ivory over his forehead, and Chris stood in the dining wing, as if to guard his manuscript.

"Let's settle this like reasonable folk," Kitchum said. "The tank and plumbing are in, the pump's in, and we just wired up a new switchbox for it in your back porch. Now. Your grandma wrote me a check for one thousand dollars, but she owes me another, and by rights I don't have to connect this thingamabob to get things going till she pays up."

"I said I'd pay him the thousand," Chris told her.

"You!"

"Nana won't want to owe us." He smiled with the benignity of Johnny Jones at this, then shrugged.

"I'll step out in the porch a minute and get the pump going, and when you see it works to your liking, ma'am, I'd enjoy having that check for another thousand."

"Can you explain why it so queerly comes out to such an even amount?" she asked.

"That's just what your grandma said! But, yes, I can. I'm cutting one-third off the bill. When we had to drill so deep, I felt I daren't charge much more than my original estimate. I suspect I'll about break even."

She couldn't believe Chris would write this man a check, but he did, leaning on the table. Kitchum took it and stared at it like an illiterate, then tore it in two.

"Say!" This came from her.

"What are you doing?" Chris asked.

"I trust you, but you aren't the ones that owe this." He shoved the pieces in a pocket and turned to her. "When you see your grandpa next, remind him of the Kitchum boy. You tell him there're no hard feelings on my part. I've stopped coveting his place. Me and my lad plan to build our own, starting from scratch like my daddy and his Indian friend did, farther down the lakeshore. Tell your grandpa that his son here, or grandson—grandson-in-law, that is, I guess—"

"I believe that's it," Chris said.

"Tell him that his grandson and you, bright beauty of a girl, should have this place. Stay here. Do."

CHRIS SAT in front of the fired-up fireplace and imagined the scene: Ellen would say she expected Nana to keep her posted on Grandpa's illness, after learning that the only doctor Nana permitted him to see, a dermatologist she was sure was about to convert to Christian Science and become a practitioner, had performed a colostomy on him. "I don't want to hear he's 'ascended' a week after he's dead," Ellen would say, as she had to Chris. "I want the truth from now on, understand?"

"You couldn't have made it clearer had your words been engraved in stone," Nana would say. "That's from Job."

There would be a question about the quotation, and both would go for the Bible bristling with its springy markers as Chris, from the corner window ledge, would say, "Chapter nineteen."

"Where did you gain your expertise?" Nana's voice.

"From whence? I believe in the holy Catholic church,

the communion of saints, the forgiveness of sins, et cetera."

"That's your perverse Catholic upbringing!"

"No, it's the Apostles' Creed. It's been adopted by every sane Protestant denomination since Luther."

"Can you tell me which one teaches healing from sickness, disease, and death? Like Jesus did! One! The Church of Christ, Scientist, founded by—"

No, they couldn't stay on, he thought, going out the front door he'd fixed, slamming it, wanting to yell back, No, not just Mary Baker Eddy. A few offshoot charismatics teach that, too, but even they don't believe you can be healed of death! He went down the concrete steps *one two three* into the dark night and could as well have stepped through the door on death into life, he felt, that quick.

He'd been dandled among the poles of forces beyond him and pulled in every direction. The portion of him that was Indian, or pure instinct, had gained ascendance and had drawn him farther down a narrowing path with no exit; the only way out was ahead. He would miss Beau; he would miss him when he saw signs of spring or heard peepers cheering across the reaches of the night like this or remembered these woods. But Beau's trek, different now than at the first, was set. A scent from the lake like the ocean overtook Chris, and he felt almost ready to welcome the insanity of New York, although he couldn't imagine sitting in a student's chair.

The screen door slapped, and in a moment he sensed Ellen close. She took his upper arm. "Don't run off now," she said. "Please don't go to town. Don't go see him."

It was the plaint of an Indian wife, and he pulled out his cigarettes with shaking hands. "No. I was thinking of another life, our other life—another." He gave her a chance to ask him to explain and finally said, "New York."

He waited for her to ask again if they couldn't stay on, but she leaned forward into his back, encircling him with her arms, and drew him into her breasts, so armorial and substantial he was shocked. "I'm in love," she said.

THE NECESSITY of packing, a whole day's sad chore. It wasn't only their clothes, which appeared outdated, but storing all the dishes and equipment they'd used. In the evening he was pressing a pile of dress shirts, still in laundry cardboard, into his suitcase, their starched fronts chilly, when he thought of the funeral. He went to their bedroom, where suitcases were lying open, and saw her at the dresser.

"El," he said. "Let's go to the funeral."

She held up the plastic bag. "What about this?"

He took it and counted the buttons through the plastic: seven. "We'll give them back to Beau."

"You said he wouldn't take it."

"Maybe if I leave it at his place."

"Do. That last was it."

He took the bag outside, unable to remember the time she was referring to, ashamed to mention the scene in the bar, and walked to the bluff. A copper channel widened across the water from the late spring sun, and the sailing shadows at the edge of the channel near the base of the bluff, miniature from his height, were hawks, back from migration and set in their prowl of the coast.

He let the peyote fall.

In the cabin the phone was ringing: Nana. He picked it up, and Beau yelled, *"Help!"* and hung up. The force of the rebuke, in imitation of Chris's call, was enough to set him back a month. He covered his face, wishing he at least hadn't tossed everything overboard. Then he heard the cry again, its plea and the way it was clopped off, and understood that it was authentic. He ran to the door, then doubled back and grabbed the rifle; it might be the kids after revenge.

"I'll be right back!" he yelled at the cabin.

He was halfway across Orin's field when light like an afterglow of sun trembled across the south. And when he broke from the trees past the Indian settlement, he saw an orange corona as if from the setting sun itself quivering above Beau's hill. Those pigeons in the barn, he thought, and a fear threaded through his ribs for Gaylin's life.

But as he came over the hill and down in a leap toward cottony, bulbous mounds like smoke that he saw were orchard trees in bloom, he noticed the upstairs windows in Beau's place lit orange. Then a spire of light flared above the peak of the roof, and he had to acknowledge that Beau's house was on fire. He floored the bus, still afraid for Gaylin—and the girl! it was where she slept!— and squalled into the far end of the drive, feeling the bus tip on two tires, then slam down, and saw Beau frantically working a pump as he stared over his shoulder at the burning house. Flames were coiling out the door toward the posts of the porch, illuminating its entire underside, and as Chris hopped from the bus where it had slid shy of Beau's Power Wagon, an explosion sent sparkling shingles climbing a geyser of flame as a porch gutter swung down at one end and crumpled in an instant melt.

Chris's legs were so weak he had to take hold of the bus to keep his balance. Beau ran toward the house with a bucket and threw—a sear of steam that appeared to agitate the flames—and Chris held up a hand against the heat. "Beau!" he yelled. "*Beau!* Is anybody in there?"

"God!" Beau cried, stumbling back from the heat, his

hair half its length and burned to a tangled frazzle. "She was! She was, but— Help!"

"Did you call the fire truck?"

"I couldn't, I was burning! I called you!"

Chris was unsure which way to turn and heard a muted *Ai-yi-yi! Ai-yi-yi!* coming in a high pitch from above and saw a shadow at an upstairs window glowing the hottest. "Ivan!" he cried. "Why doesn't he jump?"

"Gaylin put Plexiglas a half inch thick in her window— you and that gun! Ivan ran up the stairs when I phoned! To check on—" Beau sat back on the ground so hard Chris ran over and saw that his Levi's were charred and one leg burned raw.

"Don't move," Chris commanded. "Ivan!" he called, cupping his hands, and saw the dog, outlined in fire, leap against the syrupy Plexiglas. Chris bent and fumbled for a rock in the driveway as he prayed. He found one with heft, feeling the growing fire sweep over his face like the heated wind that had hit him full face on the crest of Sleeping Bear, and threw as he had then, with a tearing cry. The window blew apart, fire boiling from it with liquid force, and Ivan came springing through, onto the porch roof in a bound, his fiery body headed for Chris with a sizzling noise like burning straw. Chris held out his arms for a catch and barely felt the impact, but realized he was going over backward before he blacked out.

A STENCH OF burned hair and char overwhelmed him as he gagged to get his breath. His back felt burned, his chest crushed, and he crawled toward a far-off firelit bus. When the air grew cool enough to breathe, he rolled and sat. The house continued to burn, or its heaped remains,

a few feet high—sinking with the cookstove to the basement; black-red timbers shedding orange scales, a lightning rod draped over the stovetop—burned against the
hillside behind.

Beau came from behind the bus carrying an ax.

"It's too late!" Chris said. "You'll get hurt worse!"

"She isn't there. Gaylin's gone."

"I thought you said—"

"I was in town and came back to this. There's a note."

"A *note*? What about Ivan?"

Beau rotated the ax by its handle, then tossed it aside.
"I had to. He was burned too bad."

Chris saw the fiery body headed at him in a sizzling
rush and covered his face. "Gaylin's safe? She is?"

"There was a note in the barn where—" Beau studied
the ax. "They been sleeping there or in the tipi."

"Beau!"

"How could I tell you? Am I supposed to have exclusive
claim on her?"

"Oh, Beau, you know that—"

"Stop! I'm the one that has to live with this!"

Chris went to him, where he'd sunk beside the Power
Wagon onto a stone, head in his hands and hair melted
into clumps at its ends, and held a hand above Beau's
shoulder but was unable to lower it. "What can I do?" he
finally asked.

"Leave. Go back east. That dog was all I had. He was
the only innocent one."

Chris sensed the weight of Ivan's begging muzzle nudg-
ing his thigh and almost said, *If he was.*

"Good you freed him," Beau said.

"For what?"

"For the earth, where he won't even remember dreams."

"I wish I knew that."

"With all your Christing, you don't?"

"Beau, history turns the tables for us. We won."

"Won!"

"When you figure Europeans came here for religious freedom, look at the religion they got—transcendentalism to pantheism down to the hippies right now. It's animism, it's Indian! On the important front, we won!"

"How can you say that when my house is burned up! My dog! When I lost the only woman I—"

"Beau, you know she wasn't right."

"What's right! To be so young and—God! Here." He handed Chris a piece of canvas scrawled with charcoal in clumsy block letters: "I love hor. We left."

"Wait," Beau said, and grabbed it and studied its back in the firelight. "I knew it," he murmured, and looked off up the hill, where the hourglass of tipi poles stood. "I tried to tell myself he was just getting back to real life, but I knew he was haywire. See."

On the other side of the canvas, Gaylin had sketched rough squares, each containing a small square divided by a cross, a window, with a handprint like flame over them all.

"Arsonist," Beau whispered. "Goddamn pyromaniac!"

"Stop the Freudian stuff. Gaylin wouldn't—"

"Burning and pillaging, by God! His own parents' house five years ago. This winter the one by Indian Shores, then Jimmy Jones's, his poor uncle, who probably caught him doing it, then mine! He dropped matches on anthills, grinning, and threw them like daggers at poor Ivan."

"Five," Chris said, and Beau grabbed the canvas again. "That couldn't be . . ."

But Chris was already in the bus, backing away, when Beau called, "Wait! Where am I going to sleep?"

"Come over! Stay!" Chris wasn't far down the road when he realized the barn would occur to Beau, if his pride wouldn't allow him to stay at the cabin—if it was still there, he thought, as he pulled over the hill, panting, and studied the sky for unnatural light. He was shifting in the seat as if to find a place to rest, and saw he had to come to rest on some belief, not act out the ideas of others in his mind. And he prayed, Oh, let her be there, let her be safe, don't let anything be wrong with her. Let her be there. . . . He sped through the settlement so fast he wasn't sure the man he noticed on a porch was holding a gun, but ducked his head as he swung into the final curve and saw his lights catch somebody dodge into the woods at a sprinter's pace. Gaylin? He tore across Orin's field at the clip Beau had taken, afraid he'd seen a flicker of light coming from the cabin.

"Head for the light!" he'd yelled to Beau, and did the same, rising so high on the stems of the brushy hedge that he saw flames pecking below the window where Ellen lay asleep.

No, she was outside, dancing close to the flames—no, stomping on them, he saw as the bus slid sideways from braking, its headlights skimming past a person in a long black coat and the ski mask with yellow circles. That was how Gaylin did it, the bastard, Chris thought, out of the bus, on a run toward the hulk in black. It swung around at the lights, then took off for the back of the cabin. Once Chris got to the window and saw that the fire was nearly out, he dashed around the corner, breathing inhaled smoke from Beau's place, and had to pause. First he heard, then saw the shape, bearlike, head down the hill past the woodpile.

He got himself up to full speed in the trees and felt endangered, liable to hit one at full tilt, but angered that Ellen had been threatened. He tried to settle into the shifting considerations he'd felt in the bus, and before he got close, he knew he had their prowler, arsonist, and pyromaniac trapped. He dropped at a slant down the hill to a power-line cut through the woods. There he sprinted to top speed, drawing even with the hulk who maintained the springy strides of a gymnast, a gait he'd seen before, and then appeared to slow, afraid or unfamiliar with this area of the woods, and with the hesitation Chris cut at an angle into the trees and was whipped so badly by a branch he had to run blind through stinging tears but could hear the pant of the person, mingled with a stench of musk, and homed in on that. He pictured Gaylin's grandfather painting the stripes on Gaylin's face and in a slide of memory saw again the painting his own grandfather had undergone when he drove back into the burned-out forest and joined the man in leather leggings and a dozen others in a frenzied dance—and then Chris was there, in a thrashing stumble over slippery leaves. But the hulk dodged, taller than Gaylin, he saw, and nearly went down in shock at the realization, then heard a hurried, ragged breath of fear and knew this was his only chance.

He dove and had legs, and both of them hit the leaves with the splash of swimmers in a pool. The person pulled one leg loose and got in a kick, but Chris grabbed the boot and then the hem of the coat, oily fur, and pulled himself on top. He got hold of the ski cap and jerked, black hair flying from a face white as the moon.

"Jeez!" he cried, shocked to see feisty Michelle, who'd once threatened him and the actress. No, not Michelle, too tall. It was the *actress*. "You're the actress!" he cried.

"You bet I am, buddy," she said in the voice of the

woman they took to the powwow. "I sat a foot from your back with my hand on a pistol in my purse!" This was in her real voice. "I would have let you have it if it didn't give me such a kick!"

"What are you up to!"

"Putting out your fire! Saving her! Your little Indian bastard set it, and you, probably, in cahoots!"

"What are you doing here!"

"I've been up every night. I saw those punks rub the place with mud. I could have shot them!"

"But what are you doing at our place!"

"It's hers, you devouring sonofabitch!" She threw open the coat and bumped and wriggled, drawing down dark tights until she was naked to her ankles, where the tights caught. "There, you slick shit, that's what you're after, isn't it!"

Chris picked her up as she hit and kicked at him, padding falling from the coat, small pillows with cardboard formed over them like shoulder pads. He threw her across a shoulder and went through the woods, huffing for breath, toward the light, while she beat on his back and cried, "I'll kill you! I'll turn your balls inside out and saw them off, you dip!"

"Chris!" Ellen stood in the doorway.

"Look!" the woman cried, craning around. "He tried to rape me right out behind your place, the pig!"

"Peggy!" Ellen cried. "What is this?"

"And when he couldn't rape me," Peggy said, "he tried to sucker me into having his way with me in— Ow!" she cried as he swung her from his shoulder. He shoved her into the back porch, Ellen hurrying out of their way.

"Here's what I think of you," Peggy said, glaring at him in red-faced fury as she squatted over the welcome mat. Then a fuller redness flooded her face as a stream started dribbling from her. She bore down until it sang, and then there was a puttering of gas that caused her eyes to roll, but then she bore down harder, with a new intent, and three rabbit-sized pellets struck behind her spreading urine on the fiber mat.

Chris, sick of communal acts, stepped outside.

"All I want to do is to be alone with you, honey," he heard Peggy say. "This kid was trying to torch your place!"

"What's happening?" Ellen asked her. "What is this?"

"I been sick, bad sick. Let me explain!"

Chris went around to the bedroom window and discovered that Gaylin had used kerosene-soaked rags and also splashed logs with kerosene and gunpowder, from the smell. He ground out a piece of canvas still glowing at an edge like a racing wick. Could Peggy have done it? He turned to the moonlit sky and saw beyond it to a range of the Milky Way. Men are arsonists. *Mama! They're all in there! Get them out!* Gaylin had cried. So he set his fires in or near bedrooms to consume the one that all the others entered or came from, the one he was denied.

Chris walked to the pile of wood he had split and eased himself down on his chopping block, trying to calculate the hours he and Beau had put in together on this wood. He pulled out a cigarette, his last. Ellen and Peggy were in the living room, on the couch, he saw, realizing how easy it was for an outsider to look in from the dark and view people like images on a screen. The brutality of detachment.

No, one more cigarette, crushed and curled like a worm along an edge of the flattened pack. After it, he would give Peggy fifteen more minutes to have her say; he gave her a half hour. When he went in, they turned from the couch, a low fire trembling over the grate in the fireplace, their faces pale above the couch's back, both in tears.

"I'm taking a shower," he said, "my first in weeks. And when I step out of here"—he indicated the bathroom door, then looked at Peggy—"I expect you to be gone."

HE LAID TWO logs over the coals and sat beside Ellen on the couch, a towel around his waist like Beau, feeling old. Ellen said Peggy had told her about his "career" before they met and how the young woman, or yet another of his women, Michelle, had threatened Peggy and then one night at a party came at her with a broken bottle and tried to gouge out her eye. "She said that ended her career as an actress. Why didn't you recognize her?"

"From one night over seven years ago? Why didn't you recognize the fat lady as Peggy? She's good at assuming awful faces, and must use latex makeup to form bags for her other persona to cover that scar. She carved PIG in my window."

"What!"

"She's also Peggy, I guess, when she wants to be."

"Was it her up here all the time or Gaylin?"

"Her," he said.

"But Gaylin must have smeared that mud around."

"No, Marty's bunch. They were so mad at me the other night, it has to be for nailing them on that. You first said it was them, and they hated it that we caught them. Besides firing the rifle. The handprints were different sizes. Peggy's the nightly snooper, but they all had a crack at us, each with a separate agenda. Probably even Henderson was up. Maybe Orin."

"Peggy said she followed you since college and wanted to save me from you."

"I heard she runs a shop in Leland."

"She liked the area the first time she saw it, she said. She's kept up with you all along."

"Kept up with me!"

"She knows everywhere you've been."

"What did she intend, for God's sake?"

"Get even. Torture you. After a while, it sounds like she got interested in me. You could have at least told me!"

"How did I know?"

"I mean, about her and that shrimp you screwed!"

He wanted to say that most of her past was hidden from him, too, but kept his mouth shut.

"All those women!"

"I treated some badly, I admit. I confess it. The worst is how it's affected you. Forgive me."

"You should ask them for forgiveness! Ask Peggy!"

"We never went out. I never even knew her name, or if I did, I forgot. The one who went at her with the bottle broke up the one date we had."

"The way Peggy talked, you abused her!"

"Maybe she was thinking of Michelle."

"Who's *Michelle*?"

"The shrimp, the one with the bottle—if that's true. I didn't willfully abuse her. I was distant."

"Determined."

He recalled Ellen, when they met, resisting him with such determination he'd let her retreat in her sad sashay. "Distant and determined, then. I'm sorry."

"That won't do anymore! I'm sorry I married you!"

"Please."

"Peggy's just like my mother!"

"What's this?" Ellen always said she didn't remember

her mother, since her death in "the accident" had seemed to wipe her from memory, but over the years Ellen told him details as they came; that her parents were on a vacation they had arranged to take without her; that their car went over a guard rail in the Colorado Rockies, and there were no skid marks; that a gossip columnist at the time called it a "lover's leap"—a story Ellen found, years later, in a newspaper morgue. This columnist claimed the son-in-law was getting on less well with the head of Strohe Breweries, implying they had never got along, and was about to be fired. Ellen remembered arguments about her father's name, which was Cotler, but was changed to Cutler, and Chris could imagine the immensities (when he considered Grandpa Strohe's Germanic strain) of possible anti-Semitism. But recently, as the old man failed and Nana took over, it became clear that she was the one in control, or always had been, and Chris experienced her hate for him like a killing clot.

"Careful, gracious, and so forth," Ellen was saying. "Pumping Nana all my life, it's all I got. It only came out when I got so depressed I couldn't move, and then in platitudes. 'Your mother was a careful, lovely woman. Your mother trained you perfectly from the first. If only—' She'd close her eyes and I'd read, 'If only she hadn't married that bastard, your father, she'd be alive!' "

Ellen blew her nose, reddened and swollen from weeping.

"A man can hurt or humiliate a woman, but not the way a woman can. A woman can take another apart from the inside—a mother can. Nana was my mother the years I grew up. She did such a job I didn't have any identity. I wasn't dumb, I was fairly sure, but she dismantled me so much I *knew* I was inept. Has all my life been spent to prove her wrong? Women want power, dammit! If not over a man, then another woman, or there's no peace. I know what happened to my mother. My dad could probably stand the crap or walk away from it, but she was devoured until she had to let her mother have it. 'Let's go!' she yelled at him. 'This is it!' Or got at the wheel and drove them both over the cliff. That's how she's like Peggy. Grandpa grieved over her, he did, in his way, but Nana? She was embarrassed and shocked. Embarrassed! That a daughter of hers would do this! I mean, be dead!"

A radiance like northern lights, alien and silky, rose around the couch, as if the fireplace were putting out frost instead of heat, and Chris took Ellen's hand.

"Please," he said. "You'd never be like that."

"I might be worse! I've survived my mother and plan to survive that old—that *destroyer*, too! I'm up for this!"

"El, we have to go. We have to leave."

"I don't know how I can! I just got started, and it's another death! Peggy's destroyed it! She's destroyed the person you were to me! I wrote this book, and now it's dead, too! I wish that sick, sad kid you kept trying to adopt would have burned me up!"

"El."

"It's a murder mystery! Three dead!"

"Three."

"My parents. *Him.*"

Their child, he understood, deciding he couldn't tell her about Ivan, or even about Beau's house, yet. "No," he said. "There's also Johnny's brother, Jimmy. Four."

NO MATTER how much he showered and scrubbed he couldn't get the smell of smoke from his skin, and a ways down the highway, as the bus entered a shuttering network of shadow, he felt they were driving through fire. Then he saw the trees were all leafed out, the first he'd noticed. They were late for the funeral. Cars were parked for a quarter mile down both sides of the highway through Pshawbetown, and a crowd craning on the steps outside a wood-frame church. Chris took Ellen up to the crowd and at the edge of it saw Carlyle. Chris put a hand on his shoulder, and Carlyle turned, his chin giving; then his face wrinkled and went wide, in mocking imitation of a baby on a potty, Chris thought, then tears spilled through his slitted eyes.

The vestibule was so crowded all Chris could see past the people standing inside it and down the aisle was the head of a priest, saying, "May *his* soul and the souls of all the faithful departed, through the mercy of God, rest in peace, amen." Chris removed his fur cap and felt Carlyle grab his topcoat and press his face into it, silently weeping. The crowd was filing out now, and he tried to encourage Carlyle to back up with him to give them room. Ellen took his arm to maintain contact in the crowd already jostling them, women in beads and shawls and long dresses embroidered at the hems in primary colors—and then he saw Beau easing ahead on his game leg, a black Stetson over his chest, his eyes turned down, lids purple. The churchyard filled so fast Chris thought the service was over, but other people started walking from the waiting cars—men with blankets over their shoulders, women in sweeping skirts and shawls, turquoise and silver sparkling—and soon hundreds were in the churchyard, all silent, Carlyle gone.

Six tall men came down the steps carrying the coffin, undersized, lavender in the sunlight, covered with material stretched taut over its top and sides, draped by an

American flag, and Chris had to turn away at the thought
of Gaylin. The pallbearers swung down the side of the
church, through its shadow into raw sunlight, the crowd
beginning to follow at a distance, and Ellen slipped her
arm through his. Chris wanted to drift back, trail behind, but the crowd kept pressing him forward and finally began to part ahead, and he saw a canvas shelter
at the edge of an open field, with hazy woods beyond a
meadow graveyard.

The priest came striding past, still in his silky vestments,
the bald spot at the back of his head white in the sun,
and worked his way through people to the shelter. The
pallbearers set the coffin on the ground underneath it,
beside a mounded heap of dirt undisguised by the artificial Easter grass Chris had seen at graves. Again he and
Ellen were shoved forward, up to the shelter, and when
the crowd behind realized there was no more room, they
began to file past on either side toward the open field.
Hut. Hut. Ah, *hut*, Chris heard a hoarse voice whisper,
and five men in suits and American Legion caps came
past in a ragged march, one limping and another doing a
skip to get in step, rifles on their shoulders, and halted at
the shelter's open front. At a command their rifles went
slapping to their sides, stocks down in the grass, fists
tucked behind their backs.

The priest said a prayer at the grave, and the unnatural
quiet enveloped Chris again; he could hear insects singing
through the air, and even the children were silent. Far
off across the field where the woods began the pure
notes of a trumpet rose in taps, that mournful fanfare.
Somebody rose from a folding chair under the shelter—
Johnny, curly white head bare—and a Legionnaire
handed him the flag folded into a triangle. Johnny

stared down at it, weighing it in his hands, and Chris heard a sound and saw Carlyle in the chair next to Johnny, his head bowed and held in his hands. The rifles went slapping back up, and Chris saw that most of the Legionnaires were Indians, then that one of the five was Orin, a squirrel tail dangling from a pocket of his suit jacket, and was so taken aback he hardly heard what the voice was crying before the first volley went off—a staggering cannonade.

An oily, acrid scent of discharged gunpowder spread, and with a clatter brass casings came spinning back at him through the air. A woman cried out something in Indian, and children started whimpering. Then the woman in front of Chris sank to her knees, sobbing, and a man tugged at her shawl.

"Ready!"

"No-no," somebody said, and Chris looked around quick, sure that it was Carlyle. "Aim!"

A woman screamed, and gruff sounds went up from the men, and then, in a sudden swirl of movement, people tried to get away from the noise, toward the field. "Fire!"

Women near the shelter were on the ground with the fusillade, some with hands to their ears, shawls flying, and their wailing rose in such a chorus Chris felt the terrified squeeze of Ellen's hand. A man farther out on the field went down on a knee beside his wife, who was rocking on her haunches, and tried to take hold of her, but she threw herself flat, and he raised his face, glistening with tears, in appeal, toward the shelter. The backs of men near Chris gave and bent, shoulders leaping with sobs, and people started reaching to one another as if blinded. Then the children took off running across the field.

"Ready!"

"Boys, brothers," a voice said, too loud, and Chris saw Rio at one side raise a hand, his bald head bare and his hat at his stomach. Rio stepped forward. "That's enough now."

"Fire!"

The children screamed and hit the ground, some rolling over, others covering their heads with their arms where they lay, and the man in front of Chris bent over his wife as if to examine her as Carlyle slipped from his chair to his knees and let go with a cry above the wailing that no actor could reproduce on any New York stage. Philip stepped up and put a hand on Carlyle's back, his chest and arms twitching with unease, then stared across the field, his big bent nose pouring mucus over his trembling open lips as he wept.

CHRIS TURNED, and Ellen embraced him so hard he had to get his balance, while everywhere around the shelter and out in the field Chris saw more bodies going down and knew that his and Ellen's life had been settled by this. He was as sure now as he was of the sun that he was one who believed in a resurrection from the dead. However it might happen, it had to happen for justice to be dealt to every person down through every century until the world went up.

Johnny came treading slowly over to him, the apologetic smile on his face, glanced at Ellen clinging and giving with sobs that seemed of another kind of grief, of another age or another death, and said, "You came. Good."

"What can I do?" Chris said.

Johnny placed his hat on his head and tugged its brim, acknowledging Ellen's state. "See me in town there."

*   *   *

"WAIT," CHRIS said to Ellen, as if she'd leave the idling bus, and slid out the open door and walked among cars pulling away to where Beau's froglike Power Wagon was parked. Finally, Beau stepped gingerly across the church-yard with a cane, favoring his injured leg, and came across the highway, squinting under his hat as if the sun were against him from beneath. Beau looked out at Chris from under the hat's black brim, his face darker in its shade, and Chris recognized Carlyle in him. Beau tossed the cane into his truck box and reached out and took Chris's hand without engaging in the centurionlike underground-brotherhood handshake, and then he slowly laid his other hand on the top of their gripped hands. "Like Wounded Knee," Beau said, and stared past the truck at a shack set into a stand of trees. "You get the point about guns?"

"Yes."

"They'll have to get drunked up to live with the shame."

"Beau."

"I hope Gaylin saw it, from the woods or wherever he's hiding. He'd of had his fill."

"What do you think they'll do?" Chris asked, meaning authorities who might intervene, but he saw Beau take this another way and pictured the starlings in their tumbling fall.

"Go to high school together." Beau winced as if his leg hurt, then pulled off the hat and sailed it through his lowered window into the cab. "I won't turn him in. You?"

"Probably not."

"He might keep after you. I live in his tipi now, a true brave. What if he comes after you?"

Chris shrugged.

"Okay," Beau said, and took Chris's hand again. "Forget it."

Beau got in his pickup and backed away, one arm up on the seat, then pulled off without a glance at Chris, who wasn't sure whether Beau meant for him to forget the authorities or Gaylin or what Gaylin had done or forget everything the two of them had been through, their disputes and arguments and all the rest, or forget their entire friendship.

IT WAS THE bar Chris wasn't going to enter, but he did. Johnny was with a group of others at two tables shoved together into one, children scattered among the adults. The bartender looked up, and Chris thought this was perhaps the last person he would have to deal with, but the man stared over his head as if he didn't recognize him in a topcoat and a tie. Chris took Ellen to the table and sat her across from Johnny, then saw that the man beside Johnny was Henderson.

"Here's that guy I been wanting to talk to real good," the plump woman next to Henderson said, her flat and granular-scarred face as familiar to Chris as the face of his mother: Betty, Henderson's wife.

Henderson bristled, about to rise and swing, from his look, and Chris knew he couldn't begin this all over again. "I was careless," he said to her. "Forgive me for—"

"What's this?" Henderson asked.

"That gun he's got, he means," she explained. "No, that ain't so bad as the way you bunged my poor Dick all up."

"Yeah," Henderson said, scooting his chair back.

"But I'm sure glad you got him to the doctor and got him sewed up right off. His pretty looks wasn't spoiled one bit." She mussed up Henderson's hair. "And don't he know it!"

"Aw," Henderson said, and covered his face with a hand and turned aside, mimicking a bashful adolescent.

"See," Betty said. "This guy does anything to be the center of attention when he's got a pretty lady close enough to see." She smiled at Ellen, then shoved a bag of potato chips to a child and smiled again, pleased at her ability to dispense peace. Her eyes cocked in a merry manner Chris had noticed before—that wisp of a girl in the big bare house?—and he was about to ask Betty if she had a younger sister when he remembered the circumstances of that night and what it would mean he was saying.

He placed a hand on Johnny's shoulder, conscious now of the proper formalities, and said "You have our sympathy."

"Yes," Ellen said. "I was so torn up I—"

The door opened, and Rio walked in and saw Chris, paused with a tilting hesitation, then came to the table, pulled off his hat, and bowed to Johnny. "That was a beautiful man we laid in the ground today. He was such a quiet soul, considering all he achieved in this life. He was from a race of beautiful and gentle people, and I won't see his likes again. Us cowboys, you know, don't exist except as sots and romantics, but you beautiful people live on."

Johnny gave a nod, sighing, and Rio reached over and shook Chris's hand. "Son," he said, and that was it; he was at the bar. "Bud!" he called. "Set that table up!"

"What can I do?" Chris said to Johnny.

"You get these kids some pop."

Chris wasn't sure he'd heard right, and Johnny looked up to see if he'd been misunderstood. "Pop," he repeated.

The children were working on a tubular bag of ched-
dar corn, besides the chips, Chris saw, as he counted
heads: six.

"Orange," one boy said, and his look brought back
Gaylin's boyishness with a pang.

"Me, too," a girl said.

"Yah, me."

Chris went to the bar, and when the owner walked up,
all attention, he said, "Six orange sodas."

"And that's it," the man whispered. "Because if there's
a lick of trouble from you, you'll go flying. I'm a licensed
operator now." He reached under the bar and held something up enough for Chris to see a raspy checked-wood
grip over one side of its butt. "You get it?"

"Six orange sodas."

"That's a nice boy." The man smiled as if he meant it.

But Chris felt himself begin to give as he carried the
sodas back, bottles gritting and clanking against each
other, and saw Ellen shift to a young girl's side and place
her white hands on the table. He set the sodas in front of
the children, thinking that this was a further form of buying, a way of teaching them, and all they might remember
him by. He paused, feeling himself slow to the timing of
the world he'd been living in all winter, aware of how his
reflexes and pulse had been speeding up this past week
to accommodate the tempo of a city, the final soda swinging from his fingers like a pendulum as he pictured Beau
stepping up to each of the young men at the bar and
tapping each into place, and then his eyes fixed on the
bubbly orange liquid, struck by sunlight, simmering in the
neck of the bottle as somebody tossed a handful of change
across the table, and he heard the chirr of Sugar Bear's
bells in celebration, his dance over the ground opening
under his feet, and then an answering chorus of bells

seemed to rise from the faces aswim in Chris's vision, and he experienced again the sensation of that midnight gunshot wound deep in his chest and in a rush of breathlessness felt Ellen's shoulder under his hand and thought, *I'll be an Indian.*

About the Author

LARRY WOIWODE's fiction has appeared in *The Atlantic, Esquire, Harper's, The New Yorker, The Paris Review*, and many other publications, and has been translated into a dozen languages. His first novel, *What I'm Going to Do, I Think*, which introduced Chris and Ellen, received the William Faulkner Foundation Award; his second, *Beyond the Bedroom Wall*, was nominated for both the National Book Award and the National Book Critics Circle Award. He has been a Guggenheim Fellow, a John Dos Passos Prize winner, and the recipient of an award in literature from the American Academy and Institute of Arts and Letters. He lives in North Dakota with his wife and children.